Dear Reader:

I am so excited to see Enchanting the Lady *reissued in print!* This book is so near and dear to my heart, my first attempt at combining all the elements I love: Victorian history, magic, and romance. To have it available on the bookshelves once again, and to be able to find new readers and touch more hearts, is a dream come true.

I'm especially thrilled at the new cover design. It captures the fantasy feel of the book, without neglecting the historical aspect. One of the joys of combining genres is discovering new readers unfamiliar with one or the other. So if you love historical romances, you will find a new twist in the fantasy imbued in the story; if you love fantasy, I hope the historical aspect will add new dimension for you.

But this book is first and foremost a romance, and to be able to share Terence and Felicity's story once more is truly a pleasure. ·

My Magical Best,
Kathryne

Also by Kathryne Kennedy

My Unfair Lady
Beneath the Thirteen Moons
The Fire Lord's Lover
The Lady of the Storm
The Lord of Illusion

The Relics of Merlin

Enchanting THE Lady

KATHRYNE KENNEDY

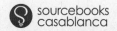

sourcebooks
casablanca

Published by Sourcebooks Casablanca, an imprint of Sourcebooks,
Inc.
P.O. Box 4410, Naperville, Illinois 60567-4410
(630) 961-3900
Fax: (630) 961-2168
www.sourcebooks.com

Originally published in 2008 by Lovespell, a division of Dorchester
Publishing Group.

Printed and bound in the United States of America.
VP 10 9 8 7 6 5 4 3 2 1

Prologue

Long ago a great wizard was born with magic in his very blood. He lived for thousands of years and went by many names, but the one we know best is Merlin.

Merlin passed his magic down through his offspring, and the power made his children rulers. Some inherited more magic than others, and eventually titles reflected their gifts. In Britain, kings and queens held the strongest power. After the royals, dukes had the greatest magical abilities in that they could change matter. Marquesses could cast spells and illusions and transfer objects but not change them. Earls mastered illusions, while viscounts dabbled in charms and potions. Barons had a magical gift, which could be as simple as making flowers grow or as complicated as seeing into the future.

And then there were the baronets. Part man, part animal, the shapeshifters were Merlin's greatest enchantment… and eventually his greatest bane. For out of all mankind, they were immune to his magic.

Merlin created thirteen magical relics from the gems of the earth, a focus for some of his greatest spells. After Merlin's disappearance, his children tried to find the relics, since these items held the only magic stronger than their own. The *relics proved to be elusive until his children discovered that the shapeshifters they so despised could sniff out the power of a relic.*

Over the centuries the relics faded to legend. But the most powerful of Merlin's descendants did not forget, and shapeshifters became the secret spies of many rulers.

One

London, 1882
Where magic has never died…

FELICITY SHOULD HAVE KNOWN THAT HER COUSIN would try to frighten her with one of his illusions on the most important day of her life. But when she opened the door to her room to fetch her wrap and saw the apparition before her, she gasped with astonishment.

The wooden floor had cracked apart to reveal a gaping hole. Felicity leaned forward and peered over the edge, an odor of rotten eggs burning her nose. Her lavender-blue eyes watered as she looked down into an abyss that glowed from a river of lava flowing at the very bottom.

Cousin Ralph's magic had surpassed his rank, just as Uncle Oliver had predicted. As a viscount's son, he shouldn't have been able to create any illusions, much less something this vivid.

Felicity swallowed and lifted her chin. Ralph's illusions usually came to her in dreams, and it startled her that he'd become powerful enough to send her one in the daytime. Still, it could only be an illusion, no matter how well crafted, and she'd have to cross it to reach the white lace shawl she needed. But she hated heights.

Uncle Oliver's impatient voice—loudly wondering what could be taking her so long to fetch a wrap—carried up the stairs. Felicity took the deepest breath she could within the confines of her corset, lifted the ruffles of her skirts and sprinted across the room, landing in a very unladylike sprawl atop her settee. Her heart pounded at an alarming rate and her hands shook when she reached for her wrap, but a smile of grim satisfaction spread across her face.

And then she glanced down.

The settee shifted, slowly sinking into the chasm.

"Blast!"

Felicity rolled, thankfully hit a solid surface with her feet, and leaped across the room, catching the edge of the chasm with her fingers. Her feet flailed and she could feel the heat of the lava flow up her skirts, and she swore she'd get even with her cousin.

She'd never been caught up in one of his illusions to this degree. But his magic kept growing stronger, and she had little of her own to counter it.

"My goodness, Miss Felicity!"

Felicity looked up into the freckled face of her newest lady's maid.

"I near stepped on ye! Whatever are ye doing?"

Felicity wiggled her toes and glanced over her shoulder. The lava burped and a fresh wave of rot hit her nose. "What does it look like, Katie?"

The Irish girl stepped back, her eyes wide, and crossed herself. "Ye're lying on the floor, miss. Wiggling like a fish."

Felicity sighed. She'd lose another maid. Again. It was hard enough to get good servants, but when only she could see the illusions, the hired help had a tendency to think she was a bit mad. Her fingers had started to slip, and her shoulders to cramp. "Would you mind giving me a hand, then? I can't seem to get up."

Katie nodded, the red hair that had escaped her cap bouncing along her flushed cheeks. Although tiny, she had enough wiry strength to flip Felicity right on her feet.

"Now, then." Felicity brushed at the dust covering the front of her white gown. "I think you should go straight away to the upstairs maid and tell her the floors must be mopped more often. Really, when one wants to wiggle like a fish, one should not be subjected to such filth."

Katie nodded again, backing down the hallway as if afraid to turn her back on her mistress. Felicity watched her bound down the stairs as if the hounds of hell were after her, and tried not to feel too sad.

Sometimes Felicity thought she might be going a bit daft. For the umpteenth time she wished she could get away from magic, find some nice untitled, unmagical man who couldn't light a fire without some ordinary matches...

Aunt Gertrude passed her in a rush of whispering silk and lavender scent, spun to a halt and narrowed her eyes. "Is that you, Felicity? I've been looking for you everywhere. Lord Wortley has become most impatient with the wait, and you know how your uncle gets when he's inconvenienced."

Lady Gertrude Wortley grasped her niece's hand

and towed her down the stairs, the feathers in her hat leading the way like the prow of a great ship. She swayed like one as well, the bulk of her thighs creating a rolling motion, her huge bustle a pendulum of silk. Felicity adored her aunt, who had been her surrogate mother since Felicity's parents had died. But Aunt was plagued by headaches, and she rarely left her personal chambers. They shared the same home, but Felicity seldom saw her.

Aunt Gertrude looked surprisingly well. Felicity could never see a resemblance to her aunt in the photographs of her mother. Aunt lacked the coal-black hair and violet eyes of her mother, and instead was gifted with mousy brown hair, watery blue eyes, and a plain face. If she'd been a beauty in her youth, it had faded with the years and her illness.

When they reached the bottom of the staircase, Aunt Gertrude bobbed her head at her scowling husband and ushered Felicity out the great door, down the marble steps and into their coach. Uncle Oliver and Ralph climbed in and sat in the opposite seat, both dressed in black top hats and double-breasted frock coats. At seventeen, Ralph looked like a younger version of his handsome father, his face just begin-ning to lose the fullness of a boy's. Ralph's mahogany brown hair was matched with similarly colored eyes, whereas Uncle Oliver's eyes glittered gray. And Uncle Oliver didn't sneer at her with disdain.

Aunt Gertrude finally let go of her hand. "Felicity, dear," she whispered. "Your palms are so sweaty. Don't tell me you've forgotten your gloves?"

Felicity shook her head and pulled the lengths of

satin from the pocket of her skirt, ignoring Ralph's snort of contempt. While she struggled to pull the cloth over damp skin, she glared at him beneath her lashes. Let him gloat over the fright he'd given her while he had the chance. If he wanted to continue to behave like a child—even though he was due to reach his majority in a few months—she would accommodate him.

Even though she had little to no magic, there were other ways she could get even: like pepper in his soup, powder in his top hat, holes in his breeches. She'd had to get creative over the years, but she just couldn't let him bully her without any consequences.

If only Uncle Oliver would do something about it. But whenever she complained, Ralph would either lie or point out that if Felicity worked harder on garnering her own magic, she'd be able to counteract any of his measly spells.

Uncle glanced at her and lifted an imperious brow. Felicity quickly turned to look out the window, staring at her reflection in the glass. She admired the three white feathers in her hair, the way Katie had done up her black locks into twists and curls, then let the back fall in waves where it flowed down her back like a river of silk. Her pale face still had a flush of pink from her fright, and her black lashes outlined the bluish-violet of her eyes, so that even in her reflection they seemed to glow.

She might have been vain, but she'd become so accustomed to people overlooking her presence that she felt sure her features weren't particularly extraordinary. Felicity knew that if she thought herself the tiniest bit handsome it was because she'd reached an age where she resembled the photographs of her mother… and who didn't think that their own mother was beautiful?

Especially when one's mother was dead.

"Do you think," she asked no one in particular, "that if my parents had lived, I would have inherited the power of a duchess?"

Stunned silence rocked with the coach over the cobblestones. Felicity never mentioned her parents; it always seemed to bring such horrible reactions from Aunt and Uncle.

Uncle Oliver scowled and cursed beneath his breath. Ralph's mouth dropped open in the most unbecoming way, and Aunt Gertrude rushed to fill the silence.

"Lord Wortley, I'm sure it's just her nerves. It's most difficult to face a presentation, especially without the support of one's parents."

Uncle Oliver looked ready to implode.

"I mean," stuttered Aunt, "when she's likely to fail at the tests, it's understandable… isn't it?" She patted Felicity gently on the hand, but her eyes glinted with a warning. "We all feel the loss of the duke and duchess, dear. Especially when one reminds us of their absence."

Felicity tried not to flinch when Aunt mentioned her probable failure. But Uncle Oliver let out a gust of breath and his features relaxed. Ralph let out a smug giggle.

"Just wait," he boasted, "until my presentation. At least then the lands will stay in the family."

"Dear Ralph," sighed Aunt Gertrude. She fingered

her pearl necklace. "That's something to be grateful for now, isn't it, Felicity? If you don't have the magic required to be the next duchess, at least your cousin might be the next duke."

Felicity tried to look grateful. She knew her lack of magic to continue the title had to be a great disappointment to Aunt and Uncle, and she shouldn't begrudge her cousin because he carried it in his veins. But she'd been duchess-of-honor for her parents' holdings for so long she felt they belonged to her. She didn't care much for Stonehaven Castle, nor their London mansion, but Graystone Castle was home. It was her parents' legacy to her...

"Look at Lord Gremville's new coach and four." Uncle Oliver's voice dripped with disdain.

Felicity stared out the window. Marquesses' powers were limited to illusions and the transfer of objects, so she knew that the white unicorns with golden horns weren't real, that the gilded coach camouflaged a plain black finish. Still, the sight took her breath away, and she longed to stroke the foreheads of the animals.

"Oh, yes," said Aunt Gertrude, still fingering the pearl in the necklace she habitually wore. "Unicorns are at the height of fashion now. Much better than those ghastly gargoyles they had last season."

"Foolish of him, don't you think, Father?" Ralph's lips thinned into a narrow line, making his handsome face look cruel. "How long can a marquess's powers last, a few hours or so? He'd have to renew the spell in the middle of the presentation, and the wards are too strong for him to get past them. It'll be interesting to see the real condition of his nags."

"Perhaps. But perhaps it would be equally delightful to have a son who could hold his illusion for even that long."

Ralph shrank in his seat, and Felicity couldn't help feeling a pang of sympathy for him. For some ridiculous reason, Uncle felt her absence of power forgivable because of her gender. But Ralph lacked that excuse. She thought Uncle had unreasonable expectations for his son; after all, Uncle was only a viscount, his powers limited to alchemy and herbs. Yet he expected Ralph to attain the power of a duke, to go beyond illusions to the actual changing of matter. Ralph's powers already entitled him to the expected rank of a marquess, or at the very least, an earl.

The coach lurched to a stop, and Felicity blinked with surprise and a sudden panic. They had reached Buckingham Palace so soon? The door opened and just as Felicity descended from the coach, the clouds cleared and the sun lit the palace. The diamond-studded walls threw prisms of color in her eyes. She squinted to admire the fanciful arches over the windows, which had been shaped into mythical beasts and ancient battles of wizardry.

Felicity averted her gaze from the warding spells that surrounded the walls. Although barely discernible, if she looked too long it always made her feel queasy.

It would be several hours before her official presentation in the palace. She had to be tested first. The guards herded their group toward a small, unremarkable building. It didn't look more important than the palace itself, but within those walls titles had been made or broken.

As they waited in line, Felicity stared at the mosaic-tiled walk. If the wards of the palace could make her queasy, the ones surrounding the Hall of Mages would make her violently ill. Designed not only for defense, but to keep the magic released inside those walls contained, the wards roiled in dizzying motion.

Aunt Gertrude patted her shoulder and murmured encouragement. Felicity lifted her chin and locked her trembling legs. They all expected her to fail. And she couldn't blame them, since she could barely manage to light a candle with the magic she possessed. But she knew she had magic; it just always seemed to be hiding from her. And lately, she'd discovered a small secret.

If she looked for her magic, it evaded her. But if she relaxed a bit, she could feel it gathering from all the tiny crevices in her body, and she'd managed, just a few times, to use it.

Felicity prayed that she could accomplish that feat again today. She endured the agonizing wait by imagining how pleased Aunt and Uncle would be to realize that she did carry a bit of her parents' power. Not enough to permanently keep her parents' title, but at least enough to hold the title of honor until another qualified for the dukedom.

"Lady Felicity May Seymour?"

She looked up into the face of a novice, his purple robes indicating his rank. He looked over her head at Aunt Gertrude, who shook her head with disgust and laid her hand gently on Felicity's shoulder.

"This is Duchess-of-Honor Stonehaven."

The novice blinked. "I apologize, I didn't see you standing there. Would you follow me, please?"

Felicity strengthened her resolve. She embraced Aunt and Uncle as if she'd never see them again, as if she went to her doom instead of a testing of entitlement. Ralph's sneer of disgust made her abruptly loosen her hold.

She followed the novice down so many hallways and through such myriad corridors that without a guide she knew she'd never find her way out again. Strange sounds issued from behind several closed doors. Green lights and blue smoke bled through cracks in the frames and seeped into the halls. Felicity grabbed a pinch of the novice's robe and held on.

"Don't worry," he said. "Not enough can get out to harm you."

"Enough of what?" she gasped.

He only chuckled and opened a door embellished with a golden crown. He pushed her through and closed it behind her, and when Felicity looked up she saw a half dozen white-gowned girls.

One-by-one they'd be called out to face their test. She hadn't thought about it, but experiencing this holding cell with other equally nervous, jittery, giggly girls felt like a subtle form of torture.

She didn't know any of the girls, but they all seemed to know each other, whispering encouragement and adjusting hair feathers. Felicity had never cared for the city, always preferring to live at Graystone Castle in Ireland. Aunt and Uncle had indulged her, though now she wished they hadn't. It might have been comforting to have a friend to talk to. But they all ignored her, so she just concentrated on relaxing. Which seemed ridiculous, considering her situation.

Felicity fought against her corset to breathe as deeply as she could. Ralph's illusions had taught her about fear from a very young age. When faced with a three-headed green monster slobbering noxious purple goo all over one's bedcovers night after night for several years, she'd learned to isolate the fear from her brain.

As she got older and his illusions became more sophisticated, her skill at managing fear had only increased.

So, she breathed, and acknowledged the pounding of her heart without thinking she'd die from it, and let the weakness in her knees flow out through her toes. She gave her body permission to be afraid, already knowing that the fear had a limit to what it could do to her. But she must let her mind relax. Must allow the little bit of magic given her to gather at her fingertips, so that when the time came she'd be able to—

"Duchess-of-Honor Stonehaven, please enter." Another novice held open a door from across the room and scanned the sea of white ruffles. His eyes slowly focused on her as she approached. "The prince is most eager to meet you." And he bowed aside, waving her through the door with an unnecessary flourish of his arm.

Two

TERENCE BLACKWELL FROZE OUTSIDE THE PRINCE'S private rooms, a frisson of anger curling up his spine. His nostrils flared and he inhaled deeply, recognizing the scent of evil power. Could it be?

Relic magic.

Here, in the Hall of Mages. And even worse, near his crown prince.

He shifted, claws scraping the tiled floor, fangs lengthening from the corners of his mouth, his muscles growing stronger and tensed to spring. A snarl of rage ripped from the back of his lion throat, and he broke down the door with one mighty leap.

His eyes scanned the room, looking for danger, while his nostrils flared, trying to catch the scent of relic-magic. The prince stared at him aghast, his eyes wide in his pudgy face, while noblemen scrambled behind furniture and women screamed. Two guards stood at the opposite end of the room, their swords half drawn from their scabbards, and several others threw spells in his direction.

"Good God, Blackwell, what's the meaning of

this?" demanded Prince Albert. The guards let their swords fall back into their scabbards, but several noblemen continued to work defensive magic. The prince gave them a look of disgust. "Leave off, gentlemen, your spells are useless."

Several of the men turned ugly shades of pink.

Terence swung his heavy mane back and forth. Where had it gone? He couldn't catch a trace of the scent anymore. His prince had been in the middle of a game of cards, which now lay scattered about the room, and two lovely noblewomen hung from each arm. The noblemen had scattered as thoroughly as the cards.

Terence grunted in confusion. The prince's expression had gone from annoyed, to decidedly amused. Terence shifted back to human, still alert for any sign of danger, but starting to feel a bit sheepish. He might've overreacted. A bit.

"Are you going to explain, Blackwell?"

"My apologies," muttered Terence. He looked up at his prince. "And to you as well, Your Royal Highness. My most abject apologies."

The noblemen started to crawl out from their hiding places.

"I assume you have a good reason for this," said the prince. "And I'll be interested to hear what it is. Now." He motioned Terence from the room, through another side door, his pudgy hands shaking only slightly. The prince collapsed on a velvet settee as soon as Terence closed the door behind them.

"You scared several years off my life, Blackwell!"

Terence lifted a golden brow. "I thought his royal highness was in danger."

"From what? My most trusted nobles? In my most warded of rooms?"

Should he tell the prince that he thought he'd smelled the scent of relic-magic? Albert already had accused Terence of being obsessed, and since a relic-user had taken his brother Thomas's life, Terence couldn't deny it. Would Albert think he'd gone from obsession to foolishness?

Terence glanced around the room, found a decanter of brandy, and poured the liquid into a jewel-studded glass. He crossed the plush carpet, and handed it to his prince, who downed it in one gulp.

"I apologize again," Terence said, arranging his face into a look of embarrassment. "There are times when I find it difficult to control the animal part of my nature. When I sense danger, I have a tendency to… let my instincts take over."

The brandy had restored the prince's color. He waved a hand dismissively. "Yes, yes. But something made you come charging into that room, Blackwell. Now, what was it?"

Terence sighed. "I thought I detected the foul smell of relic magic."

"Ridiculous," scoffed the prince, but his eyes dilated with fear, and the edges of his ancestors' portraits that decorated the walls of the room whitened with frost.

The only other time a relic had been near the palace was when a usurper used it to take over the throne. Small wonder the prince was afraid, since relic-magic was the only power that a royal couldn't defeat. "I only caught a trace of a scent," said Terence. "And it appears to be gone now."

"But here? How could that be possible?" Albert's fear had turned to anger and the frost melted, running like tears down the walls of the room. Terence wasn't sure whether the prince was even aware of what his magic was doing. The water sizzled into steam, and the marble floor beneath his feet began to shimmer with a red glow.

Terence quickly tried to reassure him. "It's possible one of the novices crafted something that resembles the odor of relic-magic—or managed to burn something that carries a similar stench."

It sounded a bit flimsy, even to Terence, and the prince snorted. "You will find the source of it, Blackwell. I didn't make you a baronet and employ you as my spy just because you're immune to magic, you know. Some of my advisors think you shape-shifters are more of a threat to the crown than the relics. Only by proving your loyalty can I convince them that they are wrong."

Terence's amber eyes narrowed and he spun, striding over to the window. His lion nature had reacted to the veiled threat within the prince's words, and he fought for control while he stared out the window at the London skyline.

The strange architecture of the nobles' mansions somehow blended with the buildings built by manual labor alone. Fanciful arches butted against tiled roofs, silver spires rose between brick buildings, and confection-like castles nestled among marble residences.

The view didn't help to soothe him as it normally would. Pall Mage looked congested, and he wondered what event caused the jam of carriages. Not that it mattered…

"There are not enough shapeshifters to overthrow the crown," muttered Terence. "Nor could we hold the throne without any magic of our own. Most baronets cannot even support their title. Do you know how many I personally employ?"

Terence heard a grunt as the prince stood, the rustle of his clothing as he crossed the room. Prince Albert clapped him on the shoulder. "Come now, man. I didn't say that those were my sentiments. And if the other baronets were as good as your family at tracking down the relics, they'd be just as wealthy as you."

"Being a predator has its advantages," agreed Terence.

"Quite. Now, I assure you that I trust you with my safety, and that of the realm. Generations of your family have always served, and never failed, this house."

His voice rang with genuine honesty, and Terence felt his muscles loosen. When only a relic would threaten a royal's absolute power over his kingdom, such trust must be difficult to give.

If only they knew more about the relics! Each stone had been enchanted with a different spell, and they'd only found six of them so far. Legend had it that Merlin had crafted thirteen stones, each with a different spell, a different purpose.

The prince dropped his hand from Terence's shoulder and sighed. Terence strode over to the sideboard, unable to feel the magical heat that made the scattered oriental carpets steam. He poured himself a small goblet of brandy and threw it down his throat, then stared at the empty glass.

The first of Merlin's stones to be discovered had been a sapphire imbedded in a goblet similar to the one he now held. It had been designed to subtly twist others' minds to the user's purpose. And the stone... the diamond that had inadvertently caused Thomas's death had been used to suck the souls of living men, to make them zombie-like creatures that would follow the user's commands. The diamond had been fashioned into a hairpin, and a woman had used its power several times before Terence and his brother had tracked it down.

The other four stones had been found before they could be used. One of lapis, in the headdress of an ancient Egyptian king; another of emerald, in the talisman of an India Mogul; a peridot in the center of a golden cross; and an African ruby embedded in a walking staff.

Merlin had been the most powerful magician of all time, and the knowledge he'd used to create the relics had been long lost.

"I would request attendance on your royal person," said Terence, "for the rest of the day. Until I discover the nature of that scent."

"Yes, yes, of course. You needn't even ask, you know. Although you might regret it. I oversee the testing today."

Terence couldn't understand why the prince enjoyed overseeing the tests for power. He personally found it incredibly boring. But until he found the source of that scent of relic-magic, he'd stay by his prince's side.

"Come on, Blackwell, let's return to the others...

you humiliated half the room, you know. Did you see the Marquess of Timberly push his wife in front of himself as a shield?"

Terence shook his head. The prince still hadn't caught on to the real reason for the rest of the aristocracy to despise not only him, but all were-kind. Assured of their loyalty, the prince had no reason to fear the baronets. Their immunity to magic provided him with a useful tool.

But it terrified the rest of the aristocracy. It not only threatened their power, but their feeling of superiority.

Terence opened the door for his prince and met the glaring hatred in the eyes of the marquess, and the open fear in the rest of the nobles' faces.

Being the prince's spy had given him a purpose for his life, a reason for being born an animal, something he'd been ashamed of until he'd realized that a shape-shifter's unique abilities could sniff out and destroy a relic. Terence raised a golden brow and stared down Lord Timberly until the man flushed and looked away.

"Come now, we had a bit of a fright, but my faithful Baronet thought my person in jeopardy." Albert sighed with dramatic flair. "If only all my retainers had such loyalty…"

That broke the silence of the room as they all rushed forward to assure their prince that they'd protect him with their lives. Terence received even more private looks of hatred. The hair on the back of his neck had just started to rise when a novice entered the room and announced that the testing would begin.

Their party assembled on the dais, facing the warding chamber in the center of the room. Most of the nobles whispered amongst themselves, seemingly as bored as Terence. He wondered why so many of the male members of the aristocracy had come with the prince today. He had his answer when a novice announced the entrance of the Duchess-of-Honor Stonehaven.

Terence could feel the nobles tense with anticipation. He overheard the whispered speculations regarding the availability of such a great title. He felt astonished when the lady in question entered the room and no one seemed to notice.

But then his entire concentration became so focused on the girl that he no longer became aware of anyone else.

Terence had never seen such a beautiful creature. The white feathers in her hair made it appear blacker than midnight, with a sheen that reminded him of the finest silk. Delicately arched brows of the same hue framed huge, liquid eyes of an unusual violet color. Her full, red lips contrasted with the pale complexion of her skin, and he wondered if her nervousness might be responsible for her lack of color. What would she look like with a blush to her cheeks from a round of fevered lovemaking?

Terence clenched his fists. He could feel his were-self trying to form a husky growl of desire, and he trembled with the effort of suppressing it. He'd allowed his animal instincts to make him look enough of a fool for one day.

But still, he could not take his eyes off the girl. She curtsied to the prince, a low sweep of such poise and grace he half expected the room to burst into applause. But conversation swirled uninterrupted around him, and it seemed that only Terence had the pleasure of the additional cleavage exposed from her bent position.

Which suited him fine.

When the Lady Stonehaven rose from her curtsy he thought he saw her glance from beneath her lowered lashes before she quickly looked down at the floor again. Her bosom heaved with a sigh, as if she'd expected no one would notice the elegance of her curtsy, and then her chin lifted almost defiantly.

Terence's nose started to itch. No, it had been itching for some time, but he'd been so intent on fighting his other bodily responses to the girl he hadn't noticed. He inhaled deeply and caught the scent of relic-magic again. It came from the Duchess-of-Honor Stonehaven.

If her beauty had held him spellbound before, the faint scent of relic-magic on her person held him in absolute thrall. Could she be a threat to the prince?

He couldn't be sure. The touch of relic-magic that she carried had been placed on her a long time ago. But how? And why?

Terence glanced at the noblemen, who still hadn't acknowledged the presence of the girl. Even Prince Albert didn't appear to see her. The onlookers in the gallery fidgeted and whispered to each other, oblivious to the girl's presence.

"Bloody hell," muttered Terence, as the truth hit him. The girl carried a spell on her that made her nearly invisible. A powerful relic-spell that only a shapeshifter would be immune to. Anyone else would have to concentrate just to see her. Who would do such a thing to her? Or had she done it herself? And if she had, why?

Terence grinned, exposing the fangs at the corners of his mouth. What an utterly fascinating creature, so full of puzzles and mysteries. What a wonderful turn of events, for the lovely girl to come here and bring him a lead to the relic.

In the space of a few moments, the Duchess of Stonehaven had not only managed to gain his admiration, but his suspicion as well. Although she appeared to be an innocent, he'd been fooled by a woman before—as had his brother—and he wouldn't allow it to happen again.

Terence threw back his head and almost allowed his were-self to let loose the howl of a hunter on the scent of his prey. He'd found a lead on another relic!

Already he'd started to form a plan. A plan that involved not only his quest for a relic, but one that would allow him to get close to the stunningly beautiful Duchess-of-Honor.

Very, very close.

Three

Felicity entered what looked like a giant bubble, which Uncle had told her protected the witnesses of a testing from any overzealous spells. When she passed through, she shivered from the wards and felt the hair on the back of her neck stand up.

She stood behind a marble table and looked up to where the prince sat on a dais surrounded by his nobles. She ignored the audience who sat behind a magically shielded wall, unwilling to meet the gaze of her aunt and uncle who were surely among them.

A nobleman leaned down and whispered something in the prince's ear. Prince Albert squinted at the bubble, his eyes slowly widening, and then they all stared. It felt odd, having so many people looking at her, noticing her, that she felt the fear creep back into her brain.

Felicity knew her attention should have been caught by Prince Albert. She'd never seen him before, and although a bit on the heavy side, he had an arresting quality that made her understand why so many women were attracted to him.

Felicity gave the prince a weak smile, but the man

behind his shoulder commanded her attention. The nobleman caught her up in his gaze and wouldn't let her go.

She'd never seen the man before, yet it seemed she knew him in some peculiar way. He bore a title—otherwise he wouldn't have been part of the prince's entourage—yet the other noblemen seemed to keep their distance from him.

His eyes... Felicity caught her breath. They glittered a pale gold, like honey in sunshine, and were shaped as round as marbles. That should've been enough—that one man bore such a striking feature. But he possessed a glorious mane of golden-brown hair as well, which cascaded over his shoulders in a thick shimmer that made her want to stroke it.

He stood as tall as the other noblemen surrounding him, but his shoulders spread almost twice as wide, and his compact body looked deceptively lazy, as if he could spring into action at any moment.

Felicity had never felt so aware of a man before. She would have been shocked at her intense scrutiny of him if he hadn't been doing the same to her.

And if he hadn't been holding her with his eyes as if she were his intended prey.

She blinked.

"Duchess-of-Honor Stonehaven? Are you well?"

Prince Albert's voice penetrated the bubble's wardings with a tinny quality, but she heard him quite clearly and opened her mouth to reply, but the tawny man hadn't dropped his gaze yet.

"I say, Blackwell," said the prince. "Quit staring at the girl. Can't you see you've terrified her speechless?"

The man responded to the name with a raised brow, as if asking whether he'd truly had that effect on her. Felicity lifted her chin.

Blackwell grinned; a flash of white, even teeth in the front, but with the longest incisors she'd ever seen. She also noted his very full-lipped mouth.

He released her finally, looking away with a blink of those golden eyes. Felicity breathed a sigh of relief.

"The baronet, Sir Terence Blackwell, has that effect on most women, Duchess-of-Honor Stonehaven." The noblemen surrounding the prince chuckled, elbowing each other. But not, she noticed, the tawny man.

Their laughter irritated Felicity. This testing, and the presentation afterward, were the most important events in a person's life. How dare these noblemen stand about and treat it as some kind of lark?

She certainly didn't feel like laughing. And she didn't want to fail. Not before Sir Terence. For some reason, she didn't want to shame herself in front of him.

"Forgive the high spirits of these men," said the prince. "It's not every day that they have the opportunity to witness the caliber of magic required of a duchess. I'm honored to meet you, you know. Your parents were particular favorites of mine."

Felicity laid both hands on the table before her. The prince had intimately known her parents? He would've been a child—

"Perhaps we will speak further at the ball tonight. After your presentation to the queen."

She nodded, not trusting herself to speak. None of the noblemen would notice her after today. If she'd had a title and power, perhaps her drab face might have been overlooked and she could have been the belle of the ball. But now she could only envision a long, humiliating evening of dancing with her cousin, if at all.

Stop it, she chided herself. You are not going to fail! Let your mind relax; let the power come to your fingers.

"Are you ready, Lady Stonehaven?"

Felicity nodded and studied the objects on the table. She reached for a crystal ball and looked up at the prince for reassurance, purposely avoiding the gaze of Sir Terence.

"Yes, very good," said Prince Albert. "Although unnecessary in your case, we should follow the orders. Place the globe in the palm of your open hand, yes, just like that."

Felicity tried to keep her hand from trembling. What would they think when she couldn't even produce a small spark inside the crystal? Felicity tried to will it to happen.

The noblemen coughed and shuffled their feet.

"Any minute now," encouraged the prince.

The ball was supposed to glow, confirming a baron's level of magic. Felicity closed her eyes and ignored her trembling arm. She just needed to focus on clearing her mind, finding the remnants of magic that she could feel in her blood.

She could feel the ball rolling on her palm with the rhythm of her shaking. She thought she heard a low growl from the direction of the dais, but couldn't be sure.

"Well now," said Prince Albert. "Do you happen to have a gift for making flowers grow? Or perhaps healing small wounds? We have one baroness who can bring down a bird with every shot—most astonishing. I say, could the thing be broken?"

He directed his words at no one in particular. She could hear his harsh breathing in the deathly still room.

A tremor ripped through Felicity's arm. The crystal rolled off her palm and hit the floor with a resounding crash. "I'm so sorry," she said, crouching to reach for the scattered shards. She avoided looking up into anyone's eyes.

"Lady Stonehaven, please don't bother. It's quite understandable. Many of our more sheltered ladies find this testing to be a nerve-racking ordeal."

His voice sounded so kind. He made Felicity feel even worse, as if she were a charlatan. Perhaps it would be better to just admit to them all that she had no magic, rather than go through with this farce.

No. She could do it. She had to do it.

"In your case, why don't we move on to the viscountess test, shall we?" The prince shifted on his throne; she could hear the rustle of the cloth. "Before you are two items, a simple charm bag and a vial of potion."

Felicity stared at the embroidered pouch and the yellowish-green liquid.

"Lady Stonehaven, what is the purpose of the charm?"

She tried to gather the magic to her fingertips as she laid it on the bag. Tried to imagine what sort of…

"It's a love charm," she blurted.

"Very good, now, what is the purpose of the potion?"

Felicity looked up. She had guessed correctly! Or had she really discerned that with magic? The prince smiled, and all the noblemen had eager looks on their faces. Except for Sir Terence, who looked puzzled.

She picked up the vial. The solution swirled inside at her touch. "It cures something."

The Prince leaned forward. "Yes?"

"Warts! It makes them fade…"

Their expressions told her that she had guessed wrong this time.

"I daresay," said the prince. "This is most unusual. But I knew your parents—a more powerful couple I have yet to meet. Surely their only child has inherited their magic."

It's what they all expected, she knew. Rarely did the talent skip a generation in the upper classes, or go to more than one child.

The golden man leaned down and whispered something in the prince's ear. The rest of the noblemen had either stuffed their hands in the pockets of their coats, crossed their arms over their chests, or transferred their gazes to the ceiling with bored expressions.

"Quite right, Sir Terence. Let's cut to the chase. We shall skip the illusion test for a countess, and the summoning test for a marchioness. If you pass the matter-change test of the duchess, it proves you carry all the lower powers anyway. Lady, er, Stonehaven. Before you lies an ordinary rock. What will you turn it into?"

Felicity knew she couldn't manage such a feat. Just because she occasionally felt a bit of magic inside of her did not mean that she qualified for the title of duchess.

"I cannot do it." There, she'd said it. Felicity wished

for Ralph's illusion, that the floor would open up and swallow her. She wanted to cry and run from the room to hide from the humiliation.

"You must try."

Her heart turned beneath her breast. That voice had not been the prince's. That voice had rumbled from a massive chest, a voice so deep, so compelling that she instantly obeyed.

She touched the rock. She calmed her mind and tried to summon the magic. Tried to see a glittering diamond materialize beneath her fingers. She despised that rock. "I told you, I cannot do it! I have no magic. I just guessed about the charm. I can't even qualify as a baroness."

At least now she felt angry instead of wanting to burst into tears. She should thank Sir Terence for that much.

"Are you sure," asked the prince, "that you have no magic at all? Not even enough to retain the title of honor until we find another?"

Felicity shook her head, no longer trusting herself to speak. The prince looked as if she had gravely disappointed him. She didn't dare turn around to see the expressions on the faces of her aunt and uncle. Would she always be destined to feel like a failure?

"This is most unusual," said Prince Albert. "It would be a shame for the title to fall from your family line, but the rules of ascension are clear. If no relation of yours tests for the power, the title will be open to another family. In the meantime…"

The prince stood. His voice had become hard, but his eyes still remained gentle. "Lady—no. Miss Felicity May Seymour, you are stripped of all rank, lands, and title. The crown will graciously give you sixty days to vacate the properties."

Her worst fears had come true. Hearing the words spoken by her prince finally made it real to her. She'd only carried the title of duchess-of-honor because no one else had come forward to claim it. She should feel grateful for that much, at least.

Still, she wanted to plead for Graystone Castle, to be allowed to live among the green hills and mossy stones. All of the rest they could have, but they couldn't just take her home from her.

And then she realized that it had never been her home. She'd only been an imposter of a tenant.

"Miss Seymour, do you understand?"

She nodded, the awful feeling in her chest so strong that she thought she might faint from it. Another robed novice waited outside the bubble, and impatiently gestured to her. Felicity gathered her skirts in her hands, lifted her chin, took a step forward and stumbled. Her elbow caught the edge of the table, and her eyes teared from the pain of it. She could hear the noblemen snicker, and then a growl silenced the room again.

Felicity stepped out of the bubble. The novice tried to grab her arm and drag her from the room, as if she were some common piece of dirt. Well, others might now regard her that way, but she would still demand the respect of a lady. She wrenched her arm free, gave him an imperious stare, and slowly, with her nose as high in the air as she could manage, strode from the room.

But she needn't have bothered with the show

of bravado, for when she snuck a peek behind her, no one noticed her leaving as the prince welcomed the next test subject into the room. Except, Felicity noted with another twist of humiliation, the golden Sir Terence.

❧

"I don't want to go," Felicity said to her reflection.

"I know," replied Katie as she brushed her mistress's long, black hair.

Felicity shifted on her vanity bench. Why couldn't Ralph conjure up his illusory hole right now? She'd gratefully crawl into it. Her presentation to the queen kept replaying itself in her mind. After the dreadful test, she'd been presented as the 'viscount's niece,' for which she should have been grateful. Otherwise, she wouldn't have been presented at all, being a mere commoner. The queen had barely acknowledged her curtsy, and the huge assembly of noblemen, except for Sir Terence, had barely glanced at Felicity from start to finish. She'd been overlooked before, but that made her feel positively invisible.

"No one is going to dance with me, not after my humiliation."

Katie grunted as she worked on a tangle. "But this is yer come-out, miss. Ye should be excited! Ye're still gentry, and with yer beauty, I'm sure many a gentleman will overlook yer lack of magic and title."

Felicity smiled at Katie's attempts to make her feel better. She could guarantee that not a single gentleman would give her half a glance. But still, she hadn't considered marriage as a solution to her situation.

Unlike most girls who dreamed of bettering their station through marriage, she'd always thought that with her title, she'd be able to marry for love.

But hadn't she always wished to live in a household without magic? Perhaps she should view this as an opportunity. What a relief it would be not to wake up every other night with some illusory monster slobbering over her, to be able to walk into a room without wondering whether the ceiling or floor might still be intact.

Katie hummed under her breath while she twisted up Felicity's hair and wove strands of pearls into her coiffure.

"I suppose," mused Felicity, "that a mere knight would have me. They don't have any magic whatsoever."

"That's the way to think, miss! Magic isn't everything. Ye can stand in front of the full-length now, so I can admire my labor."

Felicity moved to the big mirror and twirled her pale lavender skirts. She'd protested Katie's choice of a gown at first, but now she could see that her maid had been right. The color highlighted the violet in her eyes, and made her black hair and lashes stand out in startling contrast. Tiny seed pearls sewn into the bodice matched the decoration in her hair, and even though the neckline had been cut even lower than her presentation gown, she had a lovely film of lavender cloth to wrap around her shoulders.

"Oh, thank you, Katie! This just might even entice a baronet, yes?" Instantly the image of tawny hair and piercing gold eyes filled her mind.

"Ach, miss!" Katie crossed herself. "Don't even say such a thing."

Felicity tied her shawl in a soft knot over the swells of her breasts, stifling a smile at Katie's suddenly pronounced brogue. "Why ever not? They don't have magic, either."

"That's because they are magic. They're animals, and I can't understand why the prince even allows them a title."

"It's true then? That they're shapeshifters and immune to all magic?" Felicity could still hear his voice, commanding her to try, and that low growl that had silenced the other noblemen when they'd laughed at her. She shivered as she tried to imagine what his animal shape could be.

Katie's freckles stood out in relief on her paled face. "Ye've stayed in the country too long, not to be warned off baronets. Wouldn't ye be terrified?"

"Depends on the animal. A small fox now, wouldn't bother me overly much. Are there golden ones?"

Katie shook her head in disbelief.

"I'm just curious," continued Felicity. "Aren't you?"

"No, miss."

"Well, I've been told that perhaps I'm too curious about… many things."

"Please be careful, miss," Katie warned as she ushered Felicity out of the room. "Curiosity could get ye into a heap of trouble."

Felicity went downstairs alone because Aunt had one of her headaches again. Uncle Oliver and a smug Cousin Ralph met her at the front door. Both kept giving each other the oddest glances, and when they opened the door they stared at her as if expecting some reaction.

"Oh, Uncle," exclaimed Felicity. "Did you concoct a potion for this?" And she ran down the steps by lantern light, petting the muzzle of the nearest unicorn. "How long will it last?"

Uncle Oliver beamed at his son. "You'll have to ask your cousin. He's responsible for this."

Ralph puffed up, adding nearly an inch to his height.

Felicity turned and stared. Ralph had made such beautiful creatures? She thought he only had the imagination for monsters and gargoyles. "They are stunning, Ralph. How did you manage it?"

"I only changed their horns," he admitted. "The rest is still just illusion."

"But you did it." Felicity felt stunned. Her cousin's triumphs seemed to mirror her failures. "You changed matter. You can apply for the dukedom at the next presentation."

Ralph shrugged, glanced at his father, and climbed into the coach. Felicity didn't understand why he wasn't gloating, as he surely had a right to. It made her heart sink, just a little, that the magic hadn't gone to her. But having someone in the family acquire the title had to be better than it going to some stranger.

So she tried to be happy for him and even shared the same seat in the coach. "Ralph, what's wrong?"

They'd never been close. Most of the time, Felicity considered him an enemy, using his magic against her. But for some reason, he deigned to answer.

"I cannot do it all the time. And until I can, I cannot be sure I will be able to during the testing."

"Oh." Felicity thought that you either had the ability or not. She'd never heard of a nobleman who managed to change something and then be unable to do it at will, except for the rare gift that popped up in commoners. Did her family carry some curse that made their use of magic so erratic? She longed to ask Uncle about it, but wanted the truce between her and Ralph to hold for the evening. He would probably be her only chance at dancing tonight.

Uncle looked splendid in his evening clothes, his mahogany brown hair slicked back with pomade, his white cravat tied at his throat with a pearl-studded stickpin. She wished they were related by blood, not just by marriage, so she could have inherited some of his good looks.

Felicity sighed and watched the gas and fairylights flicker past her window.

Uncle Oliver patted her knee. "You will always have a place with us, you know. You should never worry about that."

"Thank you, Uncle. You are so very kind. But I had a thought."

"Yes?"

"What about marriage?"

Ralph snorted and Uncle frowned. "What about it?"

"Well, I just thought. Well. Now that I've come out, perhaps I could accept a… proposal."

"Why would anyone propose to you?" laughed Ralph.

Felicity tried not to get angry, but felt their brief truce waver. "A man with no title, or no ambition for one, might accept me given the size of my dowry."

The carriage rattled over the cobblestones. Uncle Oliver looked worried. Ralph noticed, and his eyes widened with anticipation.

Felicity's stomach knotted. "Really, Uncle, I don't have to marry a lord, do I? If I married a mere sir, I would still be called lady, and so you wouldn't be ashamed of me, would you?" She thought that might've been the reason for the look on his face. When he continued to stare at her in alarm, she hurried on. "I suppose a peer might consider marriage with me in hopes that our children would inherit my mother and father's power. It's been known to skip a generation, hasn't it?"

"You will never marry," said Uncle Oliver.

"Although, if you don't mind terribly, I'd rather marry into a household that has no magic… I beg your pardon?" Felicity's mind skidded to an abrupt halt as her Uncle's words penetrated her hopeful imaginings.

Uncle leaned forward; she caught a whiff of his cologne and suppressed a sneeze. "I'm sorry, child. I should never have spoken so plainly. The fact of the matter is that you have no dowry."

Felicity blinked. Even Ralph seemed appalled.

"Now that we've lost your parents' holdings, well, there isn't anything left. I can of course provide you with a bit of pin money, and you'll always be welcome to live with us at Fairview Manor. But as you know, that's my one and only holding, and since I don't possess the power to turn rocks into gold—"

"But my parents did," said Felicity, trying to keep the hysteria out of her voice. "Surely, they thought to provide for me beyond the entail."

Uncle Oliver shook his head sadly, and with a huge sigh, settled himself back against the cushions. "I believe your parents died too young to consider your future. So you must not blame them. They would have expected, after all, for you to inherit the power and the holdings."

Felicity's mind kept fluttering in different directions at once. This final blow following the failures she'd already experienced seem to sap her of strength, and any remaining hope of happiness. But blame her parents because they died before their time? No, she would never do that.

Uncle Oliver glanced out the window. "This traffic on Pall Mage is unforgivable. You'd think with the combined magic of the royals, they'd devise a spell for this."

Ralph nodded in exactly the same superior manner as his father.

Felicity stared at the two of them in amazement. Didn't they realize that all her dreams had just ended? Did they think the life of an untitled spinster would make her happy? Oh, why was Aunt Gertrude never around when she needed her?

To Felicity's horror, she felt tears sting her eyes, then overflow to trail down her face. She refused to wipe them away and draw further attention to them.

Uncle pulled a handkerchief from his breast pocket and leaned forward, gently wiping at her cheeks. "You know that magic exacts a price from the user. Why would your parents exhaust themselves in magically providing a dowry for you when the income from the estates is more than you could have spent in a lifetime?"

Why indeed? Felicity knew her Uncle didn't mean to remind her of her failure, or perhaps he just wanted her to realize that she'd brought about all of this herself. She'd failed in acquiring the magic demanded of her station. Another man might have thrown her out on the street.

When their coach finally reached the gates of Buckingham, Felicity had sunk into such a state of despair that she followed her uncle and cousin out of the carriage and along the glowing path with automatic movements. She couldn't appreciate the magical illusions around her with any delight.

The light of the path created multicolored pillars that rose into the night and flickered whenever anyone walked through them. Tiny dragonflies with wings that sparkled like glitter flew around the pillars. Blue light surrounded the doors opening onto the ballroom; a waterfall of color flowed down and parted as each guest entered.

Ralph elbowed her in the ribs, hard enough to make her grunt. "Smile and at least pretend to put on a brave front. Or everyone will pity me for being related to you."

Felicity pasted a smile to her mouth, retained it through the receiving line. But she needn't have bothered, for none of the highnesses gave her a glance. Uncle Oliver left for the gaming room after giving Ralph strict instructions to chaperone her. Ralph deposited her on a velvet-padded bench near the planked wall and mumbled something about getting refreshments.

I have nothing to offer, thought Felicity. Not even good-looking children. How can I force myself to carry on as if my come-out were something to be enjoyed?

She allowed herself to wallow in self-pity for a time. But really, whoever had cast the spells to decorate the ballroom had done a splendid job, and she couldn't stay downcast for very long in such a glorious place. Chandeliers of diamonds hung from stars above her, their light more brilliant than any real night sky, rocketing their natural bursts of color on the dancers below. In the middle of the floor stood the mast of the ship the huge room had been made to resemble. A rigging of gold rope stretched across the space in a spiderlike web to a sail that flapped from a magical breeze, gently cooling the heat of the throng.

For the first time she noticed that all the footmen wore pirate suits, several with eye-patches or parrots perched on their shoulders. Most had a typical servant's masklike expression, but Felicity noticed an amused glimmer in an eye or two.

The wall that Felicity sat next to shuddered, and when she looked over the wooden side, she saw an ocean that rippled with waves of silver foam. Felicity spun back around. Yes, the wooden-planked floor of the room rolled with the motion of the waves. If she'd had the power, she could've resisted the illusion. Instead she found herself getting queasy, so she closed her eyes.

And someone sat in her lap.

"I beg your pardon," stammered the lady. "I didn't see you sitting there."

"It's perfectly all right," began Felicity. "The bench next to me is empty…" Oh, how she would like not to be the only wallflower! Just to have someone else for company would help ease her humiliation.

"Lord Cushing," replied the lady. "Perhaps we might find a bit of privacy in the life boats?"

The gentleman laughed low in his throat, took the lady's arm, and steered her away from the padded benches.

That was the final straw. To be ignored so thoroughly was the cut direct, and Felicity was still, after all, a viscount's niece. She rose, determined right this very minute to track down Uncle or Ralph, and demand that they introduce her to someone suitable for dancing. It didn't matter if he had wrinkles or two left feet or crossed eyes or that he would never consider marrying her. She just wanted to dance in public for the first time in her life. Ralph should not have abandoned her this way!

Felicity wove through the throng, trying to decide which "plank" might actually be an entrance to the gaming rooms, and keeping an eye out for Ralph at every refreshment table she passed.

Some big-footed oaf stepped on the back of Felicity's dress. Her bustle stretched, then sprang back into place. The clod didn't bother to apologize and Felicity began to get very angry.

And a bit terrified.

How could this much jostling be normal for ladies at a ball? Why, they'd be covered with bruises by the end of the evening. But perhaps most balls weren't this crowded, for the presentation ball was the height of the season. When she started to pay attention to the movement of the crowd, she noticed that except for an occasional nudge or two, most people managed to move through the swell with nary a mishap. Perhaps she hadn't quite mastered the trick of it yet.

With renewed determination, Felicity moved forward again. She danced and wove, and twirled around as much as she could. She felt breathless by the time she neared the very prow of the ship.

The orchestra played on an elevated platform, beating on drums that resembled conch shells; blowing on flutes of razor clams and nautilus horns.

Felicity forgot herself for a moment in admiration of the illusion. And then events happened so fast she had but a moment to register them. A large man bore down on her, his legs so long his pace resembled a sprint. He carried a plate piled with lobster, and a glass of red claret. He concentrated on his refreshment and not on his surroundings.

Felicity could see the imminent danger but didn't have time to do anything about it. The man would collide right into her and she would be squashed beneath the tonnage.

A hand grabbed her forearm with superior speed and yanked her out of the way, pulling her up against a massive, warm chest.

"You should be more careful," growled her rescuer.

Four

FELICITY REMEMBERED THAT HUSKY VOICE, THE WAY IT
had made her tremble and how it had silenced a room
full of peers. She looked up into those golden eyes and
stood spellbound by his gaze.

"I—I'm not used to such a press of people," she
stammered.

"Ah, I see," he replied. "Perhaps I can offer my
assistance?"

Felicity mentally slapped herself. She sounded like
a country bumpkin. She must get a grip on the way
this man made her feel. She couldn't do a thing about
the way her body reacted, her racing heart and weak
knees. But she certainly didn't need to lose possession
of her mind. "You're most kind, but I'm perfectly
capable of taking care of myself."

His forehead wrinkled in the most delightful way,
and his eyes, an amber gold by starlight, softened a bit.
And then they widened with alarm. "Careful!"

His arms enfolded her, strong, warm and delicious,
and his shoulder took most of the impact of a matronly
woman's bosom.

"Dear me! I do apologize. I didn't see you standing there," said the woman. Her eyes narrowed from behind small spectacles, then widened with what Felicity thought looked like fear. "Sir Terence, isn't it? P-please forgive me. I… I… umm…"

"Apology accepted," he growled.

The matron picked up her orange skirts and moved faster than Felicity could have imagined. "Do you often have that sort of effect on people?"

His anger faded as he looked at her face, and he grinned. A simple quirk of his lips, but enough to make Felicity melt against him.

"As often as you have people colliding into you. I insist that you allow me to escort you out of this crowd to somewhere you might be safe."

"That would be most kind of you," Felicity replied, proud of herself for sounding so calm. Especially when her heart kept thrumming with excitement, and her body kept pressing against his in the most undignified manner.

Sir Terence stepped back and curved his arm under her elbow, steering her toward the side of the "ship." A footman managed to swing a tray at her head, barely missing her coiffure, but she had the presence of mind to duck.

Sir Terence pressed her closer against his side, much to Felicity's delight, moving as if they were one person. Fortunately, most of the people tended to give Sir Terence a wide birth, so they arrived at his destination without further mishap.

Gold rope had been twisted into piles that spiraled as high as Felicity's chin, just as a true ship would store extra rigging. Behind the mounds sat a collection of wooden boxes stamped with the British seal, and atop those lay satin cushions stuffed as thick as her mattress.

He'd chosen a very secluded spot.

Her body stayed glued to his side even after they sat down. His muscular arm dropped to her waist, and then he did the most astonishing thing.

He moaned, deep in his throat, and rubbed his head so hard against her shoulder that she fell on her side, his chest covering hers. She turned and looked into his eyes again. He looked more surprised than she felt.

Felicity's body sang with the awareness of the heat of his skin, the smell of his earthy cologne. She had the outrageous urge to wrap her arms around him, to feel the muscles of his back and the texture of his coat. Her body tingled with something she couldn't put a name to, and it frightened her.

"I may be a commoner now," she breathed. "But I am not common, sir. I can allow you no liberties of my person."

"Of course not. I assure you I had no intention of taking any."

Still, neither one of them moved for several moments.

He finally sat up and spent several minutes adjusting his white linen cuffs and the sleeves of his dark brown coat. Felicity managed to pat her hair and adjust her bodice. She suddenly felt very shy and a bit alarmed. Katie had seemed so terrified of baronets, and people gave this man too much elbow room, as if to get too close to him would either soil their clothes or stain their souls. What on earth possessed her to be sitting with him in such an intimate place?

Had she sunk so low that she'd welcome the attentions of any man—even one reputed to be half animal?

"What are you?" she blurted.

"I beg your pardon?"

"I mean, what type of were-animal do you become when the moon is full?"

He smiled, revealing those deadly incisors. "That is a myth, Lady Stonehaven. I change at will."

Felicity tried to stop the hammering of her heart by taking several deep breaths. Did fear make her giddy, or did her body only react to his nearness? "I am no longer Lady Stonehaven. Just Miss Seymour."

He kept staring at her, as if she presented a puzzle that he was determined to solve. Felicity stared at his mouth, wondering what it would feel like if he kissed her.

What on earth had come over her?

The music started up again, a lively Strauss polka, and Felicity nervously tapped her feet to the rhythm. "You still haven't answered me. What is your shape, sir?"

"Most women are afraid to ask."

"I am not most women."

He reached up and stroked the back of his index finger across her cheek. "I can see that. Shall I show you, Miss Seymour? Can you promise not to be frightened?"

Really, what could he be? Could he change into a mythical animal? She shuddered at the memory of some of Ralph's more creative illusions. Blast, why hadn't Uncle Oliver taught her more about baronets? That feeling of desolation crept back into her stomach. He probably thought she'd never need the information. Well, the mighty have fallen, and baronets were, by title, a class high above her now.

Felicity's curiosity got the better of her fear. And she noticed that whenever she focused her thoughts on him that desolate feeling would go away. Besides, what better way to learn about baronets than to observe their own magic?

"How can I promise not to be frightened when you have been so determined not to name your shape? But I can promise not to scream. I am quite good at suppressing screams."

His face registered astonishment. And he had such a handsome face. He'd pulled back his long tawny hair with a ribbon, making his high cheekbones even more pronounced, the square of his jaw more prominent. His eyes looked even larger, the brows above them swept up at the sides like the slant of a cat's.

With fluid grace, Sir Terence crouched on the floor, staring up at her with a hint of challenge in his eyes. Felicity gasped at how quickly he changed. Like the coming of windswept fog his edges blurred, a shifting of perception. She'd expected his bones to crack, his face to contort with pain. But as effortlessly as she changed hats, he became his were-animal.

"Oh, my," she breathed.

The look in his eyes changed. It seemed like he begged for her approval. Begged her not to be repulsed.

Felicity reached forward, and did what she hadn't dared to do while he wore his human shape. She ran her gloved hands through that glorious mane of hair. Why would anyone be afraid of him? Although the sheer size of him intimidated, she could feel the gentleness in his were-self.

Sir Terence made the oddest whuffing noise, moaned

in his throat again, and rubbed so hard against her, she went over sideways. Again. "Ah," murmured Felicity. "So that explains why you did that earlier. I must read up on the habits of lions."

She could feel the strength of his muscles beneath the softness of his fur. He smelled like wet grass, rich earth, and young plants—what she could only imagine the land of India would smell like.

"Really, Sir Terence, that's quite enough. You must let me up now."

He sniffed through her hair, making her shiver. He licked her face, his whiskers tickling her into a giggle. But really, she'd been hoping for a kiss, after all, not a lick!

"Sir, although I find you quite a beautiful member of the species, I must insist you change back into your human form. It's not at all proper for me to be sprawled out on the floor at my presentation ball."

He growled; a quick burst of air-cracking sound. Felicity couldn't help jumping. It had to be the most heart-stopping noise she'd ever heard.

He sat back on his haunches and shifted to human, rose to his feet with that feline grace and held out his hand. As if it were the most natural thing in the world.

"What happens to your clothes?" Felicity asked, letting him take her hand. He lifted her with a negligent twitch of his muscles.

"I suppose they shift into my pelt. I've never thought about it before."

Felicity sat on the cushion again, with as much decorum as the situation allowed her. "But haven't you ever shifted when you're naked? What happens then?"

He blinked those golden eyes at her. Then threw back his head and laughed. The man had a voice that could carry for miles, and Felicity hoped no one would investigate the sounds he kept making.

Although they made her shiver with delight.

"You say the most outrageous things," he finally said, flopping on the seat beside her.

"Mmm," she agreed. "You'll have to forgive me, it comes from long habit. My governesses had a tendency to forget my presence. Even my uncle and aunt would occasionally do so. Unless I said something astonishing, I'd be forgotten again. I found that if I spoke my mind, well, it was always astonishing."

Sir Terence smiled at her, incisors showing, golden eyes glowing with warmth. She felt as if she basked in sunshine.

"I hope that we will always speak our minds to one another."

Felicity held her breath. Whatever did he mean? Surely, after tonight, they'd never see each other again.

His face lowered to hers. She'd desperately hoped he'd kiss her, and now that he looked as if he might, she suddenly felt nervous. "You didn't answer my question."

"Ahh," he murmured. She could feel his warm breath against her mouth. "Perhaps my pelt becomes a bit thinner. I will pay attention next time I shift naked." He whispered the last word.

Felicity shivered. He lowered his head even more and she closed her eyes, all her senses focused on her mouth. Her, oh-blast-it, quivering mouth.

His lips touched hers with the softest caress. His mouth felt warm and surprisingly soft. She felt the heat of his hands on her back, the muscles in his shoulders as his arms tightened around her.

Felicity couldn't believe that she allowed a total stranger to kiss her.

And, worse yet, she wanted more.

She opened her mouth a bit, instinctively trying to taste him. He responded with a groan, and pressed harder against her, tilting her head back, his mouth opening and moving back and forth across her own. He nibbled her lips, then sucked at her bottom one, ever so lightly. But it made the place between her legs throb. Startled, Felicity pushed him away.

He stared at her, his mouth slightly open, panting. Her own harsh breathing sounded in her ears.

"Bloody hell," he rasped.

"Quite," agreed Felicity.

"Whatever am I going to do now?"

Felicity put her chin in the air. "You sir, are going to ask me to dance. And when this waltz is over, you shall ask for the next one. And the next."

He nodded. She had the feeling that he felt so dumbfounded, he'd do anything she asked. Well, she was not above taking advantage of his muddled senses. And proud of herself for managing that suggestion when she felt her own wits quite addled as well.

He took her hand, his palm so large she felt like a little girl, and led her onto the dance floor. Sometime during the evening it had started to rain, illusory clouds obscuring the starlight, soft petals of blue falling in drops to splash on her shoulders. It looked so real Felicity felt surprised that she stayed dry.

Sir Terence danced with a grace that had her lifting to

her toes with sheer pleasure. He whirled her around the room, never taking his eyes off her face, as if she were the most beautiful woman in the world and not a plain-faced failure. Twice he twirled her by Ralph, whose shocked expression had her laughing with delight.

Sir Terence looked as if her laughter enchanted him.

The orchestra seemed to reflect her need, never pausing more than a few moments between sets. By the thirteenth dance—she knew, because she'd counted—she decided to take pity on the baronet.

"You needn't dance all night with me," she said. "Truly, I was but jesting."

He frowned, flipping away the strands of hair that had escaped their binding. Without thinking, Felicity reached up and helped brush the tawny fringe back behind his ears. He instantly responded with that incisor-flashing grin.

"Lady, are you enjoying yourself?"

"Oh, immensely!"

He growled, and swept her up in the next dance. The other dancers gave the baronet a wide berth on the floor. Felicity had no fear about someone crashing into her. And she had no fear of being ignored, for he looked at her with such intensity that she felt as if she were the only person in the room.

Sir Terence held her close for a moment, closer than propriety would allow, and whispered in her ear. "There is nowhere I'd rather be, nothing I would rather do than have you in my arms all night long."

Felicity blushed. This golden man lit up her dark despair, and she danced with him proudly, regardless of the other guests' disparaging looks. Prince Albert valued his baronets, and let it be known in subtle ways, so how dare the other peers treat them with such disrespect?

The rain stopped and the clouds cleared, dazzling her eyes with diamond-studded starlight. He set his cheek to hers for a moment and Felicity had the strangest feeling, flutter through her. She'd thought at first—well, as much as she could think, given her body's blatant reaction to him—that he'd meant only to be kind to her. Even after he'd kissed her, she'd thought, deep inside, that he somehow knew how much she'd wanted it, and had done so to make her happy. And when he agreed to dance with her, she felt sure that after a few sets he'd excuse himself.

But he continued to dance, and now he'd made a remark so intimate that it sounded as if he meant to court her.

Felicity stiffened in his arms. It couldn't be that; there had to be another reason for his interest in her. Why would such a beautiful man seriously pursue her, when she didn't even have…

"I have no dowry," she said.

He tilted his head. "I beg your pardon?"

"I said," Felicity repeated, having to shout over the strains of the music, "that I have no dowry."

The orchestra chose that moment to end the song. Her words rang out and she winced. How many times would she humiliate herself in this man's presence?

Those golden eyes glittered. Into the silence he said, "And I have no magic."

As if neither mattered. The music started again, and those who had listened to their exchange stuck their noses in the air and frowned with disdain.

"We are social outcasts."

He nodded. "I have no use for society or its opinions. I never have. Will that bother you?"

"How can it bother me now, Sir Terence?"

"How indeed," he muttered, his lips tightening. Then he shrugged, the shoulder beneath her hand rippling with the movement of his muscles. He spun her once, twice, and then tightened his hold on her. "I wish," he whispered into her ear, "that you would just call me Terence."

Goodness, she blushed again. Felicity couldn't bring herself to even let out a squeak, much less breathe his name without the formal 'sir' in front of it, and fortunately he didn't press the matter.

The song ended, and he bowed to her. Felicity twisted her gloved hands. She couldn't help the instant feeling of dread in the pit of her stomach, no matter what she'd tried to tell herself. Would he turn his head away now, call out to some acquaintance?

"Would you like some refreshment, Miss Seymour?"

She nodded with fatalistic grace. She might as well get it over with. Now he would disappear, just like Ralph. Really, quite a tactful way for him to get rid of her.

Sir Terence curved his large hand beneath her elbow, steering her in the direction of a heavily laden table. "I would rather leave you somewhere to rest while I fetch it for you, but I fear that I wouldn't find you in one piece by the time I returned."

Felicity blinked up at him while her legs moved forward of their own accord. He wouldn't abandon her. He hadn't offered refreshment as a ploy to get away from her. Could it be possible? Did he have intentions toward her?

"There you are," hissed Ralph, grabbing at Felicity's

free arm. "I've been trying to catch you all evening. Can't I leave you alone for a few minutes without you making a spectacle of yourself?"

Sir Terence's golden eyes narrowed.

Ralph yanked on Felicity's arm and made her wince.

Terence took a step forward. "I presume you know this gentleman, Felicity?"

She never thought her name could be spoken in such a way that it made her knees melt. "Sir Terence, may I introduce my cousin, the Honorable Ralph Hugo Wortley? And Cousin, may I introduce—"

"No introduction is necessary," snapped Ralph. "I know an animal when I see one."

"You mewling little pup," growled Sir Terence.

"Ralph, how dare you?" demanded Felicity at the same time.

The look on the baronet's face made her cousin back up a step and whine his next words. "Well, it's true. And our family has a reputation to maintain. Don't you think you've blackened it enough, Felicity?"

She flinched.

Ralph smiled with victory, and his voice assumed its usual arrogance. "Come away with me at once," he commanded.

Felicity loosened her hold on Sir Terence's arm. The baronet looked as if he wanted to tear her cousin apart, and despite the appeal of that idea, she really didn't want to create a scandal.

She started to pull away from Sir Terence when he tore his glittering eyes away from her cousin and caught her up in his gaze. His amber eyes beseeched her not to go, and he grabbed at her hand. He lowered his voice to a mere purr. "I will have an answer from you before I will allow you to go."

Ralph sputtered.

Those eyes glanced away from her for a moment and pierced Ralph. "I will speak privately with your cousin, sir. I can haul her away bodily and allow you to see how much of an animal I really am…" He leaned forward and smiled, revealing his pointed incisors. "Or you can let go of her arm." She noticed the tension in Sir Terence's muscles. He restrained himself to speak civilly to her cousin.

Felicity could see the sweat on Ralph's upper lip. His bravado quickly faded, and she knew that Sir Terence had scared him witless. Her cousin dropped her arm.

Thunder pealed overhead, and lightning crackled. Women squealed with pleasure. Sir Terence guided her toward a stack of sandbags, pressed her back against it, and used the bulk of his body to hide her from her cousin's view. "I would have wished to put this to you with more gallantry, but your cousin has forced me to boldness."

Felicity nodded. It felt exciting, having both his arms pinning her between him and the soft bags. Having his eyes on her, his breath on her face. She tried very hard to comprehend what he said.

"Isn't it true that if you hadn't lost your title, you would never have given a man of my station half a glance?"

She wanted to deny it. Instead, she nodded again.

"Aah, don't look that way. I consider it a fortuitous occurrence, at least for my sake. Because you did allow me to spend the evening with you. You did allow yourself to know me… at least a little?"

Felicity smiled.

He seemed to melt with relief. "Then can you say I have some chance at gaining your affection?"

Felicity closed her eyes. The man had decided to court her, no dowry and all. She still reeled from the final certainty of it.

Her smile faltered. She couldn't deny her attraction to the baronet. And he offered her a chance at a real life.

"Yes," breathed Felicity. "Yes, Sir Terence, you have a chance."

He pushed away from her, and she missed the warmth of his body heat. He picked up her gloved hand and brought it to his lips.

"Call me Terence," he purred. "Just say it once, before I let you go."

"T-Terence."

He smiled in supreme satisfaction and led her back to Ralph, placing her hand in her cousin's. "I will call upon your uncle tomorrow, Miss Seymour." He bowed to her, a graceful movement that belied his size, and vanished into the crowd.

"Let go of me, Ralph."

Her cousin dropped her hand. "You can't do this."

"You should have thought of that before you left me without a chaperone. And I shall tell Uncle the same if you persist in your boorish attitude."

Ralph's lips twisted in the most unbecoming way. "I only sought to protect you. But if that is your choice, Cousin, I leave you to it." He leaned forward and whispered in her ear. "But I fear you may regret it."

Five

TERENCE LEFT THE BALL IN HIS HIRED COACH. HE stopped the driver once they reached Fleet Street, still miles away from his home in Trickside, and paid the man to be on his way. As usual, the horses had been skittish around him, and the driver had to fight the reins the entire trip. Terence would never experience a comfortable carriage ride, but he didn't like carriages anyway.

He would rather use his own four paws to travel.

And right now he needed to run, to feel the strength of his legs and the senses of his were-self. He needed to clear his mind of the image of lavender eyes and full lips that tasted like sweet wine.

Terence shifted, extended his claws and shook his mane. And then he began to run in the shadows, stretching full length, reveling in the feel of the wind through his fur and the spread of his muscles. When the shadows thinned he leaped up fences and lintels and continued his journey across the rooftops. He blessed the London fog that allowed him the freedom of his were-form.

He vaulted over chimneys and across the gaps

between buildings until he thought he'd managed to put the strange girl and the oddness that surrounded her from his mind. He came to a stop and let his tongue loll, catching his breath. But the moment he did, he lost himself in the memory of her scent, the feel of her lips beneath his.

Terence threw back his head and roared, the sound carrying for miles and causing shutters to slam and angry cries to ring out. With a powerful leap he took off again, over the roofs of stores along the main streets of Trickside, across the even shabbier roofs of brownstones within the residential section, until he reached his own residence within Mythical Square.

He opened the trap door expressly installed for this purpose, and dropped into the attic, sneezing at the dust as he shifted again, heading down the stairs and calling for Bentley to draw his bath.

Terence padded along the hallway and glanced at the paintings of his ancestors that lined the walls. He wondered what Lady Stonehaven—no, Miss Seymour—would think of his richly appointed townhouse decorated with treasures from his estate in Trolshire. His home stood in contrast to the neighborhood, which consisted of shabby brownstones occupied mostly by the charlatans who ran the magic shops.

The few shapeshifters that chose a London residence established themselves in Trickside not only for the anonymity it provided but because…

Terence frowned. Because no matter how much Prince Albert championed the shapeshifters, the gentry didn't want them as neighbors.

But the interior of his home would rival anything

that Miss Seymour would be accustomed to, and he grinned as he imagined the surprise on her face when she saw his bedroom.

He opened, and then slammed the bedroom door behind him. Why couldn't he stop thinking about the chit? Why would he even imagine her in his home?

He ripped off his cravat, shrugged off his coat, and untied his bound hair, shaking it loose, feeling his scalp tingle and sighing with the pleasure of it. Bentley, of course, had already anticipated his needs, and a partially full bath steamed in front of the fireplace. He finished undressing and lowered himself into the hot water, sighing again as his taut muscles relaxed.

He closed his eyes, and visions of midnight black hair and skin the color of new snow still filled his imagination. Strange, how the girl affected him.

Bentley came into the room, and Terence nodded his head for his manservant to pour freshly heated water into the bath.

He sputtered as Bentley dumped it over his head. "What was that for?"

Bentley twitched a shrug. "I dunno. Just looked like you needed it."

Again, Bentley had anticipated him. They'd fought through several wars together, battled demons and monsters in search of the lost relics, so Terence didn't feel too surprised. There were times when he felt that Bentley had managed to replace his brother in his family pride.

Terence stiffened. Bloody hell, no one could replace Thomas. He mentally scourged himself for having the thought. And Bentley—even though more friend than servant—wasn't a lion, so could never be a part of his pride. There would always be an empty place left by Thomas that could never be filled.

"I'm in trouble, Bentley."

The smaller man nodded and sat on a nearby stool.

Terence studied his manservant's face as he rose from the bath and slipped into a dressing robe. He could sometimes figure out what his master felt before Terence could himself. But for the first time since he could remember, he didn't want to tell Bentley everything. So he just settled for what the other man needed to know.

"I have a lead on a relic."

"I thought so." Bentley's nose twitched, the overly long whiskers of his mustache quivering with the movement. "I suppose you're sure about it?"

Terence narrowed his eyes.

"All right, I know you've got the nose for sniffing them out." He skittered about the room, picking up Terence's scattered clothes.

Terence grinned, grabbed up a brush and began to tug it through his thick mane of hair.

Bentley answered a knock at the door, took a silver tray from the maid and set it on the table. Terence hadn't realized he felt hungry, but obviously Bentley had.

Cheese, apples, and a plate of rare, bloody meat. Terence sat down and dug in, motioned Bentley to join him. Of course, he knew the other man would sit still for only a short time. It's why he'd given Bentley the job of manservant and the running of his household. The man had enough twitchy energy for two people, and always needed to be doing something.

Not for the first time, Terence felt grateful to be a were-lion and not some other animal.

Bentley rose and poured two glasses of brandy. Terence sipped at his, but Bentley swigged it, sat down, and sighed. The alcohol allowed him to rest a moment, and he picked up a piece of cheese and began to nibble. "I suppose," he managed to say between bites, "that you'll give me all the details when you're good and ready."

Terence smiled. "I'm going courting."

Bentley's beady black eyes widened, and his overly large ears twitched as he leaned forward in excitement. "May I inquire as to the identity of the lucky lady?"

"Miss Felicity May Seymour, formerly Duchess-of-Honor Stonehaven."

"I heard something about that... some girl who inherited absolutely none of her parents' power. Unusual, that."

Terence leaned back in his chair, watched the fire dancing in the hearth. "That's the least of it. The girl is full of contradictions. She has a 'don't notice me' spell cast on her that's so old, even I had difficulty detecting it. She's the most beautiful woman I've ever seen, and yet she appears to have no idea of her appeal. Quite refreshing, actually."

"I can see how that would be."

Something in the droll way Bentley said that made Terence shoot a sharp glance at his friend. "That spell was put on her using relic-magic. For all I know, she did it herself. Old it may be, but I can still sniff out the evil of it."

Bentley's nose twitched with doubt. Although accustomed to his friend's mannerisms, Terence started to get annoyed.

"That's why I'm courting her. To get close enough to her and her family to discover the truth, and hopefully the relic itself."

"Of course, sir," replied Bentley. "I'm sure if there was any other way to find the relic, you would have thought of it. After all, toying with some poor girl's emotions, using her without her knowledge, and ultimately dumping her after you've gotten what you want, well...I'm sure you only resorted to that decision after you'd exhausted all other plans."

Terence slammed his brandy glass down on the table. The sound of shattering crystal and the pain of gouged skin astonished him. He stared at the drops of blood that dripped from his closed fist onto the linen tablecloth.

"Bloody hell. That was an overreaction."

Bentley had already fetched him a bowl of clean water, and eased Terence's injured hand into it. "Interesting, though," he muttered. Bentley's head twitched back and forth while his sharp black eyes surveyed the damage. With quick movements, he used his nails to pull out a few shards, poured a bit of brandy over Terence's palm, and wrapped it with a napkin.

Terence frowned. "I have no intention of hurting the girl—if she's innocent of any wrong-doing."

"Of course not."

"Although I admit it might've been an impulsive plan, and I should've thought it through more thoroughly."

"But you have no intention of altering it."

Terence snatched his bandaged hand out of Bentley's. Sometimes the man overstepped himself. "Why the bloody hell should I?"

"Why, indeed."

Terence growled, a sound that struck fear in any human within hearing distance, but Bentley knew him too well, and other than twitching a bit more, regarded his employer with calm detachment.

"You think I'm attracted to her, don't you? You think her beauty so entranced me that I'm not thinking clearly? That my search for the relics could actually be overshadowed by a mere woman?" Terence panted, he'd spoken so quickly. He shook his thick head of hair and rose, pacing the room, Bentley's twitching eyes following his progress back and forth.

"She's just a puzzle, that's all. And I admit that she intrigues me. But how could you possibly think I'd be seriously pursuing a woman who is tainted with relic-magic? The same magic that killed my brother?"

"I said nothing of the sort."

"But that's what you're thinking. I know you, Bentley. The way you weasel things out of me, the way you manage to make me say what I'm thinking before I even know it myself."

"But she might be innocent," replied his friend. "If she's a pawn and you misuse her, you'll feel like a cad. Might even marry her just out of guilt."

"Perish the thought! I trusted a woman once and paid for it with my brother's life. I won't make that same mistake again. Besides, you act as if I plan to make her fall in love with me, as if a girl like her could seriously fall for a man—an animal like me. We stick to our own kind, you know that, Bentley."

"She just might be desperate enough to have you."

"She wouldn't have given me a second glance if she hadn't lost everything. She admitted as much. She would've treated me with the same disdain that the rest of her kind do. Why should I feel guilty about injuring the vanity of some shallow girl who places titles and power above men's souls?" Terence flung back the hair that had fallen into his face with an angry snap of his head. "Besides, only the relic can remove the spell from her. If we find it, and if the girl is innocent, we'll find someone who can use the magic in the relic to remove it. With her beauty revealed, she'll have no trouble receiving dozens of offers for marriage, dowry or no. Then she'll be the one to beg off because why would she want me then?"

"Why indeed? But wouldn't it be easier all around if we just searched her home this evening? Before you start courting the girl, shouldn't we discover if she can indeed lead us to a lost relic?"

Terence hated when his friend was right. But he had to agree. A search of her home would be wise, although he knew finding the relic wouldn't be that easy. It never was. But he felt sure of the taint on the girl, and no matter what Bentley said, every lead on one of the elusive relics had to be followed.

And bloody hell, the girl's circumstances intrigued him. As did her beauty, genuine modesty, and the way she'd accepted his were-form without fear. And the outrageous questions she'd asked...

Terence dropped his robe and shifted, then spun in a circle for a few moments, examining his pelt.

Bentley stared at his friend in amazement. "If we have to shift back to human sometime this evening, it might be deuced awkward for you to be naked."

Terence shifted back. "I was just—oh, never mind."

He didn't want to tell Bentley that Felicity had made him curious. He smiled at the thought of being able to tell her that shifting naked had no effect on the thickness of his pelt whatsoever.

Terence pulled on black trousers and a black shirt, shrugging into a coat of the same hue. He tied the black neck cloth in a flawless knot, in case they had to appear in public, but most of the outfit had been designed to fade into the shadows.

Terence met his friend at the attic roof door. Bentley wore clothing similar to his, except of lesser quality, and minus the gentleman's cravat. With Bentley's darker hair and skin, the man appeared almost invisible in the gloom.

"You wouldn't happen to know where the Stonehaven residence is located," said Terence. It hadn't been a question. He didn't involve Bentley in his activities for nothing.

The smaller man didn't flick an eye. "Mayfairy. Number three, Gargoyle Square."

Terence shifted and knew Bentley had as well when he felt the were-rat scramble up his fur and burrow in his mane. Terence leapt across the rooftops again, covering familiar ground in a hurry, aware of the coming dawn. Ordinarily, he would've kept to the roofs, skirting around the squares, but when he came to buildings low enough to leap from, he cut through the parks.

By the time he'd reached Pall Mage he'd given up on rooftops, the mansions too high to leap easily from, and managed to keep to the shadows through the streets of Pegasus and up through Park Lane.

Of course they weren't seen. They'd been spies for almost ten years.

Terence prowled around the mansion, impatient to get inside, and when he caught her scent he realized that he was excited to see the Seymour girl.

He'd only left her a few hours ago.

Bentley scrambled off his back and like any enter-prising rat, managed to find an entrance into the kitchens. Terence waited at the servants' door for the sound of the bolt sliding open. He shifted to human form, while Bentley shifted back to his were-self. Years of practice had shown that they both skulked better that way.

On soundless feet, Terence prowled through the mansion, Bentley ranging ahead, both of them sniffing for the telltale reek of relic-magic. Not a hint.

Terence had just followed Bentley up a stairway when he heard a woman suddenly scream. Just as abruptly the scream was silenced, and Terence caught a strong whiff of relic-magic. He shifted into his were-self and followed the smell with a speed his human body could never attain.

He burst through a bedroom door. Only the embers of the fireplace lit the room, but Terence didn't need much light in his animal form. Neither did the girl on the bed, whose eyes were wide with terror, whose black hair made her skin pale as moonlight, whose face, even when contorted with fear, was the most beautiful he'd ever seen.

Terence said her name. It issued from his lion throat as a soft growl. Felicity turned and looked at him, and he thought the sight of him would feed her terror—a reaction he would expect from any other woman when confronted by a beastly lion that had burst through her bedroom door. But surprisingly, some of the terror left her face, and she lifted a hand as if beseeching him to come to her.

He couldn't move. Something twisted inside him at her gesture, something he didn't feel ready to acknowledge yet.

The stink of relic-magic hit him in a fresh wave. It emanated from her, and Terence growled again.

Then something dark, shapeless and huge detached itself from a corner of the room and approached the Seymour girl's bed. She cringed, pulling up the covers, whimpering softly in her throat.

Terence couldn't tell if the stink came from her or the dark thing that moved toward the bed. But if the girl used relic-magic, why would she try to harm herself? Or could it be just a side effect from her use of the relic? He only knew one thing for sure: The blackness was real, not an illusion, and the hurt it could cause would be permanent.

Terence leaped forward, putting himself between the girl and the thing that threatened her.

He'd dealt with enough demons and monsters to know it was neither. It looked like the thing he saw out of the corner of his eye at night, that made his heart jump until he realized it was only the flap of a curtain or the shape of a chair made unfamiliar by darkness.

His immunity to magic protected him, but not Felicity. The blackness could smother her to death, and Terence would not allow that to happen.

The fur on his back rose in a ridge. Restraining a roar

that would wake everyone within miles, he settled for a low growl full of menace, his lips pulled back to reveal his fangs, his claws extended to lethal points. Terence looked straight into the blackness without fear.

The shape swayed, trying to stay out of his direct line of sight. Trying to make him afraid to move and unaware that Terence had the immunity to overcome it.

Terence pounced, snarling and slashing, surrounded by the stuff that had sought to terrify him senseless. It burned like hot coals; he heard the crackle and smelled the acrid odor of his singed fur. It shouldn't have been able to harm him, and for a moment he felt confused; until he realized that the blackness had mingled real flames from the fireplace into its essence.

Rage washed through Terence, and he slashed at the being with renewed purpose. The thing continued to separate from itself as his claws raked through it, until the flames of fire had been snuffed like a pinched candle, until the blackness had thinned to mist and dissolved back into the dark corners of the room. Corners that now held no fear.

He shuddered, let out a *huh* of satisfaction, then sat back on his haunches and began to lick the blistered pads of his paws.

"Thank you."

Terence looked at the girl. She remained upright, watching him, but he had the impression she still slept, so caught up in her dream that her body just acted along with it. She held out her arms, like a child seeking a father's comfort, and he approached the bed when he knew he shouldn't. When a touch from him could startle her truly awake. But he found himself with little choice in the matter, his lion-self unable to resist that blatant invitation.

She threw her arms around him, burying her face in his fur. She smelled like lavender, reminding him of the color of her eyes; and when he licked her shoulder, she tasted like sweet cream. For the first time in his life, he shifted back to human without any conscious volition of his own, his licks turning into small kisses, along her ear, across her cheek.

Her fingers stayed buried in his hair and she turned his mouth to her own. He felt completely lost, then, in the pleasure of her lips, and pressed for more, using his tongue to open her wider, his arms enfolding the warm softness of her body. She slowly lay back on her pillow by the pressure of his kiss, her hands moving to his shoulders, curving around his back, surprising him with their strength.

She held him as if she never wanted to let him go.

Terence growled low in his throat, that strange feeling blossoming in his belly again, a melting and swirling that he couldn't put name to—could only react to. Between one kiss and the next he had his body stretched alongside hers, the heat of her making him hard, until his hips moved with the rhythm, pushing against her thigh.

Her body molded to his perfectly. His shaft jumped in reaction, pulsed with anticipation. She felt so right, as if he'd been waiting his entire life for this woman, and hadn't even realized it.

Something squeaked. Terence ignored it, a minor distraction when his senses were overwhelmed with the feel of this girl in his arms. But when he felt a sharp bite on his leg, hard enough to draw blood, he sat up and stared at the furry form of his friend.

Beady black eyes glared balefully back at him. The whiskered nose twitched with disdain and Terence blinked, as if coming out of a dream.

The girl's arms had dropped when he rose. Her eyes had closed and her breathing had slowed. Her lips were swollen, and curved in a tiny smile.

He forced his own grin off his face. What had come over him? He could usually fight off the animal side of his nature, the side that still lay within him even in human form. Of course, his lion-self had never reacted like this toward any other woman. It kept screaming "mate" to him. But he still should have been able to keep it at bay.

That thing that had attacked her had been no mere illusion, and the need to protect her overwhelmed him. What if it came back? But he couldn't wake the girl and warn her. He couldn't be sure of her innocence, nor could he reveal his secrets. He'd have to think of some way to protect her and some way to keep her at a distance. Difficult, when he started courting her, but necessary. He wouldn't risk a relic-mission just because he couldn't control a physical reaction to the girl.

Bentley squeaked again, and Terence slid to the floor and shifted. The rat scrambled up and burrowed in his mane, and Terence went out the open window, grateful that the decorative ledges were wide enough to allow him to leap up to the roof. Safer up here, in case someone had been roused and searched the grounds.

He leaped homeward again, and realized that for the second time tonight, he fought memories of creamy skin and midnight black hair and soft kisses.

Six

FELICITY WOKE TO AN UNUSUALLY CLEAR MORNING. The sun cast the shadow of her billowing curtains on the wall, and she watched the play of light while she tried to sort out her emotions.

Misery hit her first, the realization that she'd lost everything. Still, she felt a trickle of relief that she wouldn't have to worry about her lack of magic anymore. And then a tiny ray of hope when she remembered the ball and Sir Terence's proposal to court her. But would he really come to call on her today? What gentleman would want a wife with no magic and no dowry?

Felicity rubbed her fingers over sleepy eyes. "Let's hope he isn't a gentleman," she murmured aloud, and then sighed. The man had proven to be much more of a gentleman than her cousin, animal or no.

She trembled when she thought of his were-form. A lion, she should've guessed it, with his amber eyes and golden hair, the way he moved with such predatory grace. She got up to splash cold water on her face. Really though, he hadn't scared her too much when he'd shifted at the ball. Only when he'd attacked the blackness, and she'd seen the glint of his razor-sharp claws…

Felicity froze, blinking water from her eyes as she stared at her reflection in the mirror over her wash-bowl. Surely, that had been a dream.

But it had seemed so real.

Felicity spun, searched the room, looking for any evidence of last night's struggle. Her carpets lay smoothly on the floor; nothing looked different. She flopped on the bed with a grunt. Of course it had only been a dream.

The sun angled across her bed, and a glitter of gold caught her eye. With shaking fingers, she picked up two strands of shiny hair. No, not hair. Fur. She remembered… her face turned red as she remembered the feel of his mouth on hers. No one had ever kissed her like that before, and she was a bit embarrassed at the thought. But it had felt delicious, and her entire body tightened and tingled with a feeling she'd never imagined.

Felicity wished it hadn't been a dream. She wanted to explore these strange yearnings he aroused in her. She didn't know that a kiss could make her forget everything but the feeling of those warm lips. That it could make her body tremble and her heart race. She sighed at the memory of the strength of his arms around her, the heat in his fingers as he explored her skin, sending tingles of pleasure wherever he touched.

Felicity swallowed and forced her heart back out of her throat. But it had only been a dream. She'd prob-ably picked up his fur when he'd rubbed up against her at the ball. Sir Terence couldn't have been in her room last night.

But when Felicity went down to break her fast, she still hadn't completely convinced herself. She brushed her lips with her fingers, and it appeared that her mouth could remember what her mind could not. The heat of his tongue licking, stroking...

Felicity blinked with surprise at her cousin and tried to control the heat of her cheeks as she sat at table opposite him.

"What's wrong with you?" said Ralph. "Your face is all red and you've got dark circles under your eyes."

She shrugged and reached for a platter of bacon. "I had a bad dream last night," she said accusingly.

Ralph gave her a yellow grin, the yolk of the egg he ate plastered to his front teeth. "You know I'll deny to Father that I sent you any illusions. If you have bad dreams, it's entirely the fault of your own twisted imagination."

The serving maid poured milk into Ralph's glass, but forgot Felicity's. Uncle entered the room, frowned at the oversight, and gently chided the girl, who quickly filled Felicity's glass with a murmur of apology.

Felicity shrugged again. She'd become accustomed to being overlooked of course, but now she realized it would continue to get worse. Not only her plain appearance—but her lack of title—would result in a lifetime of anonymity.

Uncle took his seat at the head of the table and smiled at her. Felicity hated to break his amiable mood by mentioning that a certain baronet might be calling on him today. Besides, Sir Terence would probably change his mind after thinking over his rash proposal in the light of day. It had only been a dream last night…

"Uncle, how are the wards this morning?"

His brows rose in surprise. He could be quite vain of the strength of his wards. "Not a whisper of disturbance, naturally."

Felicity stared at Ralph. "And the ones around my room?"

Uncle Oliver sipped at his tea and sighed. "Tight as a fiddle's strings."

"Are you sure, Uncle?"

"Quite sure, my dear," he glanced up and his eyes followed her gaze. "Not again? Felicity, I assure you that Ralph's magic cannot get through those wards without me knowing. No one's magic can get through those wards except a royal's."

He reached over and put his warm hand over her icy one. "I thought at first that you were conjuring the illusions yourself, but after the testing…" He gave her hand a little pat. "Well, we must assume you have vivid dreams, mustn't we?"

Ralph wiggled his eyebrows. Uncle had surrounded the house with enough charms and potions to deter anyone but a royal. He felt so proud of his wards that even if Ralph could get through them, he might not admit it. And Ralph's magic got stronger every day.

"What about baronets, Uncle?"

"Who, what?" The paper folded over and his icy gray eyes looked over the top of it.

"Baronets, Uncle. Shapeshifters. Can they get through your wards?"

"Certainly. There's nothing you can do magically to keep out a shapeshifter. Not even my wards can detect a creature that's immune to magic itself."

Felicity played with the scrambled eggs on her plate, her eyes downcast. "So, if one managed to creep into the house, you wouldn't know?"

Uncle Oliver set down his paper. "My dear, there are locks and watchmen to keep them out. They are as mundanely vulnerable as either you or I."

Felicity felt weak with relief... and disappointment. It had only been a dream, after all.

"Planning on sneaking one in?" asked Ralph.

Felicity ignored him.

Uncle didn't. "Now what in the world does that mean, Ralph?"

Ralph stood in a hurry, throwing his napkin on his empty plate. "Absolutely nothing, Father. If you'll excuse me, I'm late for an appointment with some friends."

"Don't be home late," urged Uncle Oliver. "I've purchased an old manuscript of magical codes that I think you'll be interested in deciphering."

Ralph nodded and fled.

Felicity glared at the coward's back. She'd never have met Sir Terence if it weren't for Ralph abandoning her at the ball, and he didn't want Uncle to find out. But she had no intention of announcing that Sir Terence might call. After all, what if he never came? She couldn't stand the thought of any further humiliation.

"I'm off myself," said her uncle. "Your aunt had a terrible head pain and didn't sleep most of the night. You might follow her example and take a rest. You look a trifle pale."

Felicity could only nod dejectedly.

And she tried to rest, but every time the door's bell rang, her heart leaped with anticipation. When it turned out to be either a friend of Ralph's or Uncle's, her stomach plummeted and she'd punch her pillow and roll over and try to sleep again.

After the third caller, she gave up, and Katie, sensing her mistress's mood, laced her in her cheeriest day dress, a lovely concoction of blue-gray with gathered blue roses about the neckline and hem.

Perhaps a walk in the park would cheer her up. But she knew that because of her new status, she'd receive more cuts direct than usual, and she didn't quite have the energy to face that yet.

She wandered into the parlor, a room she usually loved. It must have taken a lot of her mother's magical energy to decorate it. The entire parlor had been done in deep colors of blue and green and gold. The settee and chairs had all been molded into feather shapes, with velvet coverings printed with the likeness of the eye of a peacock feather. Gold vases supported clusters of the huge feathers throughout the room, so that wherever one sat or stood, the tips of them brushed softly atop one's head.

Even the curtains had been changed to the exact semblance of the cascading feathers of a closed peacock's tail. Felicity sighed as she parted them to stare out the window at the people walking by. She'd always concentrated on her magical studies, trying to gather those tiny sparks she felt sure existed inside.

Since her feelings always got hurt when the few friends she'd manage to make quickly forgot her, she'd quit trying. But now she regretted that, and wondered if she'd made friends, would they spurn her now?

Tears gathered in her eyes and blurred the pattern of the feathers. Really, she would have to stop feeling sorry for herself. So her future no longer consisted of marrying and having babies and producing an heir. So she didn't have any magic. There had to be other options.

And as soon as she quit weeping, she'd try to figure out what they were.

Felicity had been so sunk into despondency that when Wimpole entered the parlor and announced a visitor she couldn't reply. She just stood and stared at the butler, cheeks still wet from her tears, and hiccupped. Could it be possible that Sir Terence had come after all?

"Who is it?" asked Felicity.

Wimpole cleared his throat, glancing around the room. "A Sir Terence Blackwell, miss."

Felicity groped for support, clutching the back of a feather-chair. Her thoughts whirled, and she stared at Wimpole in silence.

He'd come… but why? She couldn't imagine a practical reason for Sir Terence to pursue her. Perhaps the baronet hoped she'd give him children with the power her parents had possessed. But surely he wouldn't gamble his future on such a slim chance? And what of her uncle? What if he shared the same feelings for shapeshifters that Ralph did? How would she ever manage to get him to accept the union?

Wimpole's upper lip started to sweat.

"I suppose—" Felicity swallowed. "I suppose you'd

best show him in. Oh, and don't bring Katie. Get one of the downstairs maids to chaperone."

Wimpole's relief at finally receiving a command cracked his usual rigid demeanor, and he surprised her with a watery smile. Felicity felt guilty that her babbling mind had caused him such anguish.

"Wimpole, have the maid bring tea. And thank you."

Wimpole nodded, his dignified bearing restored and his lapse in decorum forgotten.

Sir Terence entered the room a few moments before the maid. He looked more amazing than she remembered, with his tawny mane of hair loose around his face, those eyes of honey-gold catching her gaze with a force that wouldn't allow her to look away.

He strode across the room, took her hand in his and raised it to his lips. "Miss Seymour, what a pleasure to see you again."

His warm lips sent a tingle up her arm, a flash of memory recalling the feel of them over her own mouth. Felicity snatched her hand away. "How dare you make me wait all day."

He blinked, his face registering surprise at her tone. "I had matters to attend to before I felt free to speak with your uncle."

Felicity hadn't really thought she'd be standing here facing the charisma of his gaze. And now that he had come, she didn't know how to react.

The look in his eyes made her feel as if she'd betrayed him. He'd obviously thought to take advantage of their few moments alone in a different manner. A more congenial manner. Perhaps he'd even intended to kiss her.

Felicity stepped forward, lifted her mouth to his ear. He froze when her breath touched him. "I'm sorry. I didn't mean to snap at you. You see, I'm rather out of sorts today—"

The downstairs maid entered the room with a rattle of china and a clearing of her throat. Anna had suffered as chaperone on only a few occasions, and always made it obvious that she preferred dusting the bric-a-brac over making the aristocracy appear acceptable. Felicity jumped away from the baronet.

His voice lowered to a soft growl. "Forgive me, if my tardiness caused you any concern."

Felicity's insides shivered at the deep tone of his voice.

Anna's large bosom heaved with her sigh. "Shall I pour, miss?"

"What? Oh, yes. Sir Terence, please take a seat."

The man strode over to the smallest settee, and when she sat a proper distance next to him, he scowled and closed the gap. With the oddest little noise low in his throat, he leaned against her. Goodness, didn't he realize that the servants would talk? Felicity tried to scoot away, but the curved feather-shape of the settee had her trapped in place.

She should never have whispered that apology to him in such an intimate manner. He smiled down at her now with a confidence that bordered on proprietary arrogance. Could he sense her discomfort? If he did, it only served to amuse him.

Felicity had to admit that it felt truly wonderful, the hard heat of his shoulder pressed against hers. When Anna gave her a cup of tea, Felicity balanced the saucer on her knee and managed to partake of it as usual—as if it were an everyday occurrence to be snuggled up to a man while she did so.

The baronet ignored his offered cup and just scowled at Anna, who scuttled into a corner beneath a heavy canopy of feathers. She sniffed in her most offended manner.

"Servants will gossip," murmured Felicity, hoping he would at least acknowledge that he sat entirely too close to her.

"Then you should fire them," he replied.

Anna's eyes widened, and she suddenly pretended great interest in a speck of imaginary dirt on her sleeve.

Felicity giggled, then quickly sobered. This man could easily make her forget her entire upbringing. She'd lost the title of lady—but hopefully not the meaning.

"I've told you I care for no one's opinion but my own," he said.

"Yes, you did. But what of mine?"

He frowned, and she noticed it only made him more handsome.

"I have lost everything, sir. Would you have me give up my reputation as well?"

"Of course not."

"Then will you sit a proper distance away from me?"

He looked down in apparent astonishment, his glance moving from her squished skirts, to the empty space on the other side of him. He slowly pulled away from her, his trousers making a soft swishing sound against the velvet of the furniture, and shook his head. "I'm usually in control of my animal impulses. It seems that is not the case when I'm around you."

"Oh." Goodness, what could she say to that? She

didn't know what to think of him, of his courtship, of the entire topsy-turvy drama that had become her life. "Are you saying that my presence brings out the animal in you?"

His brows lifted in complete astonishment, and then he leaned back his head and roared with laughter. "You are refreshing," he finally managed to say. "I'll give you that."

Felicity frowned. It would be wonderful to sit here and flirt with him all day—it was such a delightfully novel situation for her. If she still had her title, a dowry, or even a beautiful face, she might even have been able to enjoy it. But too many doubts crept into her mind. She just had to figure out his reasons for courting her; otherwise, how could she trust her future to him?

"Why did you come?"

He stiffened. "What do you mean? I thought I made myself perfectly clear."

"In a muddy sort of way. You see, I'm rather of a practical nature, and for the life of me, I can't figure out what you have to gain by courting me."

"You have a suspicious nature, Miss Seymour. Why? Don't you believe in love at first sight? Can't you imagine that we are just two ordinary people with nothing to gain or lose, other than our love for each other?"

"Love? How can you even speak of such a thing? We barely know each other."

"I feel like I've known you forever."

Felicity sipped her lukewarm tea. Really, that's exactly how she felt... but she hadn't realized he'd felt the same way. Before she could comment, he rushed on.

"Wars have been fought over the love of two people who barely knew each other. There are things, Miss Seymour, that transcend rational explanation. Magic being one of them; love the other. Would you deny either?"

"Of course not."

His lips curled. "Don't you understand that by marrying me you take more of a risk than I? That you will be more ostracized by society than the loss of your title could ever have done?"

His head had crept closer to her, until his mouth was inches from her own. She could no more have pulled away from him than she could have cut out her own heart. She didn't know about love, not the kind between a man and woman, but now she knew about attraction.

Felicity stared at the promise of his lips, and her mind turned into mush. "It's just... everything has just changed so suddenly."

His mouth softened, and his eyes looked at her so tenderly she thought she might faint.

"How do I convince you? How do I make you realize you are the most beautiful woman who ever walked the earth? Shall I slay a dragon for you? Will that prove my intentions?"

He surprised a giggle from her. She wished he wouldn't make her do that, especially when she needed to be serious. "There's no such thing as dragons."

"Not since they've been outlawed, no."

Felicity could hear Anna choke from her corner. She lowered her voice. She'd been in love with the myth of dragons since she'd been a little girl, so she couldn't resist asking. "Are you saying dragons were once real?"

"Of course, but their huge appetites would make them far too dangerous to continue to create, even if we still had the knowledge to do so. Even now, many people don't believe they ever existed. But there is, however, something that might prove it to you."

Felicity tried to keep the excitement out of her voice. "What?"

Sir Terence pulled a rather large box from his pocket. It stuck at the corners of the fabric of his coat, but he finally managed to loose it and offered it to her.

"A gift, Miss Seymour. Perhaps it will suffice to prove my intentions toward you."

Her hands trembled as she placed her saucer and cup on the tea table and took the box from him. What could he have brought her, when he'd only known her for such a short time? A gift usually required some knowledge of the recipient.

Felicity sensed Anna snapping upright, leaning forward and squinting her old eyes to see what lay in the box as her mistress opened it. Felicity ignored the maid's presence as she stared at the shiny, round object on its bed of clean sand.

"What is it?" she whispered.

Sir Terence seemed in awe of his gift as well because his voice lowered to a whisper that matched hers. "It's a dragonette. A magical copy, if you will, of their larger dragon cousins."

Felicity stroked the smooth surface of the shell. "I've never heard of such a thing."

"You've lived in the country too long. Although they're very rare, you'll find that several members of the upper aristocracy have one. If you look closely at what might appear to be a particularly thick cravat, or a heavy neck scarf, you might notice it moving now and then."

"Is it a pet, then?"

The baronet shook his head, his heavy mane falling into his eyes. "Much more than that. It will protect you, you see. When I'm not around to do so."

Felicity sucked in a breath, turned her startled eyes to his. "Why would you think I need protection?"

He shrugged, but didn't break his gaze, and his eyes said more than his words. "It chases away dreams, Miss Seymour. Surely you have bad dreams once in a while?"

She couldn't breathe. Had he truly been in her room last night? Would he tell her if she asked? Or would he think her slightly mad?

"Just dreams, then?"

He leaned forward and brushed the back of his hand across her cheek. "More than dreams, if need be. He'll be a very powerful little fellow."

"Perhaps it's a girl."

Terence chuckled. "Whatever you wish. A drag-onette can only be created by a special magical license and both males and females are sterile, so that their numbers stay controlled. I should warn you, they'll eat as much as three servants. But they're worth more than a dozen."

"I can't accept this." She closed the lid of the box. "It is obviously very valuable, and I can give you nothing in return. Not even a dowry."

"You can give me yourself."

She couldn't breathe again. He was either taking her breath away or making her giggle like a schoolgirl. And he'd managed to make her believe him. For some inexplicable, extraordinary reason, the man had fallen in love with her at the ball. Why else gift her with something so valuable? She felt a bit like Cinderella.

"You can have me without the offer of gifts." She placed the box back in his hands.

He placed it back in her lap. "Then take it for the pleasure it brings me to see your face light up."

Felicity just couldn't bring herself to let go of the box again. Oh, she shouldn't accept it. But she'd always dreamed of dragons, no matter that her uncle had said they were myths. To have one of her very own, even if it wasn't a real one...

"What will it look like? What shall I feed it? When will it hatch, and will it breathe fire?"

He smiled, the tips of his incisors showing, and appeared very satisfied with himself. "It will look like a scaly worm with wings, with a very large mouth and an impressive set of teeth. No, it won't be able to fly. The creator of the spell wanted dragonettes to have prettier wings even if they weren't functional. But it will be able to breathe fire. And you shall feed it lots of meat."

Now that she had decided to accept the gift she didn't bother to contain her excitement. "What color will it be? And you didn't tell me when it will hatch."

His eyes sparkled, as if he fed on her excitement. "Do you know how beautiful you look when you smile like that?"

"If you keep up the compliments, I might just start believing in them," she admonished him.

"If people could only see you the way that I do…" He shook his head. "You won't know what color the dragonette is until it's hatched, and if you keep the egg warm, it will hatch even earlier. The best place is in the ashes of your fire."

Felicity rose and carefully took the egg from its box and placed it in the fireplace, far from the blaze kept burning there, and snuggled it in a nest of ashes. She stared at the shell, waiting to detect the first hint of a crack.

Sir Terence stood behind her. She hadn't heard him move, but she could feel his body heat. He placed one hand on her shoulder and nuzzled her hair, breathing in as if he wanted to fill his lungs with her scent. When he spoke, his voice sounded as dreamy as she suddenly felt.

"It's like a watched pot, Felicity. It won't boil until you look away."

She trembled from the intimacy of her first name on his lips, and steadied herself. "It shall," she insisted. "For I will stare at it until it hatches. I shall be the first person she sees when she enters the world."

He spun her around. "I can almost believe you're entirely innocent…"

His mouth lay next to her cheek. It only took the slightest turn of her head for their lips to meet. She wondered what he thought her innocent of, because she certainly didn't feel innocent when she kissed him back. She felt as experienced as if she'd done it before. And she had… in her dreams.

All Felicity's thoughts faded away as she ignored the protests of Anna and let him drink from her lips as much as he wanted. All her thoughts were focused on the wonder that he truly wanted her. He had given her a living, breathing dragonette, for mercy's sake, just to prove it to her. Felicity couldn't deny him anything.

As his tongue flicked across her own, she realized that she didn't want to deny him anything. Really, they'd better have a short courtship. They were known to happen, among the aristocracy, with an announcement of an heir usually not long after. Felicity had never understood it. Until now.

She barely heard the front door open, only dimly aware of the footsteps that passed across the open parlor door. "I say, I didn't know we had company—by Jove! Felicity? What on earth do you think you're doing?"

Seven

FELICITY'S UNCLE STOOD IN THE DOORWAY WITH THE most comical expression on his face. It almost soothed Terence's annoyance at being interrupted from his kiss. He had to remind himself that as the girl's legal guardian, the man could make it difficult to continue his courtship.

Terence shook his mane. How had he gotten caught up in his own deception? He courted the girl only because it kept him near the location of the relic. He sternly reminded himself that he needed to be suspicious of everyone in this household, including Felicity and her uncle. He must tread carefully.

"Allow me to introduce myself, sir." Terence walked over to Viscount Wortley with his hand outstretched. "Sir Terence Blackwell, at your service." The man still hadn't recovered himself, and Terence pumped a rather limp hand. "I apologize for the manner in which we meet. I had meant to come to you first with my request."

Lord Wortley finally snapped his mouth shut and glanced over at Felicity. "Wha—what request?"

Terence frowned. Could the man be that dense? He'd just witnessed them kissing. "Why, to ask your permission to court Miss Seymour." Lord Wortley blinked in confusion. Terence sighed. "Your niece. Felicity."

"By Jove, whatever for?"

Heat rushed to Terence's face, and if Felicity hadn't chosen that moment to interject, he might've said something he'd regret. Now he knew where Felicity had developed her lack of self-worth.

"Uncle Oliver," she said, "Sir Terence and I met at the ball last night."

"How?"

The tone of his voice startled her, and Terence surmised that Felicity wasn't accustomed to her uncle snapping at her.

"Ralph had an errand, you see. And if it hadn't been for Sir Terence, I would have suffered an unfortunate collision. I wasn't used to the press of people… so we were forced to an introduction… and well, Terence and I got acquainted."

"Closely acquainted, based on the little scene I just witnessed." Lord Wortley adjusted his cravat. "Ralph," he muttered under his breath, sounding as if he'd like to get his hands around his son's throat. His icy gray eyes turned back to Terence.

"Sir? As in…"

Terence could already see the disdain the other man held for his title. He'd been subjected to this prejudice his entire life, but this was the first time he had to tolerate it willingly. Of course, he'd never expected to be courting the daughter of a peer.

Felicity placed herself in front of Terence and blurted, "He's a baronet."

"Good God."

Anna coughed from her corner, where she'd been trying to shrink into invisibility. Terence put all of his pent-up anger into the glare he gave her and she fled the room.

Wortley collapsed into a chair ridiculously shaped like an open peacock's tail, and covered his face with his hands. He mumbled as if to himself, but Terence heard every word. "We cannot have fallen this low. It cannot be possible that my niece is seriously considering linking our family with that of an animal's. Can it?"

Terence would've growled out his rage had it not been for the glimmer of tears in Wortley's eyes, the absolutely sincere devastation on his face.

Felicity knelt on the floor and pulled her uncle's hands away from his face. "I have no magic, no dowry, no beauty to make up for it. You should be thanking Sir Terence for offering his hand to me, not bemoaning it."

"Thanking him?" Lord Wortley's voice rose. "Why should I thank him for taking you away from us? There is no reason for you to marry at all!"

"You would have me become a spinster?"

"Yes!"

At the crestfallen look on his niece's face, Wortley lowered his tone again. "No, no, of course not. Once Ralph gains the title back, he can provide a dowry for you. You'll be able to have your choice of men. You don't need to settle for this."

Terence reined in his temper. He hoped Felicity appreciated it. Wortley made him feel as if he were less than the dirt beneath the man's boots, and he'd sworn to never let anyone make him feel like that again. The urge to throttle the man so overwhelmed him that he forced his body to remain as still as a statue.

Felicity patted her uncle's face. "But I am not settling, don't you see? Sir Terence is willing to accept me just as I am. How often does a woman have the opportunity to know that a man truly wants her? He wants nothing else but me—how could any man ever offer me more?"

Wortley blinked his gray eyes at her. "That is the most incredibly naïve statement I've ever heard. And yet I see you mean it. I suppose if I do not approve, you'll run off with the man anyway?"

Felicity nodded, as if the thought had already occurred to her. Terence frowned, reminding himself that had no intention of actually marrying the girl, and he'd have to be careful not to get trapped into it by his own charade. He took two precise steps forward. "Not without your permission, sir."

Felicity's face fell. It made him squirm for some reason, that he'd disappointed her, but he forced himself to ignore it. "I may not be your social equal, but I assure you I can provide well for Felicity. My estate in Trolshire provides more than enough for her to live in the style to which she's been accustomed. And I am not without my own social connections."

Wortley winced at the reminder that shapeshifters had the friendship and support of the crown prince.

That alone should have been enough to convince the man that to refuse Terence could be a serious mistake.

Her uncle showed his intelligence by quickly realizing the implications. And his stubbornness, when he tried one last ploy. "But why her?"

"She is simply the most beautiful woman I've ever seen," replied Terence.

Wortley searched his niece's face in confusion until she blushed in shame and lowered her eyes. Terence growled low in his throat at the puzzled look on the man's face. Although he wanted to pummel the man for making his own niece feel inferior, it made him suspect that Wortley had no idea of the spell cast on Felicity. If he could've seen through the aversion spell, he should have revealed it then.

Wortley rose and shrugged his shoulders. "You have my permission to court her then." He turned to Felicity, whose cheeks still glowed red. "I will have to discuss this with your aunt, of course."

Terence frowned. It sounded like a threat. Interesting, that.

Felicity nodded, but she still couldn't meet her uncle's eyes. Terence pulled her gently to her feet and brushed a strand of hair away from her face, grazing her soft skin with his knuckles. He forced her to meet his eyes and allowed all his admiration for her beauty to show in his gaze.

She looked startled at first. Then her chin lifted, and when she smiled it lit up the entire room. Terence felt his lion-self respond, couldn't suppress the soft *huh* from his throat nor the gentle nudge of his shoulder against hers.

Lord Wortley cleared his throat. "Shall we drink on it then, Blackwell?"

Terence accepted the proffered glass and let the burn of the brandy in his throat remind him again that he had no intention of getting involved with the girl. That the real reason he was here was to find the relic and destroy it. And he would destroy her, too, if she had anything to do with the use of its powerful magic.

Now that he had permission to court her, he would suppress the instincts of his lion-self and keep his hands off the girl. He would cease to admire her beauty, wit and grace, no matter how difficult it proved to be.

He would avenge his brother's death by ridding the world of another relic.

❧

Terence stopped the hack just outside of Trickside. This time, however, it wasn't so he could stretch his paws by racing along rooftops. It would be too dangerous in the daytime. People didn't like animals running across their roofs.

Instead, he visited the shops along Illusion Row. Although most of the stores were just showcases for the gullible, there were a few real magicians scattered among them. People whose magic proved so unreliable that they couldn't pass the test for a title; or people who refused to be tested, for one reason or another.

Terence passed several windows displaying gaudy charms of feathers, beads and ribbons. Vials of colored water stood in front of placards promising everything from love potions to the removal of "any and all types of skin blemishes."

He entered the fifth shop, whose displays weren't nearly as garish, whose advertisements held no guarantees. A tinkle of bells over the door announced his arrival, and Terence blinked as his eyes adjusted to the gloom of the shop.

"Gawd, if it ain't the lion!"

Terence stifled a smile at the cackle of glee in the older woman's voice. Manda shuffled toward him, bracelets clacking and paste-stone rings flashing. The black shawl she wore over her shoulders had faded to gray, a slightly darker shade than her hair. Thin but surprisingly strong arms encircled his hips, and he caught a whiff of cats and camphor, the only perfume she ever wore.

Terence loomed over Manda. Her head barely reached his bellybutton, and she buried her face in his crotch while she hugged him.

"Manda…" warned Terence. Some women stayed sexy their entire lives, regardless of age or looks. Manda was one of them.

"I have few pleasures, lion-heart, don't deny me the simple ones."

Terence picked her up and sat her on the rickety counter. "You should be ashamed of yourself."

She cackled again. "You always come when you want a favor, or information. And what payment do I get, eh? A few shillings? What do I want with money, I ask you?"

Terence suppressed a grin. They always played the same game. "You know you'd never be faithful to me."

"What? How can you say such a thing? Why, if you shared my bed, I'd never want another."

"Who's in it today?"

Manda shrugged, her eyes drifting toward the back of her shop. "Nice fella. Thought he was too young for me, that I couldn't keep up. He's sleeping it off."

She winked at him.

Terence threw back his head and laughed, a roar that should've wakened the dead. But not the man in Manda's back room.

"To be honest, lion-heart, I'm a bit beat myself. Can we get down to business? You've found another one, haven't you?"

Terence searched her face, decided with relief that she looked tired and not ill, then nodded. One of his many sources, Manda was also a friend. He'd become genuinely fond of her and knew what she risked whenever she helped him.

A baron's daughter, she had the gift of foresight. But she had refused to marry the man her father had chosen, refused to live the 'boring life of a lady,' as she put it. She'd set up shop in Trickside and had never looked back.

"Get the book," she instructed. "And lock the door."

Terence did what she said and handed her the blank-paged book. She flipped through the leaves of it, then stopped suddenly and started to read. Her lips moved silently, and he couldn't resist a peek. But to him the page remained stubbornly blank.

"What does it say?"

"Gawd. You've gotten yourself in deep this time, haven't you?"

"Why? What does it say about the relic? Does it tell you what the jewel can do?"

Manda slammed the book shut. "Naw. I tell you every time, the book tells me what it wants to. Not what I ask it to."

Terence suppressed a curse. "Did it tell you anything useful then?"

"That you're about to head into danger. Again. As if I didn't already know that."

"And?"

A man even younger than Terence swept aside the curtain covering the back door of the room and popped his head around the corner of it. "Um, Manda? When can you, um, come back to bed?"

She winked at Terence. "In a minute. Get something to eat, you'll need your strength."

A grin cracked his face, and he ducked back behind the curtain. If Terence hadn't already been courting Felicity, he swore at that moment he would've been tempted to take Manda up on her constant offers.

Terence shook his head. He'd done it again. He was as free today as he was a few days ago. His courtship to Felicity was but a sham... why did he keep falling for his own charade?

"You've met a woman," Manda said while she watched his face. Terence shifted his feet. Sometimes it felt like Manda could read his mind.

"She's dangerous, lion-heart. Be on your guard, that's all I can tell you." The locked shop door rattled, and Manda heaved a sigh. "Between the front and the back rooms, a woman can't get any rest."

She grinned with delight, and Terence shook his head. He helped her off the counter, and unlocked the door for her next customer. A shy girl hesitantly entered, and Terence could guess what she wanted Manda's book to reveal to her.

"Lion-heart," called Manda as he walked out the door after placing a few coins on the counter. "Don't forget my offer."

Terence felt his face color and closed the door behind him on her cackles of glee.

He visited several other shops, and whether by crystal ball or bowls of colored water or mirrors of glass, they all told him the same thing. A woman had entered his life and she'd be dangerous to him. His body or soul might be in peril; they couldn't tell which.

Nothing about the relic and everything about Felicity.

Terence growled with frustration and headed home, the gas and fairylights just flickering on. Bentley met him at the front door of his brownstone, ears twitching for news.

"I managed to get the girl's uncle to accept my courtship," Terence announced.

"Was there any doubt of it?" replied Bentley as he gathered his master's coat and hat into his hands.

Terence rolled his eyes at Bentley's sarcastic tone but chose to ignore the comment. He strode across the polished floor of the entryway, again wondering what Felicity might think of his home's interior and vowing only to let her see the decrepit outside of it. Let her think his house as unworthy as himself.

Her uncle had made it obvious what he thought of shapeshifters. The girl probably had the same opinions, but she was desperate enough not to voice them. Bloody hell, it would be fascinating to marry her just to find out her true feelings. Once the vows had been spoken, he was sure she'd reveal her true colors, like most women.

Then again, what did he care how she truly felt about him?

"I asked for a tour of the house, pretending to be impressed by its magnificence," Terence said.

Bentley hung his hat and coat on the claw-shaped hooks near the doorway and followed Terence into the study. He lit candles throughout the room, illuminating the rows of books lining all four walls.

"I'm sure the fellow fell all over himself to show it off to you," Bentley replied.

Terence raised a brow. "Naturally."

"And?"

"Faint whiffs of relic-magic throughout the entire place."

Bentley twitched his nose. "Anywhere particularly strong?"

"In the kitchens. In the aunt and uncle's bedchamber. We hunt again tonight. And then we guard the girl until the dragonette is strong enough."

Bentley nodded, led Terence into the dining room where a feast had been laid out amid crystal glasses and ornate china. Terence realized he'd missed lunch and spent several minutes savoring the roast beef and Bordeaux pigeons, both of which tasted raw and juicy.

"None of my sources could offer any information on the relic." Terence wiped his mouth with a linen napkin. "Deuced annoying. They had all kinds of premonitions about the Seymour girl, and none about the relic."

"Maybe," suggested Bentley, "the thoughts of the girl lay uppermost in your mind."

Terence scowled.

Bentley pulled out the oak box that held the playing cards, and began to deal. They passed a quiet evening, Bentley winning every hand of commerce against his preoccupied friend.

After the witching hour, they donned their blacks and met in the attic. Bentley shifted and Terence felt little rat claws climb up his tail. When he thought the rat had burrowed securely into his mane, he went through the trap door and loped across the rooftops.

When they reached Felicity's residence, Terence shifted back to human and they entered again through the kitchens, searching those rooms first. The scullery maid slept next to the warm range, but to their relief the rest of the rooms were empty of servants.

Bentley squeaked softly, indicating a closed door in the muggy washroom. Terence opened it and followed Bentley's nose to a back wall that seemed to end in solid brick.

"Dead end," he whispered.

Bentley's rat body trembled, and he lifted a little claw as if he were a pointer-dog.

Terence studied the wall, running his hands along the brick. His animal nature gave him acute vision, and he thought he detected a smudge along the floor. With renewed determination, he slid his fingers into every chink or cranny in the wall, feeling for any hidden springs or levers.

A muffled pop sounded loudly in the quiet room, and Bentley scampered to the door and peeked into the kitchen. The maid must not have stirred, because Bentley returned and nudged at the crack in the wall.

Terence slid his fingers inside that slender opening and pulled. The door of brick swung into the room. He grinned with satisfaction, and Bentley scampered into the opening. Terence stifled a curse to call his friend back and studied the backside of the brick until he found another lever inside that would also release the hidden mechanism. He closed the wall behind him then and dared to light a match.

Earthen-hewn stairs, so old they had rounded at the edges, led down beneath the mansion. Musty earth tickled his nose, and he suppressed a sneeze as he tested each stair before allowing his full weight on them. This had to be the deepest cellar he'd ever seen, going so far down into the earth that he thought it might actually lead to London's notorious Underground.

But the stairs ended in an ordinary cellar, and his fifth match revealed the family's store of wine, the ancient bottles covered in dust and cobwebs, and another brick wall. Bentley traced a path back and forth in front of it, but this time Terence could not discover an entrance.

Bentley shifted back to human. "The relic went through here."

"I smell it too. But the wall isn't illusion, we'd see through it."

"There is an entrance, though. Look at all the wards."

Terence nodded. Enough wards covered this room to stop an army of magicians. Some of them particularly nasty; just a touch would shrivel skin from bone, and he felt grateful for his magical immunity.

But if they couldn't find the entrance, his immunity wouldn't be of any help.

Terence tried lifting bottles, Bentley tried poking his fingers in crevasses, but their search proved futile, and after several hours, Terence sat on the dirt floor and admitted defeat.

"They've hidden the relic here somewhere. We've only to find it."

Bentley shook his head. "I don't think so. The stink isn't strong enough. Think about it, if it lay just behind these walls, wouldn't we feel it?"

Terence agreed. He just felt too tired to consider the other possibility.

"They've got a lair in the Underground, don't they?"

Terence nodded. The last time they'd gone beneath London, into the abandoned railway tunnels that had been expanded by black sorcerers into a miniature city of its own, they'd barely made it out alive.

Bentley cursed, and he did it so rarely, that it made Terence smile. His friend wasn't particularly good at cursing. He sounded like a child mimicking his elders.

"Our best option is to wait until it's brought up and used again," Terence said. "Even if we found the entrance, we might never discover its hiding place in the maze of London's Underground."

Bentley wiped his face, leaving a black mark along his narrow cheeks. "If we had a guide, we might be able to."

"But who…?"

Bentley shrugged. "I have my contacts, you know."

Terence sighed and rose, following his friend. He didn't know how much he could trust these contacts of Bentley's, and would prefer to keep their search between the two of them. He hoped that the relic would be brought above and used again so that they could track it.

The relic-magic stink had been strongest in the cellar; only rudimentary traces drifted throughout the rest of the house. Bentley searched the reception rooms while Terence went upstairs. He opened the door to Felicity's room, relieved to find that it had very little stink in it. He hoped that meant she'd be safe from attacks tonight.

He found her lying next to the hearth, her hand outstretched toward the fender. She'd obviously fallen asleep while watching her egg. He checked for any cracks, but the surface of the shell still looked whole. The dragonette would grow quickly after it hatched, and then he wouldn't need to worry about Felicity's safety anymore.

He wouldn't have an excuse to come to her bedchamber every night.

He leaned down and brushed the hair away from her face, and before he knew it he had fallen to his knees, his mouth inches from her own. He trembled in an effort to control his lion-nature.

And then the girl opened her eyes.

Felicity's fingers curled around the back of his neck with sinuous strength. She pulled his head down and he couldn't resist the invitation. His mouth covered hers, igniting a shock of fire that rippled through his chest. Terence moaned, pushing his tongue inside her sweet mouth, undeniably lost in the sensation of wet warmth as he used his tongue to mimic the yearning his body craved. He entered and withdrew, again and again, until he growled with the need to touch her, to explore the exquisite promise of her body.

Terence fisted his hands and lifted his head, his harsh breathing the only sound in the room.

"Terence," sighed Felicity, trying to pull him back against her. "I'm not through."

"You're half asleep," he panted.

Her eyes glittered and she pouted so prettily that his gaze locked on to her mouth and he couldn't tear it away. "It's my dream and you'll do as I say."

Terence gathered her into his arms and smothered his smile against her lips. She locked her arms around his neck and thrust her tongue into his own mouth, surprising him with how quickly she learned. He held her back with one hand while the other explored her curves through her thin chemise. He traced a path from waist to neck, burying his hands in her thick, silky hair.

She moaned and threw back her head. The white, soft skin of her neck tempted him to taste it, and he trailed the tip of his tongue on that creamy smoothness, pressing kisses here and there. He gently took the lobe of her ear between his teeth, making her shiver.

She guided his palm down over the swell of her breast. It fit his hand perfectly.

He pressed his shaft against her soft thigh in a reflexive buck that took him by surprise. He'd never felt anything as arousing as the perfect swell of her breast beneath the thin material. For a moment he didn't dare move again, struggling to control his surge of passion.

Felicity arched her back, pressing her body harder against him, squirming when he still didn't respond.

Her nipple was a hard nub beneath his palm. He slid his hand back and forth and she gasped, lifting her head and covering his mouth again with a ferocity that made him grin. He held the lower curve of her breast and ran his thumb gently over the nipple, exploring the texture of it, wondering how it would feel inside his mouth, against his tongue.

Felicity gasped beneath his mouth.

Something squeaked and then bit his leg.

"Damn you, Bentley," snarled Terence. And the man had the temerity to nip him again.

Terence reluctantly disentangled the girl's arms from around his neck. He should be thanking his friend for his interference, instead of mentally cursing it. Things could have gotten entirely out of hand.

Felicity gave a cry of dismay when he shifted to his were-self, and the urge to be near her grew even stronger. Bentley quickly crawled into his mane and nipped him again, and before Terence could allow himself to think about his unusual ardor for the girl he flew out the window, scrambling up ledges, running across rooftops. Fleeing his desire.

Eight

THE DAY AFTER TERENCE HAD SPOKEN WITH HER uncle, he showed up at Felicity's door barely after noon. Most women would have still been abed, or out on calls, or at the very least, kept him waiting for over an hour.

Felicity flew down the stairs after fifteen minutes, with no pretensions about how excited she felt to see him. It took Terence a moment to speak. She looked like an angel in a white frock with layers of ruffles, her hair twined with ribbons, and loose strands curling around her cheeks and over her brow.

"Sir Terence, what a delightful surprise."

He blinked.

"May I offer you tea?"

He shook his head. This morning he'd decided that a potential suitor should call as often as he could, if not every day. He'd rushed to see the girl only because society expected a certain eagerness. But it didn't excuse him for calling unannounced this early, nor explain why he stood before her with absolutely no plans for the day.

"I thought you might enjoy… a ride in the park. Yes, certainly that would appeal to you." He didn't make it sound like a question.

"Let me fetch my parasol—and my maid."

"I have my servant as chaperone." Felicity nodded and Terence paced the entry while she ran back up the stairs. He inhaled deeply, trying to catch the scent of the relic, and casually glanced through open doorways. But he kept getting distracted by the thought of how lovely the girl looked today, and he found himself slapping his leather gloves against his thigh.

He looked like an impatient suitor. Fine, that's exactly how he should appear.

"Sir Terence? I found it."

Felicity proudly displayed a parasol as ruffled as her skirts, and when she headed for the door and the butler neglected to open it, Terence did it for him.

The poor man looked befuddled as his mistress bade him goodbye.

Terence held out his hand to assist her into the open carriage, and when she put her small gloved fingers into his own, his skin responded with a sudden surge of… something. It reminded him of the way the air felt when lightning streaked the sky. After he'd assisted her in and let go, he made a fist, staring at his hand in consternation. He shook out his fingers and quickly pulled on his leather gloves.

She took up barely any space on the seat. But when he settled beside her, he felt overwhelmed with her presence. Terence pushed back the hood of the phaeton, letting in the open sky, and Felicity smartly snapped open her parasol, the ruffles of it now framing her face as sweetly as those that framed the bodice of her dress.

He pulled his eyes away from the swell of her bosom and ordered the coachman to drive on. The mare tolerated his presence quite well. Whether from the wisdom of long years or the ache of old joints, she never shied and fidgeted at him or his coachman.

They drove through Hyde Park, ignoring the stares of the gentry as they passed by. The purpose of riding out was to see and be seen. Unfortunately, most people's gazes swept past his companion, and more than a few people gave him puzzled looks. A man riding by himself in a two-seater might look odd, and although he could care less about anyone's opinions, he wished Felicity could have the pleasure of admiring gazes. As she surely would, if she hadn't been carrying that bloody spell.

He wished he could trust her enough to ask her about it—although it would be pointless since he didn't have the relic to remove the spell. Assuming that she wanted it removed. "How long have you been in London?"

She blinked, as if surprised that he still remembered her presence. "Not very long. It's vastly different from the country." She fidgeted with the handle of her parasol and kept glancing beneath her lashes at him.

"What is it?" he finally asked.

"Would it be too much trouble if we skipped the park and drove through the city? It's just that I've barely seen much of it."

"Why not?" He hadn't meant to sound so harsh, but why hadn't her family taken the girl about?

"Oh," she waved a hand, and he made the mistake of looking at her directly. Her voice wavered when their eyes met. "I spent all of my time preparing for the testing. Not that it did any good. And Aunt doesn't get out much. She has headaches, you see…"

Her words floated away with the flower-scented breeze. Terence realized that a dark ring of violet outlined the inner blue in her eyes, making them that unusual color. The fresh air brought a blush to her pale cheeks, and it reminded him of his thoughts when he'd first seen her.

He moaned deep in his throat and leaned against her, pushing her against the side of the carriage. Her mouth opened, and she unconsciously licked her lips, making them even more inviting…

Terence fought the wildness from his were-self and jerked away, forcing his face forward, scowling with concentration.

"I'd be happy to show you the city," he growled, his voice at odds with his words. "Some of the mansions the gentry have created show quite an imagination, but many are illusion only, and if they're not renewed, they get a bit ragged around the edges."

He gave new instructions to the coachman, who turned the nag on a path that would lead back to the city, and took the roads that passed the mansions of the aristocracy. Terence began to enjoy himself, seeing the city from her eyes.

"The country doesn't have many magic-users," Felicity said. "I've never seen such use of the power before, concentrated all in one place."

Terence got caught up in her excitement, taking

her to out-of-the-way places, along streets he hadn't traveled in years. She asked so many questions, he thought he'd tire of answering them. But he didn't, and this seemed to surprise her, that every time she spoke, he answered. He wondered what it would be like to be almost invisible most of his life. It might even be worse than being despised.

"Oh, Terence," breathed Felicity, forgetting to address him formally. "It looks like a tower of confection."

He glanced at the Earl of Medusham's residence and winced. Beneath the illusion stood an old mausoleum of a house with sagging shutters and peeling paint. The roof probably leaked.

"Look," continued Felicity, unaware of the reality beneath the illusion. "There's little gingerbread men along the top of the roof, and the windows look like spun sugar, and, oh my, the shingles are attached to the mansion with gumdrops!"

Terence smiled at the excitement in her voice. She sounded like a little girl, and it made him feel incredibly jaded. He slowed the horse to a stop. "The earl is said to be in his second childhood. He's been working on that illusion for years now. Would you like to get out and see it closer?"

She shook her head. "Oh, no. I'm afraid I shall lick it."

Terence blinked. Then he laughed, like he hadn't laughed since... since before Thomas had died.

He could feel Felicity's pleasure radiate like a tangible thing. "I wish my parents could have met you," she said. "I know they would have liked you very much."

Terence frowned. Would they? He just couldn't imagine that the duke and duchess would have been pleased to have a were courting their daughter. Had they been alive, he doubted that he would have received permission to court her, whether she lost the title or no.

"Shall I meet yours?"

"My what?" asked Terence.

"Why, your own parents, of course. Surely they'd like to meet the lady you're courting."

They might have, at that.

"We seem to have at least one thing in common. I lost my parents, as well." He couldn't tell her about Thomas. That pain was too recent. And besides, this entire courtship was nothing but a charade. He couldn't lose sight of that, and exposing too much of himself to this curious girl would be a mistake.

Her tiny hand patted his arm, the glove covering her skin a thin barrier against the warmth of her touch. "Oh, Terence, I'm so sorry."

He shrugged. It had been a long time since anyone had offered him sympathy. He felt his lion-self squirming inside, battling to snatch her hand, lay it against his cheek and accept the sentiment that she offered. She appeared to genuinely grieve for him, as if the death of a couple of animals truly made a difference.

"It's getting late. I should take you home." He gave instructions to the coachman. The nag heaved a sigh, but started to walk again. Gaslights and fairy-lights began to blink on, and he shook his head in bemusement. He hadn't realized that time had flown so quickly. He couldn't remember the last time he'd spent a day in such idleness… and pleasure.

Felicity sighed and sat back in her seat, her arm pressing against his own. He fought the urge to lean into her, and instead concentrated on the road ahead, watching the traffic of carriages and horses that appeared to be nothing of the kind. Unicorns, pegasi and griffins pulled chariots of fire, silk and moondust.

"London is a magical place," murmured the girl.

Terence glanced at her. Could she truly be as innocent as she seemed?

He assisted her out of the carriage when they arrived at the mansion. Fairylight played across her pearly skin as she looked up at him, a hopeful look of entreaty on her face.

Terence knew she wanted him to kiss her. Right here, on the street. He remembered the feel of her full lips on his own, the way they moved with an experience that delighted him. If they didn't have society's eyes upon them… he couldn't stifle the purr that grew in the back of this throat, but he did step back, taking her hand in his own.

He lowered his face and kissed the back of her glove.

He muttered a good night and spun away, but not before he caught the look of disappointment that shadowed her delicate features.

The girl's nature was entirely too passionate for her own good. And for his. Terence smiled. He planned on visiting her again tonight, and then he would give her the kiss she desired.

❧

Over the next few days, Terence remembered to send over a note before he called. He didn't make the mistake again of appearing too eager to see her, but it chafed at him to beg permission.

When he couldn't be with her, the time dragged and the very air he breathed seemed flat and dull.

She'd been so enamored of magical creations, he'd decided to take her to the prince's private gardens, where she could see what the power of a royal could do.

Felicity floated down the stairs in a blue gown, making her eyes appear that very color. Terence escorted her out to the carriage, noticing that she wore gloves of such a loose weave of lace, he could see her pink flesh beneath. The thought of her hand touching him today made him catch his breath.

She chattered while they drove, as if she didn't really expect him to pay attention to her words. As if she were so used to being ignored that she'd gotten into the habit of speaking to herself. Whenever he responded to one of her comments she would start, and then apologize for rambling on so.

"I like it when you do," he said. "It makes me forget my own worries for a while. Besides, I like the sound of your voice."

He shouldn't have said that. She stayed mute for the rest of the trip, suddenly self-conscious.

When they arrived at the palace, Terence instructed the coachman to stay with the carriage. He led Felicity through the crown prince's private entrance into his gardens, and she relaxed again.

"I've never seen the like," she breathed as they walked through the living statues. "How did they get the plants to grow that way—of course, I'm being ridiculous. I just never thought magic could be used this way."

She practically skipped along the graveled pathway, her head turning this way and that, marveling at the likenesses of the royal family. "Has the queen seen this place?" she wondered aloud as she stared up at a towering bush that resembled her majesty in almost a caricature.

Terence shrugged, a smile tugging at his mouth. "Sometimes her majesty doesn't appreciate Bertie's sense of humor, but to hear the prince tell it, she nearly burst her corset strings when she saw it."

Felicity turned with a look of horror on her face. "She was that angry?"

"No, she was laughing that hard. Here now, the Master of Ceremonies. See how the roses grow from his ears and nose? He's a rather hairy man."

Felicity laughed and hurried ahead of him.

He rounded the corner, and she'd come to a complete stop, her hand half covering her mouth in surprise. "It's you," she mumbled.

Terence looked up at the huge lion, its form shaped by a golden-leafed plant that sprouted white blooms in the spring. Next to the lion grew a plant that had been shaped into the form of a man holding a whip made of a thorny vine in his upraised hand. The two plants appeared to be connected at the bottom by a growth of purple flowers, twining around the legs of the lion and man, until you couldn't tell where one began and the other ended.

Prince Albert had a cunning, insightful mind.

"It could be any were-lion," said Terence. He

grabbed her hand, breaking her enraptured gaze and pulling her onto another path. She stumbled, trying to keep up with his longer legs. With a sigh of self-reproach, he slowed his steps.

Her hand felt tiny in his. Warm and soft, the covering of lace a flimsy barrier against his skin. As he led her through a trail of roses, his attention narrowed to that small connection between them. As if the link created from her hand in his had become something that connected them into one singular being.

The sound of falling water broke the spell that Terence had been under, and he shook his head angrily. He was supposed to be enchanting her, not the other way around, and he'd best remember to keep himself in check.

"What is it?" she asked.

Terence squinted against the glare of sunlight bouncing off sheets of solid water. "It's a maze. Do you want to risk it? It might take hours to find our way out again."

Her eyes glittered, and he couldn't be sure whether it was from excitement or a reflection of the sunlight. "Oh, I trust you to find our way out."

Terence suppressed a brief flash of guilt. She'd said it flippantly, but he needed her to trust him if he had any hope of finding the relic. He hadn't realized that his false courtship would make him feel like such a heel.

He led her through the arch of water into the maze of tunnels created by the fall of liquid. He waited for Felicity to realize that the water fell upward, not down, and laughed when she stuck a finger into the flow. Sunlight through the rippling waves made patterns of multi-colored light play across her face, dance a jig over the swell of her bosom. Felicity smiled at him, all honesty and delight, unlike the coy smiles of the other women he'd known.

Terence gently tugged her hand, until she stood against his chest, her eyes looking up into his, that beautiful face so trusting. So curious to see what he'd do. He groaned and stepped back, almost stumbling in the process. He scowled and she frowned in confusion, unaware that she'd almost been... What? Ravished in the prince's private gardens?

He began to doubt his ability to keep his hands off her. His lion-self kept screaming 'mate' and made the task even more difficult.

He strode past the girl, listening to make sure her footsteps followed, and collapsed on a marble bench cunningly carved into a wave of water. He felt her settle beside him, heard the swish of her skirts against the cold rock.

"Oh, my," she breathed.

Terence pulled his hands away from his face and looked up. Across from the bench sat a round marble stone, and drops of water sprang out of the holes carved into it. The drops would hover in the air and for a split second, assume the shape of a pointed-faced water sprite, then explode into a mist of vapor.

He heard Felicity sigh with delight. He kept his eyes locked on his lap. And then she put her hand beside her, curling her fingers around the edge of the bench, right next to where his own larger hand rested. He lifted his fingers, swallowed, and covered her hand.

Again, he felt that connection, and he couldn't move. Couldn't breathe for the longest time.

He abruptly rose and continued down the pathway, trying to remember the quickest way out of the maze. He wanted to take her in his arms, wanted to ravish her as he did at night. He felt driven to touch her and couldn't stand the thought of another man introducing her to the pleasures of love.

He vowed that he'd never take her anyplace where they might be alone again.

❧

Terence arrived early the next evening to escort Felicity to a ball. He told himself that he needed to stop being distracted by Felicity, and use her to find the relic. So he'd arrived an hour early, and since he'd become a regular visitor, the butler allowed him to find his own way into the parlor. Terence wandered down the hall, determined to ferret out the scent of the relic. He'd had no success in the evening, so maybe it was brought above and used during the day.

Terence padded to a stop in front of a door that carried a strong reek of relic-magic. It had been used recently within this room! He glanced around, bumped his shoulder against the heavy oak, and the door popped open. His nostrils flared and he felt a tingle of excitement. The smell might be old, but it had once been strong. Magic had been performed in this room.

"I say," said the voice of Felicity's uncle. "Is there something I can do for you, Sir Terence?"

Illumination flared as Lord Wortley touched the

fairylight on his desk, reflecting off the glass eyes from hundreds of animal heads scattered throughout the room. Heavy gothic bookshelves held dusty tomes, and even heavier furniture made the library feel like a medieval dungeon.

Terence recovered quickly. "I was looking for you."

Lord Wortley leaned back in his leather chair. "You don't say?" He studied Terence with a calculating eye, gesturing him to a seat next to his desk. Terence took it, looked up at a large lion's head that stared directly down at him, and half turned toward the doorway.

Wortley pulled another glass from the bowels of his massive desk, set it next to his half-empty one, and filled them both. "They were my father's, you know." He waved the decanter at the animal heads. "He had a passion for hunting." He had the manners to at least appear apologetic as he handed Terence the new glass of sherry.

Terence shrugged, trying to appear unaffected by the corpses. But he yearned to bolt from the room and continued to glance toward the open doorway.

"Frankly, man, I'm surprised to see you."

Terence glanced into the slightly bloodshot eyes of the viscount. He idly wondered how often Wortley sat alone drinking in the dark. "Why is that?"

"Lady Wortley assumed you'd forget about the girl by now."

"Why?"

Felicity's uncle shrugged. "Most people seem to, anyway. 'Course, you're not like most people, are you now?" He laughed at his own lame joke.

Terence swirled the liquid in his glass. "It's odd

I haven't met Lady Wortley. When might I have that honor?"

Wortley blinked, wiped his nose with his sleeve. Terence suspected the man might be well into his cups. Excellent. If he could just tolerate the carcasses strewn about the room, he might be able to find out something about the relic.

"She has a delicate constitution, my Gertrude." Wortley sighed as if he'd borne the burden of her ill health for so long, that he should be proclaimed a martyr for it. "I'm sure she'll meet you in good time. But I didn't think it would come to that."

Terence frowned. "What do you mean?"

"I mean that Lady Wortley never expected that you'd continue your pursuit of the girl. After all, Felicity has nothing to offer you. No looks, no dowry, no magic. In fact, your interest in her may even appear to be... circumspect."

Terence saw Felicity pass by the doorway during that pretty little speech, saw her stop at her uncle's words, her eyes widening in hurt. He could just see her around the edge of the doorway. He might not have even noticed her presence if he hadn't been so intent on the exit from this chamber of horrors.

"You underestimate the finer qualities of your niece."

Wortley waved a hand dismissively. "Oh, come now. I'm well aware of her sweet, unassuming nature. But we always expected her to become a spinster, you know. She's such a comfort to her aunt."

"I'm sorry to disappoint you," Terence replied, anger simmering to the surface. Bad enough that the girl received such treatment from strangers, but for her own family to be ignorant of the girl's appeal to any eligible man…

"Come now, Sir Terence. I'll make it easy for you. Much to her surprise, Lady Wortley feels you may have some sense of honor toward this courtship. Have no fear, we won't accuse you of being a rake. Should you happen to tire of this ridiculous notion of pursuing my niece, we'd let you walk away with no slander from our quarter."

Terence felt the hair on the back of his neck rise. His were-self reacted to those words with an inner snarl of rage. He barely managed to suppress the urge to throttle the man. "How… kind of you," he muttered.

Wortley thrust his chin out. "I don't know what game you're playing or why. But don't try to fool me into thinking that you're actually going to marry my niece. You haven't approached us with any negotiations, you've made no attempt to secure a license—"

"Aah, but Lord Wortley," interrupted Terence, "that's precisely why I sought you out this evening. To formally discuss the contract of marriage with Felicity."

He heard a gasp from the doorway, glanced in time to see the bloom of Felicity's smile before she turned and darted back down the hallway.

What had he done?

Nine

FELICITY SWEPT AWAY A PEACOCK FEATHER AND
stared out the parlor window. Had it only been a few
weeks ago that she'd stared out this same window with
tears in her eyes? Fearful of being snubbed by society
and feeling sorry for herself?

Now she felt the happy flush of her cheeks and
couldn't suppress a smile of anticipation while she
waited for Terence. Her betrothed. She shook her
head, still unable to get used to the idea.

Of course, it hadn't been easy. She'd never seen
Aunt Gertrude so upset. It hadn't disturbed her that
Terence was a shapeshifter; rather, she seemed to be
distraught over the fact that Felicity would marry at
all. Aunt seemed to feel that only she could take care
of her niece properly and had questioned her in detail
about where she would reside and with whom.

Felicity knew that if her aunt met Terence, she
would realize what a wonderful man he was, shapeshifter or no, and not be so concerned.

The arrival of a peculiar-looking carriage brought
Felicity's musings to a halt. What had Terence

managed to surprise her with this time? She let the curtain feathers drop, picked up her maroon skirts, and fled to the door, Katie suddenly appearing and following close on her heels.

Terence ducked out of the coach's door, his golden hair loose around his shoulders, those amber eyes meeting her own with such intensity that it took her breath away for a moment.

"He's so handsome," breathed Katie in her ear.

It took a moment for Felicity to realize that Katie was speaking about the coachman, not Terence.

"Where'd you get it?" Felicity asked Terence, nodding at the coach.

He shrugged, as if the cost of a floating coach shaped like a seashell and pulled by four matching seahorses had only been a matter of a few shillings. "I borrowed it from a friend."

Felicity's heart turned over. She hadn't managed yet to get used to the effect the sound of his voice had on her. It rumbled from his chest to her ears, then spread through her body with a ripple effect.

He reached for her hand and she backed away, making him frown with annoyance. But she couldn't help it. Looking at him made her heart flutter. Touching him made her want to kiss him. She feared that she'd throw herself at him and that he might push her away. Over the past few weeks he'd been so dreadfully proper with her, only kissing her hand good night when they parted.

And he'd been very careful never to be alone with her. She might have thought the man she'd first met—the one who'd kissed her senseless—no longer existed. Except at the oddest moments, he would push against her, making those soft *huh-huh* sounds deep in his throat.

Katie scrambled up next to the coachman, her nervousness at being near the baronet apparently forgotten in her eagerness to flirt with his coachman. Felicity took Terence's hand and ducked into the coach. Felicity felt like the pearl within the oyster-shaped carriage as she nestled into the velvet-padded seat. Terence settled beside her, the breadth of his shoulders squashing her between his warm side and the smooth walls. When he didn't pull away, she breathed a sigh of relief.

Not a moment went by in the past few weeks without her feeling a curl of dread in her stomach. She wondered if he'd realize he'd made a mistake. That her drab appearance had finally bored him. That kissing her had been so unpleasant, he couldn't find the nerve to do it again.

If it hadn't been for her nightly dreams, his behavior might not have bothered her. But he'd come to her in the moonlight, wearing his lion-shape and guarding her against her nightmares. She had only to call his name and he would shift to human and make her feel such incredible sensations…

Felicity wanted the man that came to her at night, not the one who sat so stiffly formal beside her. She wanted to make her dreams a reality and had been working up the courage to confront him.

She shivered.

"Are you cold?"

Felicity froze with indecision. If she said yes, would

he put his arm around her? And then, unable to resist the temptation, would she rest her head against his shoulder, placing little kisses against the hard softness of his neck? Would he pull away in disgust, or as usual, freeze until his muscles tightened from the strain?

She sternly reminded herself of her decision. Fear of rejection would not stop her. "It is rather chilly, isn't it? I mean, since the sun's going down."

She sounded foolish. Terence blinked and stared out the rounded window, as if just realizing that the sun had started to set. He pulled a cashmere blanket from under the seat and settled it around her lap.

Felicity grimaced. "You think of everything, don't you?"

He shrugged, his arm rubbing against her silken sleeve. "Since what I want to show you is only seen at night, I thought it prudent to bring you a blanket."

Felicity rubbed her fingertips against the soft material. "Where are we going? You've been awfully mysterious this evening."

He finally turned and looked at her. And then he continued to stare at her for the longest time, in the same way she felt she stared at him. In awe of his beauty, longing to touch that perfection.

"Against my better judgment," he replied, "I'm taking you to Spellsinger Gardens." He turned and stared out the window again.

Felicity had heard of the place, although she'd never been there. Proper ladies didn't go to the Gardens. Wine and song and every form of ribald entertainment made it quite unacceptable. Not to mention the rumors of lovers' trysts.

Felicity's heart fluttered. "Then why are you taking me?"

He spoke to the window. "There's a new exhibit that I knew I had to show you as soon as I saw it. Your reputation will not suffer, however. It's why I borrowed this coach."

"You are overly concerned with my reputation," mumbled Felicity. She purposely ignored the fact that she'd chastised him about it in the first place.

He didn't answer, continuing to stare out the window. Felicity felt the rumble as they crossed Spellsinger Bridge. The illusion that they floated was obviously only that, for the true wheels clattered over every bump. And occasionally the seahorses neighed.

But they were a joy to watch, their tail fins fluttering and their large eyes growing more luminous as night fell. The shell opened in front, so she had an unrestricted view. The coachman and Katie rode behind them, an occasional giggle from her maid the only reminder that she wasn't truly alone with the baronet.

As they neared the entrance to the Gardens, Terence touched off the fairylights inside the coach, pulled the curtains across the two round windows, and pushed some lever that closed the opening to the shell. Her view narrowed to a slit and both of them were plunged into shadow.

Felicity could barely see a thing. She could hear the music, though, boisterous strains that made her feet tap. And laughter and scattered applause. She couldn't resist peeking around the edge of the window's curtain.

Open buildings, too large to be called gazebos, sheltered crowds of people. In one sat tables piled with mounds of food and drink. In another, couples lay on couches and pillows scattered across the floor, some of the bodies so intertwined that they looked like one form. Entertainers swallowed fire and juggled balls of swirling light. Women walked among the throng, some of their gowns cut so low, Felicity could swear she saw the rosy tint of nipples.

They passed fountains of colored water surrounded by statues of mythical creatures engaged in activities that involved impossible contortions. When they neared a huge pavilion, she gasped when she saw many of those same creatures seemingly alive.

Terence put his arm around her to pull her away from the window. "You don't need to see any of that," he said rather gruffly.

"Whose pavilion is the big one?"

He sighed. "I knew this might be a bad idea, but I couldn't resist... That's the prince's. Only the royals could change people into creatures of myth."

Felicity gasped. "Why would anyone—"

"For entertainment and profit. Ask no more, that wasn't what I brought you here to see."

She snuggled into his side, the weight of his arm over her shoulders a comfortable one. "You didn't tell me not to look."

He pulled her closer as if offering comfort, his voice gentling to a purr. "I should have been more attentive. A girl of your innocence shouldn't have seen any of that."

"I read books," Felicity said in her defense.

"That's different."

"Perhaps. Did you know this is the first time we've

been alone together for some time?" She felt him stiffen. Her stomach dropped to her toes. But she gathered her courage and hurried on. "Why is that? You have seemed so preoccupied…"

"Have I been neglecting you?" His voice whispered at her ear.

"Of course not. It just seems that, well, that you may have regretted your decision to marry me." There, she'd said it. She'd made herself vulnerable to him and risked being torn into pieces.

Her eyes had adjusted to the darkness, but she would have felt his frown anyway.

"Regret it? What have I done that's made you feel that way?"

Felicity took a breath. She couldn't stop shivering and he tightened his arm around her. "Your proposal was so sudden. Now that you have gotten to know me better, I just thought that you may have regretted your rashness."

He sighed. A great release of breath that seemed to melt the wall that he'd held between them. "Now that I have gotten to know you," he murmured as if to himself. "Ah, don't you see it's only made it more difficult for me?"

Felicity shook her head. She didn't have the slightest idea what he meant. She leaned toward him, breathing in his scent. Clean earth, musky animal.

His full lips curved in a smile, the tips of his incisors showing at the corners. His eyes roamed her face, as if suddenly freed of some restraint. "You laugh at my jokes," he whispered. "You defend my kind to your aunt and uncle's friends. When my temper flares, you soothe it with a look. When I'm sunk in gloomy thoughts, you tease me until they fade. How can I resist you? How much longer can I fight the impulses of my lion-self?"

His mouth drew closer to her own. Heaven help her, but her lips ached to be touched by his. "Why must you fight it?"

"Don't you know what would happen if I gave in? Shall I give you a glimpse, Felicity? Just a taste of what would happen if I allowed myself to make love to you?"

Felicity only knew for certain that she wanted him to kiss her the way he had in her dreams. That she wanted his hands on her, making her body feel all of those frightening, exhilarating things.

Her reply flew from her lips like a sigh. "Oh, yes."

His arm around her shoulder tightened and his other wrapped around her back, his hand pushing her toward him, arching her spine while his mouth captured her lips. Oh glory, much better than her dreams! Every nerve in her body tingled; her lips burned from the fire in his. His raspy tongue swept through her mouth, and she felt as if her world had narrowed to that one part of him. Awake, aware, conscious of the way his tongue curled around hers, then swept along the inside of her lips, teasing her mouth open even farther.

Felicity forgot to breathe.

He pulled her closer. Her neck arched back. Her mouth had opened to his skillful probing, and now he captured her tongue with his lips and suckled, gently, but oh, so swiftly. Until she became aware of more. The place between her legs began to throb along with the beat of her tongue being pulled in and out of his mouth.

The shock of it allowed her to become aware of the pounding on top of the coach.

Terence growled and abruptly let her go. Felicity melted like butter against the cushions.

He opened the small hatch that allowed conversation with the coachman. "What is it?"

The coachman blinked at his master's tone. Felicity heard Katie give a startled squeak of alarm. "We're at our destination, Sir Terence."

Terence softened his reply. "Very well." He snapped the little door closed, pulled a lever, and the shell opened to reveal a fog-shrouded lake. He spoke without looking at her. "Most of the spectators are on the other side of the water, so we won't be seen. It should start very soon now."

Felicity couldn't seem to focus on his words. They rang against her numbed senses like gibberish.

She fought the urge to squirm in her seat. She'd only known this man for a few weeks, yet he'd shown her more warmth than she'd ever been given since her parents had died. Her eyes filled with tears.

His arms went around her again. "Ah, Felicity, I'm sorry. I forget how young you are."

His voice gentled to a purr, filling her with a deep longing. He kissed the tears from her face, gentle touches that warmed her.

His hand turned her head to look out over the lake, his cheek against hers, stray tears trapped between their skin. When he spoke again she could feel his jaw move. "Watch the water, dearest girl."

Why would she care about a lake, when she just wanted to think about that kiss? She'd been foolish to tempt him. No wonder he'd tried to keep his distance. He'd been trying to protect her chastity. If she dared glance down... oh yes, she couldn't resist. And she saw the evidence of his desire. Had they not been interrupted, she would be a ruined woman.

A horrible little part of her mocked her for her prudery. So what, she'd already lost everything. Wouldn't it be nice to at least willingly give something away?

A disturbance in the water fortunately halted that dreadful train of thought, and Felicity blinked the remaining tears from her eyes. A fountain spewed upward, and in the wake of that outpouring grew a figure of light. It swirled like millions of fairylights tossed in a storm, then coalesced into one mountainous form of luminescence.

Sparkles of lavender, green, and blue formed a scaly head. Glowing reds shaped a tongue and maw that spat gouts of orange and yellow fire. Wings? Oh, yes! Large, open wings batted so realistically that Felicity could imagine being buffeted by the gusts of air they created. She leaned forward and heard Terence chuckle.

"The tail," she whispered, willing it to emerge from the water as well. Coaxing the magician who'd created this wonder of light to finish the illusion.

A glow of blue-green-gold highlighted the ridges on the tail. The dragon hovered above the water in all its glowing brilliance, its tail slapping against the surface of the lake, sending ripple-shocks to the shore. Right up to where their coach sat.

With a speed that made the breath leave her lungs, the shining dragon shot up into the air, circled the lake, spewing ribbons of orange-yellow fire into the trees. Felicity could hear startled screams float from across the water. But she didn't feel afraid, knowing that the dragon wouldn't shoot its fiery breath at her.

"It's only an illusion," she reminded herself.

"But a very good one," said Terence.

"Oh, yes."

Three more times around the lake it went, and Felicity craned her neck to keep it in her sight. Then it shot into the air again, turned snout-first to the water and dove, spiraling like a top, flecks of iridescent light exploding from its core and floating lazily down after its passage.

It hit the water with a clap of sound that made Felicity cover her ears. The water folded over it, the lake gentled to its former lap of waves, and she sighed.

"I knew you'd like it." His voice held a trace of smugness.

"It's the most amazing thing I've ever seen."

His hand pressed against her now-dry cheek and turned her head to face him. "I think I'm jealous."

"Don't be ridiculous," sighed Felicity, getting dangerously lost in the softness of his eyes. "It was only an illusion of light."

"But if it were real," he said, "I think you would love it, more than you could any man."

"Not true," she countered, "for only to a man could I do this." She kissed his mouth. "Or this." She leaned up in the seat and placed feather kisses along his neck. She felt him tense.

"Or this." She ran her hands across his temples, down the silky mane of his hair, gathering in great handfuls and pulling it over his broad shoulders. Her hands wouldn't stop; they continued to caress him, move across the hardness of his chest.

He moaned when her hands reached the waist of his trousers. It made her feel brave and shamelessly powerful. This strong, feral man felt afraid of plain, little Felicity.

"I already brought you to tears once," he panted. "Are you sure, dearest, that you want me to do it again?"

Felicity nodded. Really, her sensible side kept battling with her heart, and she wished one of them would give up the fight.

His eyes gleamed. Still, he didn't move, as if battling some inner turmoil of his own. Then he turned with a jerk and opened the little hatch. "Take her for a walk," he commanded.

Felicity heard Katie's muffled protest, then a moment of silence. The coach rocked and Felicity felt their chaperones climb down from their perch. Bushes rustled, Katie giggled, and Felicity tried not to feel too ashamed of her maid's easy abandonment. After all, Katie had said that she thought the coachman most handsome.

Terence moved the lever, and the shell collapsed again to a mere slit of an opening. Starlight filtered in, muted and soft.

"This is madness."

His voice sounded very far away. Felicity didn't answer, afraid of what that statement might mean. Instead she took his face in her hands, turning it toward her with ease. Her heart had won the battle.

She'd always been ignored, easily forgotten. But never with this man. She pulled his head down to her mouth, forcing it open, until she felt his tongue. Felicity played with it until it relaxed enough so that she could suckle it, in the same way he'd done with hers earlier. He'd taught her so very much.

He felt so... pliable in her hands. He allowed her to undo his cravat, peel his coat from arms and back, unbutton his shirt. Until the glorious feel of his warm skin lay against her hands. Sparse, downy hair covered his chest. It surprised her, that lack of coat.

Terence hadn't moved of his own volition. "Don't be afraid," she whispered.

The baronet shuddered.

Felicity's heart soared. "I have no idea what to do next."

He laughed, but it sounded more like a groan. He put an arm around her back and one beneath her skirts, sweeping her up in his lap, moving so swiftly she gave a startled gasp. Terence silenced it with his lips, the taste of him like salty honey. She lifted one arm and wrapped it around his neck, pulling him closer, sighing into his mouth.

Terence used his tongue with that same skill, and Felicity felt the same answering response between her thighs. She wiggled on the hardness she could feel even through the thickness of her skirts.

"Woman," he growled, one arm supporting her head, the other starting to fumble with her skirts. The cashmere blanket slid to the floor. When his hand touched her ankle, she suppressed a moan of desire.

He laughed, deep in his throat, the rumble in her

mouth feeling quite delicious. He'd managed to bunch her skirts around her waist, running his hands up her stockings, hesitating where her drawers met her garter.

Felicity's awareness drifted from the delightful sensations in her mouth to the heat of his hand. Her heart hammered so hard she thought it would fly from her chest. She fought against the fear that threatened to overwhelm her desire.

She felt his hesitancy as a silent request for permission to continue. Little did he know it was already too late. As soon as she'd realized that he felt just as afraid of her as she did of him, that his aloofness the past few weeks had nothing to do with regretting his decision to court her... well, her heart was no longer her own. And since she'd already given him her hand and her trust, her body seemed but a minor thing.

Felicity wrapped her other arm around his neck and pulled her upper body closer to his. The bodice of her dress exposed the top of her breasts, and for the first time since she'd become a woman, she was grateful for it. The heat of his chest felt wonderful against her skin.

Terence caressed the inside of her thighs with light strokes, each one drawing closer to her center. The pulse between her legs turned into a throb, and she gasped in astonishment. He growled and covered her aching flesh with his hand. Felicity bucked beneath him; she couldn't help it.

He released her mouth and her head fell back like a doll's, arched over his arm. Felicity panted for air while his fingers stroked and fondled her, while his mouth kissed and sucked at the skin of her neck.

She'd never imagined such a feeling existed. That her body could be made to feel such exquisite pleasure.

Terence's hand emerged from her skirts, and she gave a whimper of dismay. He chuckled, his intentions clear when he began to pull down her bodice to bare her breasts. Felicity felt her face flood with color from embarrassment, then chided herself for being a nitwit. He'd already done—well, at this point, what did it matter?

He buried his hand back beneath her skirts, and she groaned with relief as he continued his earlier attentions. She marveled, though, at what he did next. His mouth strayed from her neck, he lifted her higher in his arms, and began to kiss her breasts.

Felicity started to squirm again as his fingers stroked and caressed the flesh between her legs. When he latched on to one of her nipples and began to suckle it, she felt herself becoming even more swollen, more engorged with… something. Some want, some need that she hoped he would soon decide to fulfill.

"Terence…"

"Ah, say it again."

Felicity moaned. He thrust a finger inside of her.

"Terence!"

She felt a burst of wetness and then an explosion of sensation that ripped through her body in waves of indescribable pleasure. Her head flew up and her eyes flew open. Terence lifted his head to meet her gaze.

His pupils were so dilated that his eyes looked like pools of blackness. But they glittered with tenderness while a lazy smile spread across his face.

"Oh my," breathed Felicity.

"Quite."

"But… that isn't all, is it?"

He leaned forward and kissed the tip of her nose. "Not quite."

Felicity smiled. He blinked at her as if startled, then growled a laugh. He lifted her up, grasped her waist and plunked her on his lap, facing him, her knees on each side of his hips. With a grunt of annoyance, he cleared her skirt and petticoats from between them, until only her drawers and his trousers separated their bare skin.

Felicity looked down, raised her eyebrows, and cocked her head at him. He chuckled again and started taking pins out of her hair, until it lay in a jumbled mass over her shoulders. He grabbed up handfuls of it, brought it to his nose and inhaled deeply. When he finally looked at her, their gazes locked for a timeless moment.

"You're so beautiful," he murmured huskily.

Before she could reply he cupped her face and brought her lips to his. Felicity's heart fluttered with something the very opposite of her earlier fear.

"You have no idea of the restraint I've used with you, dearest." He spoke between kisses, his lips moving against her own with his words.

She dared to sneak her hand down to his lap and feel the hardness there. He jumped and growled, and Felicity swallowed hard. He was so very big.

"Don't worry," he reassured her. "I'll be gentle. I can still control the beast. It will only hurt for a moment."

"Hurt? There is pain involved?"

"I never should've—only a bit, and only the first time."

Felicity shifted, and he groaned. He reached down to the waistband of his trousers, began to unbutton them, his eyes fixed on her face, waiting to see if she showed any fear. She lifted her chin.

His eyes widened. "Go away," he snarled.

Felicity jumped, almost fell backwards, but for his hands catching her. "What is it?"

"Nothing. Oh for—I suppose I should be grateful. This is the second time tonight I've been saved from folly. I can't hope for a third."

"Terence, what are you talking about?"

"There's a messenger sprite hovering near your shoulder."

Ten

FELICITY SPUN, STARED INTO A TINY FACE WITH A sharp chin and an even sharper nose. "Not now!" The messenger nodded once, stuck her tongue out at Terence, and disappeared through the slit in the clamshell in a shower of sparks.

"What is it?"

"Oh, Terence! It's the dragonette. I've had a messenger ready for the moment it began to hatch. It's finally time!" She bounced in her excitement and frowned at his groan. "I'm awfully sorry. They say these things do happen at the worst possible times, don't they?"

He didn't seem to share her excitement, but for some reason he took it rather well. Frustration warred with relief on his face.

Felicity bit her lip. "We shall be alone again soon, won't we?"

He gave a brief nod as he picked her up and placed her on the seat next to him. Felicity started trying to fix her garments. Terence managed to get himself clothed even quicker, and opened the shell. He bellowed for

Katie, and she emerged from the bushes, pushing and covering this and that, just like her mistress.

Terence instructed Katie to fix her mistress' hair on the ride back to Felicity's mansion, while he rode with the coachman.

It seemed like a lifetime, yet only a moment, before Felicity reached her front door. With a wave at Katie's continued fussing about the condition of their clothes and hair, Felicity sprang out of the coach and up the steps, leaving the big front door open behind her.

She skidded to a halt in the parlor at the sight of Anna with her finger over her lips. Really, she should never have given the older woman charge of her egg whenever she went out. Even though Anna had cared for the egg with as much concern as she'd raised her own children, Felicity felt herself bristling at the woman's possessiveness. And of constantly being told that she had no experience raising younglings and Anna knew best.

As if Anna had ever birthed a dragonette!

Still, Felicity tiptoed into the room and lowered her voice to a whisper. "Why do I have to be quiet?"

"Now, miss. We don't want to be disturbing its concentration, do we?"

Felicity shrugged.

"Leave us," growled Terence from behind them.

Felicity smiled. Anna left. She'd really have to learn how he did that; making the servants obey without question.

With Anna out of the way, she could see the egg now, cradled in its nest of ashes. Felicity knelt down next to the hearth and laid a finger on it. She didn't see any cracks—could Anna have been wrong and interrupted her outing for nothing? Or maybe the older woman had some kind of sixth sense about things. When Anna had passed Katie in the doorway she'd taken one look at her maid's flushed face and sniffed in disapproval.

The egg moved. Felicity suppressed a yelp as she jerked backward. She would've fallen with unladylike grace right onto her derriere if Terence hadn't been behind her. He braced her shoulders and whispered into her ear.

"It won't bite."

His voice sounded low, husky. A lover's voice, she realized with a little thrill… and a flush of heat to her face. "What do we do?"

"We wait."

Felicity touched her egg again. "Have you ever been at a hatching before?"

"No. Very few people can say they have."

"What if something goes wrong?"

He grunted with exasperation. Felicity felt his breath on the back of her neck and shivered. Goodness, her reaction to his nearness made her even more giddy than before they had… well, perhaps if they'd finished what they were about to… best she didn't think about it at all.

The egg moved. Felicity held her breath. It moved again, toward her hand, then sort of wiggled. She started to breathe again when the first small crack appeared. Then a small piece broke away and revealed a dark little form inside.

"Oh, Daisy," she murmured.

Terence's voice sounded startled and annoyed. "What?"

"That's her name."

"You named a dragonette Daisy?"

Felicity turned and looked at him. His eyes widened at her glare, and truly, if he hadn't been so incredibly handsome, she would've snapped at him. But his eyes were amber-gold in the firelight, and still shone with memories of their evening, so she couldn't speak harshly to him. She settled for a soft rebuke. "And what's wrong with Daisy? It's my favorite flower."

He snorted.

"And it never fails to lighten my spirits. Why shouldn't I name the second most precious thing to me after something that gives me such joy?"

Terence opened his mouth, closed it, then settled for a charming grin. "Second most precious thing? Tell me, dearest, what's the first?"

Felicity blushed, glanced at the doorway where Katie hovered, as if guarding the door to the parlor from any intrusion.

"You know," she whispered.

"But I want to hear you say it," he teased.

Her eyes burned. When she had to say something so close to her heart, why did tears well up and the words stumble out of her mouth?

"You are. You're the first most precious thing in my life."

The grin faded from his face. For a moment Terence stared at her, as if he tried to see into her soul. Then a brief flash of—guilt?—crossed his face, and he made that little *huh-huh* sound, and rubbed against her shoulder. His chest rumbled, like a cat when it purrs, and he leaned down and kissed her breath away.

A tiny squeak made Felicity turn back to her egg and blink with surprise. Daisy had managed to break off a piece large enough for her to crawl through, but she'd gotten stuck. "Oh, you poor dear," said Felicity. With shaking fingers she reached out to break away the remaining shell.

She received a rather dry lick for her efforts, from a tongue as yellow as the inner flame of a fire. Her baby's scaled hide shone as white as a pearl, and the most gloriously faceted eyes stared up at Felicity. The dragonette squeaked, and Felicity smiled, fighting off another bout of tears. She'd been weeping a lot lately for a girl who rarely cried.

"Daisy," she said with delight, and scooped up her baby, holding it before her face, each of them looking into the other's eyes. "Oh, welcome to the world."

Eyes the color of yellow sapphires blinked at her, with an intelligence in their depths that startled Felicity.

She'd expected Daisy to burn her hands, but the little dragonette felt only slightly warmer than her own flesh. Felicity held her up to Terence in triumph. "And you made fun of her name—look! Isn't she exactly the colors of a spring-fresh daisy?"

Terence nodded his head in reluctant agreement, a puzzled frown on his handsome face. "That's the oddest thing," he said, reaching out to pet the scaly little head. "You'd almost think she colored herself that way on purpose."

The dragonette turned her gaze on Terence, and he smiled. "I'll bet you did."

"No, look," Felicity pointed out. "There is color in her hide—as much as the dragon of light you took me to see. Like an opal, she has hidden colors beneath the surface."

He squinted. "Hmm. Could you move your hand?" The color of Daisy's scales swirled with the movement. "I have to agree. She's most astonishing, even for a dragonette."

They both beamed down at her baby, almost as if, yes, almost as if she were both of theirs. Joy flooded her heart. Love for this man, and the gift he'd given her, overwhelmed her for a moment. When she'd had all of her inheritance intact, she'd never felt as rich as she did right now.

Felicity kissed him, flat on the mouth, and Daisy hissed. "Jealous, are you? Well, we must break you of that right away. You can't be hissing every time I kiss your papa."

Terence made a sort of choking sound, and when she glanced at him, he gave her a rather weak smile.

"You'll be safe, now," he said, almost as if to himself. And then louder, "I... I have to go away for a while."

Felicity stopped crooning over her little charge. Her stomach dropped. "What do you mean, go away?"

"Oh, not for long. But there are some matters I have to attend to at my country estate. I meant to tell you earlier, but..."

"For how long?" Felicity tried to keep the note of anxiety out of her voice. Just when she'd thought everything was so perfect...

"Two, maybe three weeks."

She nodded. She understood about responsibility. She'd had it all of her life with her own properties. She just wished he didn't have to leave now. "When?"

"Tomorrow. The sooner I go, the quicker I can return to your side. You won't forget me, will you?"

Felicity started to feel a little better. "Perhaps."

"Then I shall have to make sure you don't. Daisy, remind her that you're a gift from me, will you? At least every minute of every day." His voice lowered. "Because that's how often I will be thinking of you, dearest."

The endearment made her world start to glow again.

⤳

Felicity stared in the mirror while Katie plaited her hair for bed. It had been thirteen days, four hours, and too many moments since Terence had left for his estate in Trolshire. She'd received two messages from him, one to say he'd arrived, and another that he missed her. She knew some men couldn't bear to convey intimate messages to a smirking sprite, but his were terse to the point of rudeness.

Felicity released a plaintive sigh.

"Ach, miss," said Katie, "He'll be back before ye know it."

"Not soon enough for me. It's hard to comprehend that I'd miss him this much, after knowing him for only weeks."

Katie smiled, her up-turned nose crinkling with the gesture. "Love is like that sometimes. Like a load of bricks falling atop yer head."

Felicity nodded. That's what it felt like, this sudden falling in love. And she did love him, helplessly. She'd trust him with her life.

Felicity studied her maid. "And how is your coachman?"

Katie tied a ribbon on the end of Felicity's braid.

"He's not my coachman, yet." She patted her own red locks, which curled out from beneath her frilly cap. "But he's a bonny fine lad."

Felicity giggled while Katie pulled back the covers from the bed. The maid jumped a foot backward when she exposed the slumbering form of Felicity's dragonette.

Felicity pretended not to notice her maid's fear. "Daisy likes to warm the sheets for me before I get in. Isn't she a dear?"

Katie nodded, a bit unconvincingly, and stared at the lizard. "Look how she's grown in only thirteen days…"

"…three hours and too many moments," finished Felicity. She sat on the bed and petted Daisy's petal-like ears. Her baby had grown amazingly fast. She'd written to Terence, asking him if her growth was normal, but hadn't received a reply. Of course, given the amount of food Daisy consumed, she shouldn't be surprised. She could down a haunch of meat the size of her own body and spend hours in half-lidded repose digesting it. Thank goodness she'd stopped growing when she'd reached half an arm's length long, or Felicity would've had to start bribing Cook for more meat.

"Uncle Oliver isn't very fond of her," Felicity said with a sigh of dismay. "I think he's afraid of her."

"As is most of the household, miss."

"Including you?"

Katie blinked and studied the dragonette a moment. "Not fear exactly, miss. More of a healthy respect."

Felicity smiled with relief. She studied her pet. Daisy only weighed perhaps five pounds, although that doubled right after she ate. Her snout, including an impressive array of pointed teeth, comprised a third of her body, and her ridged tail perhaps the other third. Beautiful, petal-like wings draped the top of her luminescent body, and her yellow-sapphire eyes dominated the small form.

"I can't imagine why anyone would be afraid of her."

Katie muffled a sound behind her hand. "Daisy does breathe fire, miss. Scorched Wimpole's new shoes, she did. Makes a body a wee bit nervous. But if it makes ye feel any better, I don't think Lady Wortley is afraid of her."

"No, oddly enough, I think Daisy is afraid of Aunt."

Katie straightened the items on the vanity and banked the fire. "I just think Daisy's smart enough to avoid her."

Felicity frowned. She'd given her maid explicit instructions to speak freely in her presence, but sometimes she didn't understand Katie's view of people. "Oh, you mean because Aunt gets headaches and can be cranky. Well, everyone avoids her then."

Katie sighed and rubbed her back. "Will that be all, miss?"

"Oh, yes. No, wait a moment. There's been something I've been meaning to talk to you about." Felicity averted her eyes and took comfort in her dragonette's loving gaze. "Katie, when I marry Sir Terence, will you come with me?"

Katie didn't answer right away. Felicity's maids had never stayed for long; in fact, Katie had been the most loyal of them all. But Felicity knew Katie had a fear of baronets. Felicity glanced up.

The freckles stood out on Katie's pale face. Then she shook herself and looked her mistress square in the eyes.

"Thank ye, miss, for the offer. I'd hoped to stay with ye. Ye'll need someone like me looking out for ye."

"Oh." Felicity felt a wash of relief. She wouldn't have to go live in a strange home without someone familiar with her. It also would be helpful to have someone who noticed her most of the time. But she had to be fair to Katie. "What about, well, the matter of my husband being a shape-changer? There's bound to be other animals, er, people in his household."

"After getting to know his coachman and seeing the way Sir Terence is with ye, I have changed my opinion of shapeshifters."

"Have you?"

"Yes, and pardon me for saying, I think the way the rest of the aristocracy treat them is shameful. And why they continue to spread the vilest rumors…"

"I think it's fear, Katie. Because shape-changers are immune to their magic and they hold no power over them. The elite do not like to feel vulnerable."

Katie looked thoughtful for a moment, then nodded agreement. She turned down the gaslights. "I think ye may be right, miss. Good night, then."

"Good night, Katie." Felicity sighed as her maid closed the door of her small, connecting room. How comforting to know that not only would she have Terence and Daisy, but Katie too.

Felicity crawled beneath the linens, waited until Daisy had burrowed down to her feet, then touched off the small fairylight on her side table. She lay awake for a time in the glow of the banked fire, thinking of Terence, like she'd done every night since he'd left.

But she didn't dream of him anymore. Perhaps now

she didn't need her dreams of his passionate kisses. Because she had them for real. But she missed Terence the lion, who'd fought off her dream demons and made her feel so safe. When he returned, she'd have to ask him to shift for her.

Felicity fell asleep to thoughts of her fingers buried in rough fur and the feel of a sandy tongue across her cheek. When she woke sometime later, she cursed herself for even thinking about bad dreams. For surely that's why she imagined the fearsome thing at the end of her bed.

Or maybe Ralph had decided to take advantage of Terence's absence by sending her this illusion.

Felicity blinked at the slimy, dripping apparition at the foot of her bed. Illusion or dream, she just wished they didn't look so real.

"Go away," she whispered. What on earth were those ghastly things growing out of the slime? She closed her eyes against the sight, but opened them when she heard something splatter against the floor.

The linens near her feet erupted, and a small, hissing lizard emerged to face the thing at the foot of her bed. Felicity couldn't believe that the snarling, snapping ball of fury was her own sweet Daisy. Why, she looked positively vicious.

Funny, how dreams distorted things.

The slime backed up. Daisy spewed a burst of fire. The slime retreated a bit farther, the things growing out of it dropping in random bursts of vapor. They hit the floor with a sound that resembled ice cracking, even though they seemed to burn a hole through the wooden floor.

Daisy snorted. The slime wavered a moment, as if coming to some decision, and lunged forward, straight over the dragonette toward Felicity.

One of her suppressed screams broke loose. Daisy seemed to swell in size, opened her mouth until Felicity could see her uvula, and belched out a stream of fire at the slime. The sound it made as it shattered caused her to cover her ears. Cold flakes settled on her bed panel, and melted softly against her cheeks.

"You made it snow, Daisy."

Flame-yellow eyes blinked at her, and Felicity would swear those scaly lips curved upward into a grin.

Felicity sighed, her eyes already closing, and sank back into her bedding. She tried to stay aware, to praise Daisy for her courage, to think about how her little baby had protected her. But all she could manage before a deeper sleep overcame her was the fleeting thought that, even far away, Terence had protected her.

By giving her Daisy.

❧

Only when the sun lit her curtains did her eyes open. She stared around the room, thinking that she'd forgotten to do something the night before. Gracious, what could it have been?

But the sound of doors slamming and footsteps pounding through the halls distracted her from her thoughts. She rose from bed wondering what on earth all the commotion was about.

She called for Katie to help her get dressed, but her maid wasn't in her room. She looked for Daisy beneath the linens, but her dragonette had already gotten up as well. By the time Felicity went through her morning ablutions, a breathless Katie managed to appear to help her dress.

"What in heaven's name is going on?"

Katie puffed her answer. "We're packing, miss."

Felicity frowned. "Who's packing?"

"We are, miss. All of us. We have instructions from Wimpole to move the entire household to Lord Wortley's estate in Sussex."

"To Fairview Manor? Why?"

Katie shook her red curls. "He didn't say, miss. But one of the servants overheard the master saying that the crown had decided to cut short their leave to allow ye to stay in the manor. And to clear out anything of a personal nature from yer parents' seats of Stonehaven and Graystone castles because it wouldn't be necessary for ye to return there!"

Felicity's head spun from the shock. What had she done to deserve such callous treatment? Why wouldn't they let her say her farewells to her home in Ireland? "I must talk with my uncle. Hurry, Katie."

The girl nodded, and with nimble fingers swept Felicity's hair into a neat chignon, buttoned up the front of her peach muslin dress, and even managed to stab in a comb of peach-colored pearls at the top of the coil of hair.

Felicity passed Ralph in the hallway. At the black look on her cousin's face, she decided to keep going, grateful that he didn't seem to notice her. She knocked on Uncle's study door, hoping she'd find him hiding within, and was rewarded with a reply to enter.

Uncle had left the heavy, fringed curtains closed.

The dim light added to the oppressive feel of the room, with its dusty bookcases and medieval-type furniture. Felicity averted her gaze from the stuffed animal heads on the walls; their glass eyes always seemed to stare at her with resentful intelligence.

"Uncle, what is happening?"

Lord Wortley rose from his favorite overstuffed chair, a frown of concern on his face. "Now, Felicity, there's no cause for alarm. Come, wipe those tears from your face." He handed her a handkerchief that had her father's initials embroidered in the corner.

Felicity tried to catch her breath in the stuffy room. "Why would they treat me this way? What have I done?"

"My dear girl, you've done nothing wrong. Try to be sensible for just a moment. The title is gone, there's no need for us to stay here. Your aunt has the desire for some country air, that's all."

Felicity sniffed. "So the crown isn't forcing us to leave?"

Uncle Oliver pulled on the lapel of his favorite smoking jacket. "By Jove, certainly not. Whatever gave you that idea?"

Felicity wasn't sure if he was telling her the truth, or trying to protect her. But from what, she couldn't even hazard to guess.

"Besides, I've had nothing but snide remarks behind my back at every gentlemen's club I belong to. It will be a relief to return to the country for a while… and check on my plants."

Felicity blinked. Plants. Of course, she'd forgotten about Uncle's garden. He may only have the magic of alchemy and herbs due a viscount, but Uncle had reputedly become one of the best at his craft.

He cleared his throat. "Best go pack a light travel bag. The family will take the train to Fairview, and the servants will follow with the rest of our belongings."

She nodded, still stunned by this abrupt change in her life. She'd best get used to the idea that she no longer had any control over—

"Terence! Oh, Uncle, how will he know where we went? He's expecting me to be here when he returns. I must send him a message before we leave."

"Dear girl, don't you worry yourself. I've already taken care of it for you. I've sent a messenger sprite just this morning to his Hall in Trolshire, informing him of our change of residence. If he wants you, rest assured, he'll be able to find you."

Felicity nodded in relief, her mind already frantically thinking of what she must bring with her. Daisy must have her meat, perhaps some dried beef would do for a snack. And she must pack her mother's picture, her box of mementos, and perhaps a change of clothing. Who knew how long it would take the servants to arrive with the rest?

It wasn't until one of the servants bumped into her as she hurried up the stairs that she realized what her uncle had said. What did he mean if he wants you? Had Uncle heard from Terence? Maybe he'd changed his mind about their engagement...

Felicity stubbornly shook her head. Not again. She would never doubt his love for her again. Hadn't he proven that he wanted her that night in Spellsinger Gardens? Hadn't he given her the priceless gift of Daisy to chase away her bad dreams?

No, she wouldn't let an offhand remark bother her.

She trusted Terence with her life, and no one could make her doubt him again.

Felicity had never felt so rushed. The moment she had her valise packed, Aunt hustled her into the carriage, narrowing her eyes at Daisy, who'd wrapped herself around Felicity's neck and refused to budge. Aunt then proceeded to ignore the dragonette, firmly stating that this sudden upheaval had caused a dreadful head pain. She closed her eyes, covering her head with a shawl.

Ralph glared accusingly at Felicity all the way to the train station. When Felicity scrambled into their private railcar, she shrank against the cushions, fearing that her cousin could be right. Despite what Uncle had said, they'd never have had to leave the London mansion if Felicity had kept her title. Uncle, however, smiled at her reassuringly, in between his complaints that their private car needed reupholstering.

Between one blink and the next, Felicity's surroundings had changed, and it made her feel a bit lost. She soon found herself looking out the window of the coach that had been waiting for them at the train station in Sussex, and inhaled the salty tang of the ocean air. White birds wheeled and screamed above cliffs of rock beneath a sky so blue it hurt her eyes. Low grasses rippled from gusty sea breezes along the side of the road, and the wind-shaped trees finally gave way to taller, straighter versions as they traveled slightly inland toward the manor.

Felicity sucked in a breath. "Oh, Uncle, it's beautiful."

Uncle Oliver quit complaining about the bumpy road and followed her gaze. "I forgot, child, how long it's been since you've visited Fairview. This beats all the wards we had in London, doesn't it?"

"The plants are wards?"

Ralph snickered. "'Course they are."

Aunt emerged from beneath her shawl for a moment. "Ralph, dear. Be nice to your cousin." Her breath shook and she spoke barely above a whisper.

Felicity looked at her aunt with concern.

"Don't worry," whispered Uncle. "She'll be fine as soon as we get her to the manor. Her delicate constitution makes travel difficult for her."

Felicity fought another twinge of guilt and quickly turned back to the view out her window. Plants and trees of unimaginable beauty surrounded Fairview manor. Blossoms of red and purple and snowy white sprouted from every branch and stem. Vines hung like ribbons between the plants, displaying their own pink flowers with petals so long that they draped like scarves all the way to the ground.

"How will Sir Terence…" she wondered aloud.

Aunt let her shawl drop, fiddled with her necklace, and then patted Felicity's skirts reassuringly. "Don't worry, your uncle has seen to everything. The moment your young beau sends word, the plants will be parted for his arrival."

With a sigh of relief, Felicity continued to gape, sticking her head partway out the window, amazed to see the greenery curl itself back to reveal a smooth gravel road. The coach slowed to a crawl, waiting for more of the plants to give way before them, until finally the manor itself came into view. Ivy lay so thickly over the walls that it obscured most of the windows, giving the illusion that the manor had been crafted of leaves instead of stone.

"You must be the most gifted botanist in all of England," Felicity whispered in awe.

Uncle Oliver smiled with pride.

"Father's herbal potions are the strongest ever crafted," Ralph boasted. "I wouldn't be surprised if the mere art of a viscount could counter the spells of even a royal."

Felicity smothered a grin. She didn't think that had come out exactly the way Ralph had intended. Uncle frowned at his utterance of the word "mere," and silence reigned in the carriage until they reached the manor.

At least Felicity's old room looked exactly as she remembered it. Dark and decayed, with holes worn in the upholstery and bed hangings, the wood-planked floor scuffed to rough splinters. This beautiful old place showed its neglect and age.

After a silent evening meal, with Ralph throwing her evil-eyed looks and Uncle reading his herbal at the table, Felicity retired to her room with dragging foot-steps. She struggled out of her dress, grateful that Katie had thought to dress her in one with buttons up the front. Her maid wouldn't arrive until tomorrow at the earliest, and Uncle kept a skeleton staff at the manor, so she'd best be prepared to take care of herself.

She'd just finished weaving her hair into a single braid for sleeping, when Daisy hissed out the window from her perch on the sill. The dragonette turned and gave her a hopeful look of entreaty.

"I don't know if that's such a good idea," she mused.

"Uncle warned me not to go wandering in his new gardens. There's spikes on some of those vines and leaves that make you itch if you brush up against them."

Daisy hissed again, her eyes shading from yellow to red.

Felicity sighed. "I suppose with your scales and fire-breath, I shouldn't be afraid that anything would harm you. And uncle didn't say *you* couldn't get out of this musty old manor."

Daisy flapped her wings. Felicity unlatched the window, pushed the frame against the vines growing over it, until it opened enough to allow her little dragonette out.

Daisy had gotten into the habit of wanting out before they settled for the evening. Felicity suspected that she supplemented her meals with her nightly forays, and since the neighbors didn't seem to mind the reduction in garbage rats, she saw no harm in it.

Daisy blinked a *thank you* and slithered over the sill, disappearing into the thick mat of vines. Felicity peeked her head out, watching her pet's progress by the movement of the greenery. "Be careful of what you eat," she called. "Gracious knows what's living amongst such plants. And don't be long, for I'm lonely without you."

She wanted to call out more instructions, but Daisy had already reached the ground. She heard a squeal and saw a spark of fire, and wondered if her dragonette would be able to crawl back up to her window with a full belly.

Felicity sighed and lit a candle against the encroaching darkness. The fairylights wouldn't work—the spells probably hadn't been renewed—and gaslights hadn't been installed in this old place, so she left the candle burning while she waited for Daisy to return.

She worried foolishly that Terence might not receive her uncle's message, or that he'd think they'd left on purpose to avoid him. She berated herself for her uncontrollable imagination and crawled beneath the linens. The ocean breeze trickling through the open window made her tremble, made the candle dance shadows on the walls.

She imagined her lion watching over her and replayed the memories of the night Terence had brought her body alive. Absorbed in curious imaginings of what might have transpired if they'd not been interrupted by Daisy's birth, her eyes drifted slowly closed.

When the sound of an unnatural gurgling woke her, the candle had burned down, leaving her room in darkness, and Daisy had still not returned.

She bolted upright in bed. Daisy had never left her side for more than an hour or two. Worries of what horrible calamities might have befallen her pet in these strange new surroundings made her leap out of bed.

An inky blackness covered the floor and curled around her bare feet like thick molasses. She stumbled and pitched forward.

Felicity turned her face sideways, so her cheek landed into the ooze, instead of her nose. She pushed and rolled, but couldn't rise. The blackness held her down like glue. She tried to tell herself to wake up from her own nightmare, that the black mess covering her floor was only an illusion and couldn't really harm her. She opened her mouth to scream for Daisy, and instead heard her voice calling out Terence's name.

Then the blackness rolled into her mouth and up her nose, a thick, viscous substance that tasted of cod liver oil. When she took a breath to scream, she felt it flow into her lungs. Into her ears. With merciful swiftness, the stuff enveloped her entire body, and Felicity knew no more.

Eleven

TERENCE STOOD WITH LEGS BRACED, HANDS CLASPED behind his back, and stared out the window of his tower room in Blackwell Hall. He tried to concentrate on the view. Usually the sight of the windswept moors, with their purple blooms of heather and occasional rocky crags, filled him with a sense of freedom and peace.

But he couldn't shake the feeling of being trapped. He couldn't stop imagining black, tumbled hair and trusting lavender-blue eyes and a beautiful face so aglow with passion that it would bring a lesser man to his knees. Terence cursed.

He'd never run from anything in his life; yet he'd run from Miss Felicity Seymour. He'd told Bentley to find a guide to the Underground and to contact him at Blackwell Hall, and then he'd taken the next train out of London. At the first station that touched on the moors, he got off and shifted, running through the grasses as fast as his lion's paws would take him.

He'd fought his were-self the entire way. It told him to go back to his mate. It told him to turn around and take what belonged to him. He growled in frustration, a full-throated roar that echoed across the moors for miles.

And he'd run on, until his haunches ached, until his tongue lolled from his powerful jaws and his head hung with fatigue.

His instincts took him home, through the crags of rocks surrounding Trolshire; their distorted human shapes resembled the mythical trolls that had given this land its name. His lion-self had taken him past the Hall, into the small grove of trees that clustered around a natural spring. He'd shifted into human at the foot of Thomas's grave.

"I need you," he'd demanded, his voice cracked and sore. "I never could understand why you went all cockle-headed over that woman. And now I do."

Terence shook his head, his dusty hair flying into his face. He strode to the pool, filling his mouth with the sweet water, letting it soothe his parched throat. He bathed his face, smoothing his wild hair back with the water, and went back to Thomas's graveside, blinking drops from his lashes.

And he'd spoken to his brother again. As if Thomas could've answered.

"What am I going to do? I can't keep up this charade anymore... because I'm no longer pretending... if ever I had been. I think I fell in love with this girl the moment I saw her, and what madness is that?" He collapsed onto his knees by Thomas's headstone. "Am I to repeat your mistake? This girl is just as tied up in relic-magic as the woman you fell in love with. And she killed you."

He'd pounded his fist in frustration against the smooth marble. "When I'm with her, I'm assured of her innocence. Did you feel the same way about the woman who murdered you? Is that why you trusted her? Well, you were a fool, Thomas. And I'm afraid... Bloody hell, I'm afraid that I'm a fool, too."

Terence sighed and rubbed his face to pull him back to the present. Of course, Thomas hadn't answered him. He knew he'd never hear his brother's voice again. That woman—Alicia—had used Merlin's diamond to steal other men's souls, to manipulate them for her own greed, and when Terence had exposed her, Thomas had been reluctant even then to condemn Alicia. It had cost him his life.

Terence had protected the sovereignty of the royals yet again, but the price had been too great. The world broke when Thomas had died.

Terence braced his hands on the windowsill, popping tendons in his shoulders. How did ordinary humans continue to live with such sorrows and worries? At least he had the reprieve of becoming his lion-self, to just live in the present on instinct alone, with little thought for his human concerns...

A scuffle at the door, interspersed with giggles, interrupted Terence from his thoughts. Everyone knew not to disturb him when he retired to his tower, but he couldn't help feeling grateful for the distraction. He forced thoughts of Thomas from his mind and turned toward the door.

What was left of his family and pride—his two little sisters, Lonna and Rianna—entered the room. Since both his parents had been shapeshifters, and even more unusual, were-lions, all their offspring had inherited their abilities. Six-year-old Lonna held the door open for her twelve-year-old sister, whose arms were laden with a tray of food. With careful precision, Rianna put the tray on his open roll-top desk, placed her hands on her slender hips, and flipped back her mane of tawny hair. "Cook says you haven't eaten all day."

"And that gives you leave to disturb me?"

A little bravado left her stance and she shrugged, briefly shifting into her lioness form, proof of her discomfiture.

Lonna's eyes widened and she turned a glare on her older brother. "S'not fair. You been here more'n a week and we hardly seen you a'tall." She fully shifted into her lioness form—so that whatever she'd been about to say next turned into a tiny roar.

Terence felt his lip quirk. He couldn't wait until they learned to control their shifting. How had his parents managed to discipline him and Thomas when they kept turning into their were-selves? He sighed at the thought of his mother and father. He'd lost so many of those he loved... how could he not cherish those still left to him?

He crouched and held out his arms. Lonna gave a little squeak, then pounced on him, snarling in mock-play. Rianna quickly gave up her adult-like demeanor, shifted and leapt on him too. Terence spent the remainder of the evening rolling across the floor with his little sisters, sometimes in human form, and sometimes in lion. He culminated the night by letting them crawl on his back, little human hands clenched tightly to his lion's mane of fur, and loping through the halls and gardens and moors of Trolshire.

Much later, he smiled when he tucked them into their beds, their cheeks still pink from their ride. He hadn't come to any decisions about Felicity, but he hadn't done wrong in coming home. He'd forgotten how much his sisters needed him.

And how much he needed them.

"Lonna," he whispered. "You look more like Thomas every day."

She answered with a sleepy grin. "I know. And Rianna looks kinda like you. Funny, huh?"

Terence tousled her red-gold hair. "Yes. Poor Rianna."

Lonna giggled and rolled over, her breathing slowing into the deep rhythm of sleep.

"I'm glad I look like you." Rianna's voice drifted from across the room. "And when I grow up, I'm going to be a spy just like you and hunt the evil relics that killed Thomas. And I won't let nothing stop me. Not family, nor love… nor nothing."

Terence stood dumbfounded. Is that how his little sister saw him? Abandoning his family for revenge? And what could he say? She was right, and they both knew it.

He bid her good night, but she ignored him, pretending to be asleep. As he walked to his room, he vowed to spend more time at his home, until the girls could control their shifting and could be brought to London with him.

He entered his own room, grateful for the big blaze in the hearth, and stripped off his clothes. He slid beneath the cool linens naked, as he preferred. He wondered what Felicity would make of his sisters and their constant, uncontrollable shifting. She'd probably smile with delight, and cuddle them to her just as she liked to cuddle his mane...

Warmth flooded Terence's chest; a soothing that he often felt when he thought of her. The heat fled to another part of him as he remembered that night in Spellsinger Gardens when he'd almost...

He growled. He'd have taken Felicity then, if not for that timely interruption. And then what would he have done? Married her, of course. No gentleman could do otherwise. And then what? She could just be a brilliant actress, using the relic to try to regain her title. What if recovering the relic destroyed her? The jewel had a tendency to bond with the user, and to part them might kill her. Could he murder his own wife?

If only he knew what magical power the relic possessed! It might help him figure out if her nightly monsters were a backlash of using the relic, or if someone was using the jewel against her.

Terence tossed and turned, still unable to make a decision about the girl. When he'd left London, he'd ordered Bentley to find a contact to help them search for the relic Underground. He didn't relish the idea of going beneath London into the abandoned railway tunnels. It was a haven to the scum of humanity and practitioners of the black arts. Sorcery had expanded on the old tunnels until the Underground had become a city almost as large as the one above it. But without any logical design and evil permeating throughout, it had evolved into nothing more than a maze of hell.

Yet he had to know the truth about Felicity. He realized that his desire to find the relic was prompted now by more than just revenge. He needed to know whether her goodness disguised a black heart.

Something crashed into his window. Terence sat up and squinted in the dim light. If he didn't know any better...

He got up and slipped into his trousers, opened his window and frowned at the message sprite that lay stunned on the sill. Terence picked up the winged creature and carefully set him on the bed.

The sprite opened his eyes and rubbed his forehead, muttering about the bane of clean glass. "You can never tell that there's something there."

Terence crossed his arms over his chest and leaned against the fireplace mantel. "You could stop and look first."

The message sprite gave him a lopsided grin. "That wouldn't be as dramatic as swooping into your room though, would it?"

"No, but a lot safer." Terence's smile dissolved as he studied the sprite's haggard appearance. "What message do you have for me?"

The little winged man narrowed his eyes thoughtfully. "I have a message from Bentley. It's a bit confusing."

Terence lifted a brow. Bentley didn't trust message sprites, nor fairylights, nor anything else the royals provided with their magic for their less fortunate subjects. There were too many political factions within the palace that would seize the chance for a relic, or any knowledge of them. His friend suspected that the message sprites might not keep their messages private.

Which meant Bentley felt the message was urgent enough to use one.

"What is it?"

The sprite waved a hand. "Long flight, that. Throat's a bit parched. Wouldn't happen to have any brandy?"

Terence refrained from rolling his eyes. The regular post might be slower, but at least he wouldn't have had to deal with an ill-tempered sprite. "Just spit it out."

The little man tapped his fingers against his throat. "Really. Very dry."

Terence schooled himself for patience and rang for the maid. The girl came quicker than he would've thought, even for a were-rabbit, and bobbed her head at his request. The sprite continued to grin at Terence until the girl returned with a tray of crystal and brandy... and a thimble. Her hands shook as she set it on the Chippendale table, for although her human side said master and friend, her were-self told her lion and predator.

The winged man took the thimble Terence handed him and swirled the amber liquid as if pondering the quality of the alcohol. He finally took a sip. And then another. Slowly.

"I've often wondered," mused Terence, "if a lion could digest the wings of a sprite, or if they must be spit out first."

The man froze in mid-sip and gave him a weak grin. "Bentley says he found a contact to guide you to the dark place."

"Ah." Terence poured himself a glass of brandy and savored the burn on his tongue. The dark place must be the Underground. Bentley had purposely made his message vague.

"Oh, there's more," taunted the sprite.

Terence growled.

"Just something about a girl. He wouldn't tell me her name or why you would care about some destitute—"

Terence strolled to the bed and grabbed the man by his wings, lifting his little, pointed face to within inches of his own. Terence gave him a friendly swing.

"What is the message?"

"What's the matter with you? Ouch! Sorry, never mind. Bentley said to tell you that the girl is gone. He's fairly sure she went with her family to their estate in Sussex. But their departure was sudden enough to make him suspicious. Can you let me down now?"

Terence grunted and carefully set the sprite back on the bed. He'd come to Blackwell Hall to put some distance between the girl and his desire. So when Felicity had stopped sending messages, he'd been privately relieved. Now he silently cursed himself.

She wouldn't have made such a move without telling him. He was certain that she loved him... or at least thought she did. She would have told him where to find her. Unless she couldn't.

"Fly back to London," snarled Terence, "quicker than you came. And tell Bentley to meet me at the station in Sussex. Can you do that?"

The sprite grinned, flapping the creases from his wings. "Sure. What if he wants to know why?"

Terence snorted. He wanted information to dangle in front of Bentley's nose. Well, why not? "Tell him— after he has to drag it out of you, of course..."

"Of course."

"That he's to meet me there because I said so."

Terence smoothed back his wild hair. He told

himself not to worry about the girl. He had no reason to believe her disappearance might be anything sinister. Bentley always had suspicions about everything.

But Terence's were-self urged him to rush to her side and make sure she was all right.

The sprite studied Terence's face with both pointed eyebrows raised. "She must be some girl." Then he flew out of the room, but swooped back in for one go-round. Terence ducked, then shook his head. He supposed that made up for the little man's disappointment over his earlier entrance.

For the first time, Terence felt guilty when he said goodbye to his sisters. They shouldn't be left alone without family around them. Why hadn't he realized that sooner?

He would give it some more thought as soon as he assured himself that Felicity was safe. His anxiety for her made the journey to Sussex seem long, with all kinds of questions to ponder. Terence met an equally withdrawn and silent Bentley at the station, who had already secured them a gig. They barely exchanged a few words until they reached Lord Wortley's estate.

Bentley pulled back on the reins of his rented horse. "You think this is it?"

Terence shrugged. "The old man from the village said the place was overgrown with plants."

"This isn't overgrown, it's a bloody jungle! How are we going to get in?"

Terence studied the tangled foliage. Had Felicity's uncle decided that separating the girl from her intended would change her mind? That if given enough time, he could talk the girl out of marrying him? Or did he think that Terence would drop his courtship and forget about her? Well, despite what Wortley might think of the girl, he'd find out soon enough that Felicity wasn't a woman that could easily be forgotten.

And that nothing could keep Terence away from the woman he'd claimed.

Terence leapt out of the carriage and shifted, lifted a paw and revealed his razor-sharp claws. He slashed at a vine that had glaring orange streaks along its length. Orange-green muck oozed from the cut and the plant shrieked like a demon. Terence woofed and froze.

Bentley suddenly appeared at his side and pulled a knife from his boot. "Bloody hell, what was that? Are the things alive?"

Terence wiped the orange stuff off his claws by raking the ground. He pushed forward again, cutting through a fuzzy-leafed bush. At least the thing didn't scream. He heard Bentley following him, muttering under his breath.

"Lord Wortley's only a viscount. Dabbles in potions and charms. Heard they grew their own herbs, but this is ridiculous."

An hour later, Terence had cut them through to a little clearing. In the center of it sat a spiny-tipped plant, the middle of it sporting a style as thick as a sapling, the stigma at the top resembling the flowing skirts of a woman's dress. It looked harmless, but he gave it a wide berth anyway, sticking to the edges of the clearing.

Bentley studied the plant with a frown. "Do you think Lord Wortley used relic-magic to create these monstrosities? I shudder to think what kind of potion this would be used for."

Terence had started swiping at foliage again, cutting another path, when he heard his friend give a startled yelp. Bentley stood frozen with the style of the plant curved toward him, swaying its stigma over his head, the gauze-like petals of it brushing the top of his friend's brown hair.

Bentley dropped his knife, a slow smile spreading across his narrow face, and petted the billowing stuff. He gathered up handfuls and buried his nose in it.

Terence leapt. The plant shuddered and contracted, wrapping Bentley with suffocating gauze. It pulled his friend toward its spiny center. Terence swiped at the style, trying to cut it in half, succeeding only in scraping its green skin.

He roared, and Bentley blinked, the dopey smile on his face fading to one of bewilderment. Bentley tried to move, and the gauze squeezed tighter. Terence leapt again, this time aiming for the stigma, slicing through the film of it. With an abrupt shudder, it let Bentley go, sprang back to its upright position, and fluttered its skirt-like stigma as innocently as a debutante.

Bentley crouched, retrieved his knife, and scuttled after Terence, who used his claws with renewed enthusiasm to hack their way out of the clearing.

"I was foolish, sir."

Terence grunted.

"But you have no idea how good she—it smelt. Like the finest perfume. I've never experienced anything like that. If Lord Wortley markets it as an aphrodisiac, he'd make a fortune."

Terence shifted back to human and sat, his aching arms resting on his legs. "It tried to eat you, Bentley. I doubt Wortley created that thing with a love potion in mind."

"But it shouldn't have been able to harm me." Bentley twitched his nose. "I mean, it's magic, and we're immune."

"The plants are real," replied Terence. "Magic was only used to alter their growth. We're just as susceptible to them as we are to any other mundane threat."

"This place needs to be burned to the ground."

Terence nodded in agreement. "We'll tell the prince about it. If we ever make it out of here."

Bentley's nose twitching escalated. He pulled another knife from his other boot. "Give me a good old monster any day." He began to hack double-handed through a screen of bushes. The leaves were coated with white powder, and soon it looked as if his friend stood in the middle of a small snowstorm. He sneezed.

Terence got to his feet, shifted into lion, his heavy fur coat protecting him from the white fall. By the time they'd made it through the growth to a small stream, red welts had appeared on Bentley's skin and he shifted into his rat-self to escape the torment. He crawled into Terence's mane and stayed there.

Terence washed himself and his friend thoroughly in the stream before moving on. He trod through the water, hoping it would be a safer path to Wortley's manor.

The quiet unsettled him. Other than the sound of the wind shushing through the trees, and the splashing of his paws, the forest-jungle lay silent.

He might not have heard the hissing otherwise; or if

he had, it would have been drowned in the cacophony of noises from any normal forest.

He dropped to a crouch, nose searching and ears straining. He never would've caught the faint scent of scorched wood or the sound of muffled hissing if he'd been in human form.

The sound could have been made by a snake. He tried to convince himself of that. But it sounded so much like the noise he remembered Daisy making that his heart turned over. Could it be the little dragonette? And if it was, that meant…

Terence crashed through the jungle, leaping over lichen-crusted logs and squeezing through twisted branches, only pausing long enough to slice through vines if they formed a weave that he couldn't penetrate.

The odor of burnt wood hit him like a wall. Terence shuddered to a stop between two saplings, his tongue hanging out. He felt Bentley part the hair of his mane to have a look-see.

The saplings formed a ring in front of them. Their branches—no, not branches. These were too supple to be true branches. They resembled nothing more than green, tubular arms. And those arms wrapped around each other, forming a prison-ring in their center. The end of each arm tapered into a point, and several of them poked and prodded the dragonette trapped in the center of the ring.

Daisy fitfully breathed bursts of fire. She looked like she'd been trapped for some time and had reached the end of her endurance.

Terence leaped into the middle of the ring, hoping those arm-branches might be as vulnerable to his claws as human ones. Bentley shifted in midair, twisting to the side as they landed, pulling out his knives in one fluid movement. Terence fought off the spear-like arms while Bentley hacked at the prison of roots.

Bentley had more success. The roots seemed tender, giving way to the bite of cold steel, whereas Terence did more dodging than damage to the arms.

"Almost got him," grunted Bentley. "Almost got him… out! He's free! Terence, let's—"

Terence spun, barely missing a green spear that shuddered as it impaled the ground next to him. The roots had rallied, encasing Bentley's feet. The dragonette snapped at them, but couldn't burn them without scorching Bentley. The saplings pulled more roots from the earth and Daisy turned on those, shriveling them as they approached.

Terence growled. Bentley shifted, the roots that had encased him unable to tighten quickly enough to catch his rat-form. As soon as Terence felt him clamber up his mane, he leaped forward, grabbing the fighting dragonette gingerly in his jaws. With Daisy burning a path in front of them, Terence carried them out of the circle, dodging spears from above and roots from below.

Terence headed doggedly for the stream they'd passed, feeling Daisy go limp in his jaws. He wondered how long the dragonette had been trapped within that deadly circle. Daisy would not willingly leave her mistress's side for very long, but the creature looked half starved.

Terence set Daisy on a sun-warmed rock by the stream and shifted. Bentley clung to his collar, staying in his were-form. "Daisy, where's your mistress?"

The dragonette opened her eyes, those yellow sapphires piercing him. She could no more answer than he could speak in his were-form. But she understood what he said, for he saw her shudder with alarm and try to rise, only to flop back on her belly, her legs unable to support her.

"She's not—she wasn't in that circle of trees, was she?"

Daisy shook her head.

"She's safe at the manor?"

Daisy blinked at him.

At the manor, yes. But he could tell that Daisy wasn't sure of her safety. The dragonette pleaded with her eyes.

"I'll take you to her. Will the stream lead us there?"

Daisy seemed to smile, those scaly lips curling up at the corners. Terence shifted back to lion-form, clasped the dragonette in his teeth again, and bounded through the water. He didn't know how long Daisy had left Felicity unprotected. What if something had happened to her?

Twelve

Felicity drifted in and out of her dreams. Sometimes she heard Katie's Irish lilt and felt warm broth trickle down her throat. She had enough strength to swallow it and to wiggle a finger or two, but the effort to open her eyes always made her sink back into a fog of blackness.

So she'd stopped trying. She would just lie there, listening to the sounds around her, daydreaming about her lion. He would stop the black thing from filling her, fighting it off with his claws, and then she would be able to breathe freely for a while, without black ooze filling up her lungs.

When she smelled the musky scent of wet lion fur, she didn't feel surprised, just grateful that her daydreams had become more real. When Katie gasped with fear, followed by the sound of dishes crashing to the floor, Felicity felt tempted to open her eyes.

But then she heard that voice, the husky tone of it making her shiver, and she didn't want this dream to end.

"What happened?" he asked.

"I-I'm not certain." Katie sounded frightened. "When I arrived, she just wouldn't wake up. Lord Wortley says 'tis the fever, but I've never seen the like. She's cool to the touch."

Felicity felt the warmth of a large palm atop her brow. "I feel no fever. Did she have another bad dream?"

"I canna say, sir. But I asked Master Ralph to send for a physician when he reached London. He… he went there for his testing, ye see, the very day Miss Felicity fell ill."

"What do you think, Bentley?"

Felicity thought this an interesting development. She'd never met anyone named Bentley and couldn't imagine why she'd dream him up. Especially his voice. It seemed to twitch.

"Never seen the like. She's not enspelled, but she reeks of—"

Terence interrupted. She remembered his name now, and that he was her lion-turned-human. "I smell it too. Did she overexert herself, or has someone used it against her?"

Felicity wrinkled her forehead in a frown. Had she not been so perplexed, she might've been elated that she'd managed to move her facial muscles. What were these two talking about? Used what against her? She must still be dreaming, for this appeared like all of her other nightmares, making little sense.

She heard Terence let out an explosive breath. "It doesn't matter anymore. I've got to get her away from here, for her own good." His voice sounded oddly resigned.

The Bentley man squeaked. "Sir! You can't mean to take her back through that jungle."

The hand on her forehead moved away, and Felicity groaned. She wanted him to keep it there. Then she felt the heat of Terence's body move closer to her, felt his breath near her face. Smelled the musky, clean scent of him. His fingers smoothed the hair away from her cheeks.

"Felicity, are you awake? Can you open your eyes?"

She groaned again. She wanted to do it for him, wanted to see his handsome face, but she feared the blackness.

His voice gentled to a whisper. "I am here now, nothing will hurt you. And I've brought Daisy with me. Surely you want to see your dragonette?"

Felicity fluttered her lashes. Her baby had come home? She'd been so worried when Daisy hadn't returned. Felicity's eyes flew open and she gasped for breath. She knew the black ooze didn't fill her lungs now, but she could remember the pain of it. In a panic, she kicked at the linens covering her, trying to get even that little weight off her chest.

"Look at me," demanded Terence, his commanding voice penetrating her frightened mind. Her eyes flew to his, and then the oddest thing happened. Like so often, he mesmerized her with his gaze, but this time, instead of making her heart beat with a wild anticipation, the warmth in those golden depths soothed her.

A dry tongue licked her face. Felicity lifted a shaky hand and smoothed the scales on top of Daisy's head. Those sapphire-yellow eyes swirled, looking guilty and scared and relieved all at the same time.

"Daisy," she sighed. The dragonette burrowed her snout against the back of her neck, and settled herself around her shoulders.

"I had…" Felicity's voice cracked from disuse. "I had the most dreadful nightmare."

The worry wrinkles on Terence's forehead smoothed out, and that lazy smile spread across his face, exposing his incisors. "I bet you did. How do you feel?"

Felicity sank back into the pillows. "Stronger now, I think. I've just been so very weak."

Terence exchanged a look with another man— Bentley, she presumed. He twitched his nose, and most remarkably, his ears, while at the same time scratching at his neck and arm. She'd never seen such extraordinary dexterity. The man finally shrugged.

Katie frowned at Terence. "It's shocking enough that you're in her bedchamber, sir, but a strange man as well…" Katie was right. Felicity should be appalled. But all she managed to feel was a weak curiosity.

"May I introduce you to my manservant and friend, Bentley Poole? Bentley, this is Miss Felicity Seymour, and her maid, Katie."

The thin man jerked his head in a nod at her and her maid, then resumed his furious scratching. Felicity noticed the red welts along his face and arms. Had he stumbled into some poison ivy?

"Terence," said Felicity. "What are you doing here? Certainly my uncle didn't allow you upstairs."

His lips curled. "No, we came into the house through a different route." He gestured at the open window.

"I don't understand."

"We had a bit of difficulty getting through the surrounding jungle."

Daisy hissed in her ear.

Terence frowned at her dragonette. "It made me doubt my welcome."

"But Uncle said…" Felicity's eyes closed. She still felt so very tired. "Uncle said he'd sent you word when to come, and that he'd keep the road to the manor clear." She tried to remember his exact words, but failed.

"Felicity. Open your eyes. Good. I suspect that your uncle may have brought you here to keep you away from me."

She opened her mouth to argue, but he put a finger across her lips.

"You know he thinks I'm not good enough for you. Perhaps he thought you'd change your mind about me, if given enough time."

"I would never," Felicity muttered beneath his finger.

"I know, dearest. But I think I have a solution to all this. Will you trust me?"

He'd called her dearest. She knew she'd do whatever he asked, when he called her that. She nodded.

"Will you come away with me?"

"You mean elope?"

Katie gasped, and Bentley sounded like he swallowed a choke. "Are you sure about this, sir?" he sputtered.

Terence turned and fixed his manservant with a baleful stare. "Do you see another way to protect her?"

Bentley scratched his armpit and shrugged.

Before Felicity could ask what Terence thought he might be protecting her from, he turned back to her. "We intend to marry soon anyway, why wait? And once the deed is done, your uncle will come to accept it."

Felicity glanced at Katie. Her maid's eyes shone with dreamy romance. Well, it did sound rather romantic, but not very respectful of her aunt and uncle. And what about her dress and all the lovely wedding preparations she'd planned?

She looked back at Terence. He had the most worried frown on his face. What was more important: him or her silly desire for the fripperies of a wedding?

"You didn't receive a message from my uncle?"

Terence shook his head.

Felicity didn't understand it. She glanced again at Bentley, noting the dirty state of his clothes, his disheveled hair, and several scrapes and bruises. They had indeed fought their way to the manor.

"I've heard of several couples," interjected Katie, "who have eloped because their parents were opposed to the match. It's not uncommon, miss, if ye don't mind me saying so."

Terence looked surprised by her maid's support and gave the redhead a nod of appreciation. He seemed to be aware that Felicity wavered on a decision, for he pushed the advantage.

"Felicity, you must choose between me and your uncle. It's as simple as that."

Was it? She couldn't be sure. But she had resolved to never doubt Terence again. "Do you really think it's best?"

He nodded, that golden mane of hair tumbling over his brow and cheeks. She reached up and smoothed it back, savoring the silky softness of it. "Then I will allow you to steal me away."

His face split into a smile that brightened the room. Bentley made that choking sound again, and Katie clapped her hands.

Terence took Felicity's hand, and pulled her from the bed. "Can you stand?"

Felicity's knees wobbled, but they held.

Terence turned to Katie. "Pack a light bag."

"Now, sir? It's almost dark."

Felicity giggled, feeling lightheaded on her feet.

"Yes, now. Tell her uncle that she's not to be disturbed this evening. I suppose you'll want to go with her?"

A stubborn expression crossed Katie's freckled face that dared him to deny her, but obviously Terence had no intention of doing so.

With a speed that left Felicity breathless, her maid pulled her behind the dressing screen and helped her into her favorite blue serge traveling costume, an amazing feat since Daisy refused to be budged from her position around Felicity's neck. Felicity managed to pack her own valise and write a note to her aunt and uncle, while Katie went downstairs to let the household know that her mistress didn't want to be disturbed.

Terence's manservant Bentley only offered one argument. "At night, sir? In that god-forsaken—"

"Enough. We'll follow the creek most of the way. If we travel at night, the ladies won't be able to see anything that might, er, frighten them."

Bentley's brow smoothed in apparent under-standing, and he nodded.

Felicity hadn't had an opportunity to explore the inner portion of her uncle's garden, but surely Terence didn't think her so delicate that plants and flowers would frighten her? Perhaps she should tell him about her dreams sometime.

Felicity held her breath when Terence and Bentley went out the window in their were-forms, Terence practically leaping to the ground and Bentley scampering through the vines like Daisy had. When they reached the ground they shifted back to human, and Terence told her to jump.

"Are they mad?" whispered Katie. "Best let me go first, miss, to test it out."

Felicity laid the note to her aunt and uncle on her pillow and nodded tiredly. Her legs simply had no strength, and that first surge of energy had quickly left her. After Katie jumped safely into the men's arms, she followed her maid more by falling out of the window than by leaping.

Although she had resolved to leave by her own two feet, Felicity only managed a short way into the garden before her strength completely left her. Terence scooped her up into his arms, and though she desperately fought against it, his comforting stride soon put her to sleep.

❦

Felicity slept through most of the journey back to London. She remembered exchanging vows in a small village chapel, her eyes heavy with sleep. But she'd managed to stay awake long enough for the ceremony. She didn't regret the lack of a large wedding; the kind minister and his sweet wife treated them like royalty, and Katie had managed to gather flowers from Uncle's garden for a lovely bouquet. Bentley eyed the plants suspiciously, and although she had wanted to save them to press into a book, they mysteriously disappeared after the ceremony.

Terence had sealed their union with a kiss that left no doubt of his passion, making her legs crumple beneath her again. Unfortunately, even though they'd secured a private car for the rest of their homeward journey, Felicity fell back to sleep as soon as her head hit the cushions. She didn't wake again until the train jerked to a stop at the London station. The warmth of Terence's body as she snuggled up to him filled her with joy, and she realized that since they'd left her uncle's manor, she hadn't had a single bad dream.

After a quick meal to break their fast, Terence hired a coach to take her home to his London residence. Felicity couldn't suppress a feeling of excitement.

"You truly live in Trickside? Where all the magic shops are?"

Terence nodded, the worried frown between his brows disappearing when he looked at her face. "Will you mind living there for a while? I'll look for another place, in a better area that might tolerate shapeshifters."

"I will make my home wherever you are. It doesn't matter to me one whit if it's not acceptable to the aristocracy—don't you recall I'm no longer one of them? Besides, it all sounds vastly exciting."

He picked up her hand and kissed her knuckles. The gesture gave her a tremor of delight. Goodness, she just realized that the man who'd kissed her hand was now her husband. And that they only had part of the day left before they'd retire to his bedchamber.

The coach slowed to a stop in front of a rather decrepit brownstone building. Felicity tried to hide the chagrin from her face. So, it was even less grand than she'd imagined. It was still her new home, and perhaps she'd be able to redecorate the inside. By non-magical means of course, but her husband didn't lack for money, and she'd manage it the same way the lower classes did.

Terence took her hand to escort her out of the carriage and continued to hold it while he took her up the steps to the front door. Bentley and Katie had hurried on ahead to prepare for them. When Terence opened the door, Felicity could see that the entire household staff had been assembled to greet her.

She blinked in astonishment. Every one of them, from the scullery maid to the footman, noticed her. They bobbed their heads or curtsied, shyly mumbling their welcomes, never once looking over her shoulder or narrowing their eyes at her as if she were difficult to see. When they dispersed to go about their duties, not one of them accidentally bumped into her.

Daisy stretched and grumbled, and Terence told Katie to take the dragonette and instruct Cook to provide her with the finest slab of meat in the kitchen. Daisy refused to budge until Terence reassured her that he would protect Felicity. That she would always be safe here.

Felicity decided she would very much like being mistress of her new home. That as Terence's wife, she held such a position of importance that she might never be overlooked again.

"Shall I show you around?" asked her husband.

Felicity nodded, her eyes widening as Terence led her from room to room. She realized that redecorating would be entirely unnecessary. Treasures filled every nook and cranny, vases and carpets and furnishings that had the patina of museum pieces. Other than adding her own personal touches, she couldn't imagine disposing of any of his exquisite belongings.

"How did you come by these?" she said, running a finger across an ancient carving of ivory. Tiny figures in pointed hats bent over some type of labor, and even tinier animals frolicked in the foreground.

"My father brought them back from China," he replied. "Most of this house is filled with the overflow from Blackwell Hall. My parents... traveled quite a bit before they died."

"I see. I'm sorry, Terence. I miss my mother and father, too." Felicity squeezed his hand, and although he stared straight ahead, he returned the gesture.

"This is my," he said, stumbling over the words, "I mean, our, bedchamber."

He led her through a double door into a large, airy room. Felicity trembled, feeling the blood rush to her face as she stared at the massive poster bed. He'd given her a healthy curiosity about what it would be like to consummate their marriage, and yet she suddenly felt terribly shy.

Terence studied the room with a worried frown. "You'll probably want to make some changes. Make it more ladylike for you."

Felicity's lips tried to smile at him in reassurance. He thought she might be worried about fripperies, when that bed shouted its implications at her? But she reminded herself that she had gotten quite good at suppressing fear.

"If you really don't mind? I'd like to make the parlor a bit more to my taste as well."

"Whatever suits you." He dropped her hand. His face looked oddly disappointed.

"Of course," she hurried on, "it's quite elegant enough as it is. The entire house is much larger on the inside, and one would never guess that the interior could rival any of the finest mansions in the West End. I would only add, as you say, 'ladylike' things. Oh, flowers, and cushions and such."

Terence's face looked less grim as she spoke. He tossed his mane of golden brown hair, staring into her eyes, until her words just floated to silence, and she drowned helplessly in his gaze.

"You like it then? My house?"

She licked her lips and nodded.

With two strides he stood a breath away from her, and placed his large hands lightly on her shoulders. "You're not disappointed? You're used to much grander things."

Felicity realized that he still felt inferior to her, and she silently cursed the society that had made him see her in that way. It would be a struggle to get him to overcome that.

"I must assure you, h–husband, that I have never felt more at home than I do here." And she realized that she spoke the truth. The moment she'd walked in the door, she'd felt as if she finally belonged. For the first time since her parents had died she was safe and significant, and she'd never be overlooked here.

Terence stared into her eyes as if he longed to see into her very soul. Then he lowered his head and kissed her with such tenderness tears stung her eyes.

Felicity threw her arms around his massive shoulders and kissed him back, trying to show him how much he meant to her. If not for him, she'd be a lonely spinster, and now she had her own home, his protective love, and the promise of children...

Her eyes flew open and saw the empty, massive bed. She started to tremble again.

Terence pulled away and stared at her. "You're still not well. I've made you jump through windows and suffer the rails and turned your life upside down. I'll send for Katie, and I want you to rest, understand?"

Felicity opened her mouth to object. She'd been sleeping for the past twenty-four hours already. The last thing she wanted to do was rest. But the worried frown on his forehead made her snap her mouth shut.

She'd been hardy enough to jump through a window, after all. But she supposed she must get used to the whims of a husband and let him pamper her when he felt inclined. So she let him go fetch Katie and lay obediently on the bed, breathing in the scent of him that branded the pillows. Her eyes shut of their own accord, and despite all the excitement of finding herself in her new home, she drifted off to sleep.

When she woke, she smiled ruefully at the paneled ceiling. Perhaps her husband had been right, after all. She hadn't thought she could sleep any more, and had managed to anyway. Felicity tried not to jostle Daisy when she rose. The cook may have gone a bit overboard. The dragonette's stomach still bulged from her meal, and she lay in a contented stupor.

Felicity searched the room for the bell-pull, smiled at the woven design of lion cubs at play when she found it. She wandered the room while waiting for Katie, studying Terence's choice of books and knick-knacks. She should've felt like a stranger, but instead she kept finding herself sighing with contentment.

Katie arrived followed by a maid with buckteeth as large as a rabbit's. They poured a bath and Felicity would've soaked longer if she hadn't been so eager to join her new husband. Katie surprised her by pulling a new gown out of her husband's clothing armoire.

Felicity greedily pulled it on, feeling like a bride at last, in the layers of white lace that covered the bodice and skirt of the gown. It was woefully out of fashion, but had tiny seed pearls stitched along the low-cut neckline, around the hem of the sleeves and across the narrow waist. Katie gathered up Felicity's thick, black hair and twisted it loosely in the back, sprinkling pearl-topped pins throughout her creation.

Daisy hissed and Felicity gathered her up, letting the dragonette wrap her scaled hide around her neck. Now it looked as if she wore a choker of opals to highlight her gown.

"Sir Terence will have his bride this evening, at least," announced Katie with satisfaction. "Don't get me wrong, miss. The ceremony in the village was perfectly romantic. But rather rushed. Tonight, his lordship will understand the true value of the match."

Felicity sighed at her reflection. The face that looked back at her was the same as always, except for the happy sparkle in her lavender-blue eyes. She had a sudden flash of memory of her sixteenth birthday, when Aunt and Uncle had come to Graystone Castle with all their fine friends. She'd been so excited about her first presentation into society, and had vainly thought that she looked just as beautiful as her mother with her hair up and dressed in a fancy, blue silk gown.

Her governess had stiffly reminded her that a keen mind would take one farther than a pretty face, but Felicity had ignored her. After all, her governess had been the most homely woman imaginable; what would she know of beauty? And nothing could have squashed her enthusiasm.

Except walking into a room full of people who ignored her very presence.

Felicity sighed. She wished she could be a little less ordinary looking, but perhaps Katie had managed that feat with the dress.

"Where did you get it?" Felicity thought to ask.

Katie winked. "'Twas Sir Terence's mother's wedding dress. He told me to make use of his mother's trunk for ye, until he could provide ye with a proper wardrobe."

Felicity marveled at her new husband's thoughtfulness as she floated down the stairs of her new home. She could easily get used to being the center of attention.

Out of long habit, she kept to the walls, leaving the steps clear. A servant started up the steps, carrying a bundle of linens, and Felicity stopped, pressing herself even closer to the wall, waiting for the maid to pass her.

The servant stopped and bowed her head, waiting for her mistress to pass first.

They both stood in such indecision that Felicity finally laughed, swept up her skirts again, and proceeded past the girl.

She found her golden man in the dining room, dressed in black trousers, waistcoat and jacket. The white of his shirt and gloves stood out in stark contrast to the rest of his formal garb. He rose when she entered the room, his mouth open to say something, and then he just froze, staring at her.

Felicity didn't quite know what to do, so she stood and stared back. He'd brushed his hair away from his face, but left it hanging loose in the back, as he seemed to prefer. The candlelight reflected off the sharp planes of his cheekbones, and his eyes glimmered with golden fire. She made herself breathe. She'd have to live with him, after all. She couldn't go around all day feeling flummoxed every time he gazed at her.

"Thank you," she managed to whisper. "For the loan of your mother's clothes. I'm sure I don't do them justice."

He swallowed. With careful precision he placed the crystal goblet that he'd held in his hand back on the table. "It always astonishes me that you don't realize how beautiful you are."

Terence refused to let her sit at the opposite end of the table, and instead held out the velvet-upholstered chair next to his own. His attention stayed fixed on her throughout the meal, as if she were the only other person in the world. He found little excuses to touch her and sometimes no excuse at all. His gloves barely shielded her skin from the heat of his fingers when he smoothed imaginary hair from her cheek, caressed her arm, or touched the back of her hand.

He made her feel as if she were the most important woman in the world. What else could possibly matter?

"You haven't touched your peas."

Felicity looked down in surprise at the lamb cutlet on her plate. Out of habit, she had chased all the little green vegetables off to the side. "I'm just not partial to peas."

One golden brow rose. "Do you hear that, Bentley?"

"Very clearly, sir," replied his friend as he inspected another dish that the maid had brought into the room. At his nod of approval, the girl smiled and set it on the table, giving another shy smile to Felicity.

"Tell Cook that her new mistress is not partial to peas, and that they shall never be served in this house again."

"Certainly, sir," replied Terence's manservant, and apparently went off right then to do his master's bidding.

Felicity took a sip of wine. How could she not love this man? She felt safe with him, and protected, and cherished. Had she harbored any doubts about her feelings, they would've been dismissed as soon as she'd walked into her new home.

Happiness overwhelmed her and she smiled at her new husband. He jerked back as if he'd been struck, and then grinned sheepishly, pulling his chair even closer to her.

Ah yes, she thought she might have loved him from the moment they'd met. And now she was in danger of completely adoring him.

Thirteen

FELICITY WIGGLED IN HER CORSET, HER STOMACH uncomfortably full. Terence had encouraged her to eat too much of their wedding feast, even feeding her tidbits from his own fork.

"Dessert?" he asked, waving a hand at the chocolate cream.

Felicity groaned. "No, thank you. Even my favorite couldn't tempt me to eat another bite."

Terence's eyes lit up. "Did you hear that, Bentley?"

"Yes, sir," sighed the manservant. Felicity hid her grin behind her napkin.

"Tell the cook—"

"To make sure it is served every night," finished Bentley, already halfway out the room.

Felicity lowered her napkin. "Really, Terence. It's not necessary to make Bentley tell the cook every little thing I like or dislike. He looks quite worn out from running to the kitchens."

"Hmm, perhaps you're right. The best way would be for you to make a list, all at once, and give it to the cook."

Felicity blinked.

"And if you find that the meals she prepares are not to your standards, you must tell me at once, and I will hire another cook."

"It's really not—"

He leaned forward, placing his gloved hand over hers. "It is, and I will hear no objections on this. Not when it involves your comfort in my, er, our home."

She should argue with him, but all the attention made her feel so happy, she didn't want to. If only she hadn't been aware that his actions sprang from a fear that his home wouldn't be good enough for her...

"Terence. Your home is grand, the food is excellent, your servants equal to those of the royal family. Had I married a king, I couldn't have asked for more."

He leaned back in his chair, a smug grin on his handsome face. "Naturally. But wait until you see Blackwell Hall. It would rival even your Irish castle, I'm sure."

Felicity picked up her napkin and hid another smile. How quickly he'd turned arrogant! And how delightfully handsome he looked, with that satisfied smile curving his full lips and that broad nose tipped haughtily into the air.

"—and my two sisters, Lonna and Rianna, occupy the west wing, where Thomas and I were raised—"

"I beg your pardon?" Felicity had not been listening, in complete absorption of her husband's good looks, but her ears had pricked at the word *sisters*. "You have... that means I have... sisters. Why have you not mentioned them before? And who is Thomas? You never mentioned him before either."

Terence paused, as if he just now realized what he'd been saying. He shrugged. "It's never come up."

Felicity tried to tamp down a surge of anger. Daisy woke and hissed. "I had assumed that you were an only child, like me. Don't you think it would have been appropriate to mention the rest of your family?"

He growled. Softly, under his breath, but she heard it quite clearly. It didn't scare her in the slightest. He owed her an explanation. She had sisters-in-law! All her life she'd wished for a sibling to ease her loneliness.

Felicity realized that she'd married a complete stranger. How could she have vowed to trust a man who kept so many secrets?

"Perhaps, madam," interjected Bentley, who'd silently returned to his post, "I should mention that he lost his brother quite recently, and perhaps that's the reason…"

Terence sprang to his feet, his chair screeching across the wooden floor, and turned to his friend, tawny hair flying around his face. "Stay out of this. Better yet, leave us to our privacy."

Bentley's nose twitched, but he calmly gave his master a bow and waved his hand at the maid and footman to precede him out of the room. He paused before closing the double doors behind him. "Sir, may I have a word with you before you retire, then? It concerns an urgent business matter."

Felicity frowned. One minute Bentley acted like Terence's equal, the next as his servant. She wondered how many years they'd been together and what they'd experienced, to create such an odd relationship.

Terence raked his fingers through his thick hair. "Yes, of course."

Bentley dipped his head and closed the doors firmly behind him.

Felicity tried to suppress a shiver. Terence paced the room like it was a cage.

"Is it true?" she asked. "Did you lose your brother recently?"

He refused to meet her eyes. "Yes. But that's not why I didn't mention my sisters. I just thought…"

He stopped behind her chair, as if he hid from her. As if he were going to say something else, and had changed his mind. She could feel his body heat warm the back of her, his breath stir the hair on the top of her head. He tossed his gloves on the table, and settled his bare hands on her shoulders. Daisy hissed, but didn't snap at him.

"I thought," he continued, "that we should have time alone together first. Even though I feel like I've known you my entire life, we haven't really even begun to understand each other. I thought that should come first, before we involved my sisters in our life. I only thought of them, and not how you might feel."

Felicity closed her eyes and leaned her head back against his body. Of course they had to consider how the girls would feel. But he had it all wrong. "Who takes care of them? A governess? Or do you have any more family you haven't told me about?"

"I have cousins, and you'll meet them all. But only my two sisters are left of my close family."

"Then let me tell you how it feels to be raised by a governess. To not have the love and support of a family. It is lonely, Terence, lonelier than you could imagine. And no matter how well meaning the servant, they can never love you like true family can. I cannot imagine that the girls don't want to be with you. Why have you not brought them to London?"

His hands tightened on her shoulders. "They cannot control their shifting yet. It would be difficult for them here. And I am often gone on business anyway. But recently I have come to doubt my decisions concerning their welfare."

Felicity tilted her chin up to look at him. Perhaps she might never know everything about him... except that he loved her. Shouldn't that be enough? "Then will you bring them here?"

He bent over her face and gave her an upside-down kiss on her forehead. "There's some business I must attend to first."

"But after that?"

He bent a little farther and kissed her lips hungrily, as if he'd wanted to do it all evening, and had just now loosened his restraint. Felicity enjoyed the novel sensation of his bottom lip over her top and lost herself in the warmth of his mouth.

Really, how many ways were there to kiss? And would he show them all to her?

"It seems," he murmured, "that I cannot deny you anything. I will fetch new sisters for you, as soon as possible."

Felicity reached up and buried her fingers in his hair, tilting his head sideways so that he could kiss her deeper. He complied with a low growl, his hands sliding down her shoulders until his fingers caressed the tops of her breasts. Daisy hissed and Felicity smelled the faint scent of smoke.

Terence pulled away. "Daisy's right, you know." He laughed a bit shakily. "This is not the time or place, and I have no restraint where you're concerned."

Felicity's cheeks warmed. Yes, it would be enough that he loved and wanted her.

He came around to the side of her chair and held out his hand. She took it and rose, keeping her eyes lowered from his. Terence put a finger under her chin, and forced her to look at him. His eyes burned with something that fascinated and terrified her at the same time.

"Leave Daisy with Katie for the night."

"Y-yes, of course."

"You look flushed, dearest. Perhaps you should retire early."

Felicity's heart pounded in her ears. She knew very well what he truly meant.

He leaned forward and kissed her again, a possessive quality to it, as if he branded her as his own. "I will join you shortly."

Felicity could only nod. With sudden clarity she remembered what he'd done to her body in Spellsinger Gardens, the way he'd made her explode with pleasure. She'd dreamt about it, had even been eager to experience it again. Yet, at the same time, she felt slightly fearful of what might come after. She'd caught a glimpse of him and didn't know how she might properly manage it.

She forced herself not to flee from the room. She hesitated a moment, with her hand on the doorknob. She had to ask, before she left him. But his face had shown such pain that she didn't want to force his confidence. "Will you tell me about Thomas sometime?"

He frowned, and she felt a twinge of regret. She needed to give him more time, to stop pushing to know every little thing about him. But she so longed for his confidence.

"Sometime," he finally replied.

⁂

Katie fluttered around the bedchamber, making Felicity even more nervous.

"Katie, do stop fretting."

Her maid flushed. "I just worry, ye not having a mother to advise ye and all. But perhaps that night in Spellsinger Gardens…?"

"Shameful of you, the way you abandoned me so quickly."

"Well now." Katie gave a saucy grin. "That boyo could charm the angels from the heavens, what chance did I stand?"

Felicity laughed. Katie didn't look one bit repentant on that score. She watched the Irish girl pull down the linens and fluff the pillows. Maybe she should accept Katie's offer to give her some advice.

Then again sometimes it was better to not know what one was getting into. So she let Katie draw her own conclusions about what had happened that night in the Gardens.

"Turn off all the gaslights," instructed Felicity. "And just light candles around the room. Oh, and take Daisy, let her hunt for a while. And are you sure about this nightgown?"

Felicity plucked at the sheer material. The moment Terence walked in the room, she'd likely expire from embarrassment. She could see the rosy tips of her breasts perfectly, and the mirror reflected the perfect triangle of dark hair between her legs.

"'Twas all I could find, miss."

Felicity raised her brow.

"Trust me, mistress, ye look like a vision. Ye'd set any man's blood afire."

"I don't need it on fire, Katie. I'd be content with a low smolder."

Katie laughed, the musical sound calming Felicity more than words ever could. Tonight would be fine. She'd manage it… somehow.

After Katie had fussed around the room some more, she gathered up Daisy and asked, "Do ye want me to wait with ye, miss?"

"Heavens, no."

"It's taking him an awful long time."

Felicity's heart sank, and she collapsed into a chair by the fire. Could he have forgotten about her?

"Do ye want me to find out what happened to him?"

"No. Yes."

Katie slipped out the door, returned a few moments later without Daisy, and with her apron curled up into a pouch. She began to pull out handfuls of spent rose petals and toss them across the bedding.

"He's in the study with Bentley. I could hear them arguing."

Felicity let loose a breath. "What about?"

Katie gave a moue of disappointment. "The walls are too thick. Couldna hear a word. But I don't trust that Bentley. He's too twitchy for the likes of me."

"Well, they're probably arguing about business, so

it may be a while." Although, hadn't Terence told her he'd join her shortly? "They do have an odd relationship, although I think it rather resembles ours, sometimes."

Katie giggled, and Felicity ushered her out of the room, eyeing the petal-strewn bed with doubt. Whatever would Terence think about it? It smelled heavenly though, when she crawled into the linens, so she resisted the urge to brush them off.

Felicity sat upright for some time, listening to the crackle of the fire, holding the bedcovers up to her chin. She prayed he hadn't truly forgotten her. Had she not taken a nap today, she'd already have been sound asleep.

If only she were more memorable. What if he came into the room and didn't even notice her in the bed? That, she decided, would be more dreadful than him not coming at all.

Felicity lowered the bedcovers. She leaned back on her arms, thrusting her breasts against the sheer cloth of her nightgown. She did have a nice figure, surely he remembered that from their night in the Gardens. A nice face wasn't everything, was it?

She crawled out from beneath the bedcovers and smoothed them flat. Then she tried several different positions, hoping to gain his attention when he walked in. He'd yet to forget her—but the longer he took, the more she doubted.

Felicity lay sideways, hand propped on her head, gown billowing around her body, outlining the curve of her hips. She lifted her leg and pointed the toe. With a grimace, she rolled onto her stomach, propped her head again, and looked at her back. Yes, the gown draped her behind in an enticing manner—she could just make out the dark line between her cheeks. But would he like that sort of view?

She grimaced again and rolled onto her back. Perhaps if she propped the pillows behind her, yes, and spread her hair out like a halo, and then flung out her arms like so…

No, that wouldn't do. She should sit on the edge of the bed, and then put her arms behind her, and look over her shoulder with a smile of wicked invitation…

She flopped backwards, her legs spread and hanging down the side of the bed, her arms flung wide in agony. She couldn't find a single position that didn't make her feel like a fool. Still, she got up to try again. Maybe if she stood on the…

The door edged open with a soft creak, and Terence slipped into the room. Felicity froze in mid-pose, having been so involved in making herself look desirable that she'd forgotten all about him.

Terence glanced at the bed, and his mouth dropped open. The look of utter amazement on his face made Felicity look down at herself. She couldn't even recall how she'd managed this latest arrangement. Somehow her gown had gotten tangled around her waist, and she was on all fours, her long, black hair cascading down her back and over her shoulders, her bare bottom exposed to his gaze.

Well, she needn't wonder if he'd like that sort of view. His eyes glittered with appreciation.

Felicity wanted to crawl beneath the covers in humiliation. But it would draw even more attention to her predicament, so she settled for completely ignoring the situation, as if exposing her bottom to the air was an everyday occurrence for her. "Hello."

The shock on his face faded to a lazy grin. "Hello, yourself."

"Um. Your meeting with Bentley took a very long time." Felicity tried to keep the annoyance out of her voice. But, really, this was their wedding night. Couldn't his business have waited?

"I know. I thought... I thought you might have already gone to sleep. Lord, you're a gorgeous little thing, aren't you?"

Felicity sat on her haunches, the gown sliding down her skin and covering her bottom half. Not that it mattered, the material didn't hide much, but she did feel a bit more comfortable. His golden-brown eyes burned across her body, his gaze not straying for an instant.

Felicity swallowed. And she'd been worried that he wouldn't notice her.

She continued to speak as if she'd done nothing out of the ordinary. He just might believe that she cavorted like that every night and wouldn't realize that he'd just caught her trying to make herself more enticing.

"I've been sleeping for the past few days. I doubt if I shall be able to sleep a wink tonight."

"So do I," he replied, his voice lowered to a husky growl.

Felicity stopped reaching for the linens to cover herself. All night?

Terence took a step forward, his hands fumbling with his tie. His voice slurred the words. "It might have been better if you'd already been asleep with that delightful body hidden beneath the linens."

"Why?"

He threw his cravat on the floor and started shrugging off his coat. "Because now it's too late and I can't stop this from happening."

Felicity dragged the top of the bedcovers closer to her. His words sparked a kernel of fear in her belly. Was it so dreadful then, that he'd try to spare her from it? Why did he act so strange? "Are you drunk?"

"Certainly not." Terence threw his coat over a chair. "Slightly foxed, but never drunk."

Felicity's hands finally closed on the edge of the bedcovers, and she started to drag them over her.

"Don't do that."

She froze at the snap in his voice, at the glitter in his eyes. A thrill went through her as she realized that not only did he see her, but he appreciated the view. She just wished that her uncertainty about what he might do to her—would it really hurt?

Felicity couldn't stop babbling in nervousness. "It was kind of you, to try to spare me this. But it's necessary, isn't it? I mean, if we are to have children. And truly, it was quite pleasant... what we did in the coach. It's just, well, you're rather—"

"So, you like to talk?" His voice had gentled to a purr. "All right, we'll talk. Had any bad dreams lately?" He started at the buttons on his shirt, slowly releasing them one at a time.

Felicity's head spun. Tonight of all nights he had to ask her about her dreams? "No, not since the one I had at Fairview Manor. Why?"

"It got you that time, didn't it? What was it, a fog of black, a slimy monster, a mist of knives?" He stripped off his shirt and let it fall to the floor. His skin gleamed gold in the candlelight, the hairs of his chest made a pattern that sharpened to a point near the top of his trousers.

Felicity tried to concentrate on his words, but the more skin he revealed, the more difficult it became. "No, it was like black molasses, sticky and suffocating..."

He started on the buttons of his trousers. Felicity wanted to close her eyes, but continued to stare in fascinated curiosity.

Her mouth continued of its own accord. "How did you know, about the other monsters? They are remarkably like the ones I've seen in my nightmares."

His trousers slid down to his ankles. He didn't wear anything beneath them. Goodness, he was even bigger than she remembered. It stood out from his body like a tender weapon. He stepped out of the puddle of his trousers with fluid grace, and took a step toward her. Felicity sucked in a breath.

Terence lowered his head, tawny hair tumbling over his face, his eyes looking up at her beneath his brows. "Haven't you realized it yet? I know your monsters, dearest, because I've fought them off for you. My were-self protected you every night since we've met, until Daisy grew large enough to guard you for me."

"Then it wasn't a dream! It was you after all. Why didn't you tell me sooner?"

He'd reached the edge of the bed. Felicity tried not to stare at his lower half while she spoke, but found her gaze riveted to his shaft. How would he... and where would she...

"Look at me."

She met his eyes. He still kept his head lowered, as if attempting to dampen his predatory stance. Terence searched her face, as if he sought to discover some hidden truth. He held out his hand.

"Come here."

Felicity would have to lower herself again to all fours and crawl the short space to the edge of the bed. Trying to keep track of their conversation had started to become impossible, with him naked and his eyes glowing with promise. She wanted to ask him how he'd gotten into her room, why her dreams had become more tangible since she'd met him. Had her dreams of kissing him been real as well?

How many other secrets did he conceal?

But it seemed that her mind ran on one track, and her body on another, for regardless of her thoughts, her limbs moved of their own accord and she found herself upright before him, kneeling so that their eyes were almost on a level.

Terence reached out and cradled her face in his hands, running his thumbs across her cheeks. "Do you know where your dreams come from, Felicity?"

"Ralph. He likes to scare me with his illusions." Her breath trembled from her lips as she spoke.

"Are you sure?" The pressure of his hands tightened. "Have you ever heard of relic-magic? Do you know what happens when a sorcerer uses magic that is too powerful for her? Without full control, it rebounds back on the user."

Felicity could feel the tension in his body, the hidden strength in his hands. "I... no. But you know

I don't have any magic, Terence. This relic kind, or otherwise." She shivered—whether from his veiled accusation or the flush that ran through her body at his nearness—she couldn't be sure. She realized that although she'd vowed to trust him, he hadn't reached the same decision.

Hidden depths lurked in this conversation that she couldn't fathom. She wondered if marriage would always be this difficult. How long would it take before they really knew each other? "What have I done, to make you think I would even hide something like that from you?"

His chin lifted, and he studied her intently. "It's not you, it was someone else…"

Felicity's heart sank. Someone else, perhaps another lover? Had he been betrayed by a lover? Had he looked at that other woman as he did her, had he taken her to this very room, had he seduced her on this very bed? She didn't feel the wrath of jealousy, just a horrible disappointment. No one could love him the way she did. No one could appreciate him. He had wasted himself on this other woman. Or women.

To her horror, Felicity realized that tears had begun to fill her eyes. They spilled over the curve of his thumbs and seemed to suck the tension out of his body. His hands slid over her shoulders to her back, and he pulled her against his warm chest.

"Shush. I'm sorry, it doesn't matter now anyway."

Felicity sniffed. Did that mean that he trusted her, after all? Or that it didn't matter that he'd been with other women? She imagined that if she'd been with another man, it would certainly be of consequence to him.

How would she compare to all his other lovers?

"Have you been with another woman in this bed?"

He pulled his head back and stared at her. "What?"

"You heard me."

He laughed, a low rumble of sound that she could feel vibrating in his chest. "Is that what's been going on in your pretty little head? You're concerned about... ah, if only you could be as innocent as you appear."

Felicity narrowed her eyes. "I will have you know that I have never been intimate with anyone other than you."

The smile remained on his face. "Really."

"Yes, really. And I think it's fair for me to know whether you've shared this bed with anyone else."

His hands drifted down her back, their heat suddenly covering the rounds of her bottom. He pushed her toward him, so that the swollen rigidity of his shaft pressed itself against her.

"Do you?" he asked.

Felicity tried not to flinch. She had the feeling that he made fun of her. "Stop it, Terence. Will you answer my question or not?"

"Bloody hell, you love to talk, don't you?"

His mouth covered hers, taking her words away, taking her breath away, his lips firm and soft, his tongue sharp and searching. By the time he pulled away, Felicity could only gasp.

"That's one way to keep you quiet, I suppose. Let's find others, shall we?"

Before she could protest, he'd grabbed the hem of her nightgown and lifted it off her body. She shouldn't have felt so vulnerable then; after all, it had only been a sheer piece of cloth, but suddenly her fears returned.

Terence took a step back, his eyes raking over every inch of her. "You're perfect, aren't you?"

Felicity sank back on her bottom, surprised to hear the sincerity in his voice. She should've taken off her clothes years ago. No one would have ignored her then. She choked back a slightly hysterical giggle.

He leaned forward, nuzzling her hair with his mouth. His breath tickled her ear as he whispered, "I have never brought another to this bed, Felicity. And I won't do anything you don't want me to."

She started to babble again. "Truly? That's a relief, for I'm not quite sure I can manage…"

His mouth covered hers again, and Felicity grinned. She may be ignorant but she learned fast. What a delightfully easy way to get him to kiss her again. She wrapped her arms around his shoulders and let him lift her back up onto her knees. He tasted sinfully good, like heady wine and a hint of something else. Something that she tried to identify.

Ah, the taste of Terence.

When he pulled his mouth away, she felt tempted to start talking again. Until he licked her earlobe, and traced a wet path down to her neck, and lower, until he circled the taught nubs on her breasts. It made her impatient, but she couldn't imagine for what, until he sucked one of her nipples into his mouth.

Felicity shuddered, wrapped her hands in his thick mass of hair, and pressed him closer to her. The place between her legs throbbed, and she remembered how he'd touched her before. Suddenly she needed more than anything for him to bring her that same release.

"Please, Terence."

She didn't know what she begged for, but he did. Terence pushed her knees apart, and Felicity leaned back on her arms. She could feel the heels of her feet digging into her bottom, the cool air tingling across her breasts as he moved that wayward tongue down her belly. Down between her thighs.

Goodness, it felt better than his fingers. Oh, so incredibly much better.

Felicity never could've imagined such a thing. She'd thought he'd already shown her the pleasure he could tease from her body, but this felt different somehow.

When he suckled, Felicity held back a scream. She was grateful that she'd become exceptionally good at suppressing screams, as wave after wave ripped through her body.

Terence raised his head, his eyes burning with a golden fire as he watched her tremble with release.

"Beautiful," he mumbled. He pounced—Felicity could only describe it that way—and picked her up, unfolding her legs, laying her flat on the bed. The sweet smell of roses drifted between them as he covered her body with his own.

"It won't hurt. You're ready for me."

Felicity smiled dreamily. "I don't want to know what you're going to do. Just do it."

He growled, the sound of it reminding her of his lion-self. She realized that he'd held himself back, that even now, his muscles quivered with the control he had to exert over them.

Terence spread her legs. Felicity caressed his shoulders, marveling at the feel of his muscles, the smoothness of his skin. He gritted his teeth, she could see the tremor of his jaw, and something pushed between her legs.

His shaft. That huge thing that would surely tear her apart. If felt so odd; soft and round and hard. Threatening, yet welcoming at the same time.

He pushed, then stopped, groaning.

Felicity felt herself stretch to accommodate that part of him. A kernel of panic swelled in her chest, but before it could blossom into full-fledged terror, Terence covered her mouth with his own and plunged inside her.

She swallowed a whimper. He froze above her.

"Dearest. Are you all right?" He panted, speaking against her lips.

Felicity didn't know if it was his sudden painful entry into her, or the sweet way he called her dearest, but her eyes stung with fresh tears. She sucked on his bottom lip in answer, not letting him say any more, wrapping her hands in his hair and pulling his mouth harder down on her own.

Terence pulled himself out of her, the long, heavy length of him, and then slowly slid his way back inside, but not all the way. She sensed that he kept himself tightly in check. It didn't hurt this time. Rather, she felt it build something within her. Similar to the way he made her strain for the release that his fingers—and tonight, his mouth—had brought her.

Slowly, he built up a rhythm, until Felicity became swept up in it, felt that striving toward some unknown thing build until she thought she'd go mad for want of it. She swept her hands down the ridged muscles of his back, grasped at the hard swell of his bottom, and tried to push him deeper inside of her.

But he continued his slow, purposeful rhythm, ignoring her pitiful strength, holding the full length of himself back. He lowered his head and captured her mouth again, their breaths mingling into one. Then he traced a path of hungry kisses along her cheek and to the back of her ear, soft shivers coursing through her body from that sensitive spot. He dipped his head even lower and she felt his hot, wet mouth cover one nipple, and then the other, suckling each in turn, to the same rhythm of his thrusts. Felicity tossed her head, arched her back, until a deep release of pleasure flooded her body.

Terence gasped her name and shuddered. She could feel his own release inside her, feel his shaft convulse in wave after wave. A warmth spread in her womb, and Felicity prayed for children.

For children of a man who was half animal.

A man who loved her more than she had ever imagined being loved.

Terence rolled on his side, bringing her with him, keeping her tight in his arms. "God help me, but I love you."

Fourteen

FELICITY WOKE THE NEXT MORNING WITH A SMUG little smile plastered to her face. As soon as she became aware of it, she tried to erase it, but when she stopped concentrating, her lips would curve back up again. She gave it up and snuggled closer to her husband, his muscular body spooned behind her own.

She felt like a woman now, a rather grand feeling. Not that the loss of her virginity itself mattered. It was the love behind the act that made her feel so incredibly altered.

Still, she'd thought becoming a woman would feel different somehow. That perhaps the world would change because suddenly she would know all the answers.

She knew nothing except the love of her man, and somehow, that satisfied her more than anything else she could have imagined.

Felicity wiggled her bottom. His shaft lay against it and half rose in response. Terence growled, and his hand shifted from her hip to her breast.

"Good morning," he rumbled, lightly stroking her nipple.

She wiggled some more, and he sighed in her ear. "Keep that up, dearest, and you shall sorely regret it."

"Why?"

"You'll need to recover, and I can't let you do that if I stay in bed with you a moment longer."

Terence rose, all muscle and golden skin in the morning light, and padded over to the wash basin. "Go back to sleep. Your body could use the rest."

Felicity pretended to close her eyes. Now that he mentioned it, she did feel an uncomfortable stiffness between her legs. But surely it would go away soon…

"When do you think we can do that again?" She never imagined that she would ask a man such a thing. She never imagined that she would have done all the things that she had already done with this man. But then, she never thought she'd trust another human being the way she trusted her new husband.

He wiped the water from his eyes with a cloth and smiled. "Perhaps tonight. If you take it easy today. I have to attend to some business, and while I'm gone, I want you to keep to the house, do you understand?"

If she hadn't been so happy, Felicity might have gotten annoyed over his bossiness. But she'd been peeking beneath her lashes, watching the way he moved about the room, admiring his rippling muscles and predatory grace.

She sniffed. "Why?"

He strode over to the bed and placed a kiss on her forehead. "I see you peeking. You don't have to hide it, you know."

Felicity's eyes opened wide, and he chuckled.

"I intend to fill my sight with your beauty every

chance I get," he promised. "And I refuse to peek. How can you be so shy after last night?"

Her cheeks grew warm at the memory of the way she'd behaved, and he chuckled again. He grabbed the linens and with one quick flick of his muscles, stripped her of them. Felicity felt the rush of cold air across her body but refused to move. She allowed him to gaze at her as long as he wanted, relishing in his newfound awareness of her.

"You're even lovelier in the daylight," he murmured. He glanced down at himself and growled. "That was a mistake." Terence covered her up again, pulling the bedding up to her chin. "Until I can announce our marriage, it's best you stay indoors. I don't want to risk your reputation by any chance encounters with society."

"I don't care what society may think. How much worse can I be treated than what I've already been subjected to? Why, when I think of the way I was given the cut direct more than—"

Terence leaned down and kissed her breath away. Gracious, she could really get used to that. She wrapped her hands in his hair, loving the way the silky strands flowed through her fingers, and kissed him back. She used her tongue to mimic their lovemaking, and he pulled away with a groan.

"You're a shameless hussy," he teased.

Felicity colored. "Only with you."

"And you'll keep it that way, do you hear?"

She nodded. His voice had made it sound like a request, not a command, but she saw a flash of alarm in his eyes. It made her realize that he felt just as vulnerable as she did.

"Terence, you know I love you, don't you?"

He lifted one golden brow and gave an arrogant nod. "I know it. Now, go back to sleep."

Felicity obediently closed her eyes, but continued to peek as he washed himself all over, then dressed in his usual black attire. He left the room while wrapping his tie in a knot, still admonishing her to stay close to home.

She really didn't want to face any of her peers. She wanted to explore her new home and catalog the changes she would make. And perhaps do a little snooping, she admitted to herself. Maybe the house would reveal some of her husband's secrets, and she could banish that small kernel of fear that underlay her feelings for him.

She sprang from the bed with barely a wince from soreness and yanked on the bell-pull, requesting a bath for her morning ablutions. She would have to see about installing a permanent one in the water-closet— gracious, how ridiculous to have maids trudging up and down the stairs with buckets.

The bath soaked most of her soreness away, and by the time she'd wrapped herself in a clean cloth, she felt like her usual self.

Felicity told the maid to fetch Katie to help her dress and pondered the assortment of clothing that had belonged to Terence's mother. She'd have to get a new wardrobe right away. Although the dresses fit perfectly, she felt uncomfortable wearing them.

Thank goodness, though, that they all had enough cloth in the back to create a decent sized bustle. A lovely black day dress of flower-patterned silk damask would set off her hair perfectly and make her complexion appear even paler. A bit formal for morning, but Felicity wanted to wear it anyway. The skirt comprised yards of fabric gathered up into sweeping folds, and the sleeves had a puff at the shoulder, lacking the severe tailored look currently in fashion.

She would feel quite feminine and a bit grand. It suited her mood perfectly. She slipped into an embroidered linen chemise, pulled it through the back of her knee-length drawers to help support the bustle, and wondered what might be taking Katie so long. Felicity always appreciated help with her corset.

As if she had summoned her, the door flew open, and Katie barged into the room, preceded by a hissing Daisy. The dragonette flapped her wings in ecstatic greeting, and she quickly wrapped herself around Felicity's shoulders.

"It's a beautiful day outside, miss," said Katie as she started the struggle of lacing Felicity into her whale-boned corset. "There's a lovely park across the street, where all the tradesman set up little tables, and they sell the most fascinating things there."

Daisy hissed when Felicity laid her on the hearth to finish dressing. The dragonette eyed her sorrowfully until she stood clothed in the black damask and allowed her pet back around her shoulders.

"My husband thinks I should remain indoors," said Felicity.

"But ye look so lovely in that dress, miss." Katie let out an exaggerated sigh. "'Tis a shame no one but the house servants will see ye in it."

Felicity laughed. "No one notices me anyway." She

picked up the folds of silk and swished them back and forth. "I don't suppose any of the aristocracy would be at the park, do you? It sounds like a walk would be a perfect way to start the day."

Katie's face lit up. "I do need to collect a bit more gossip."

"Katie!"

"Truly, miss, it's necessary. How am I to know which merchants are honest or not, before they cheat us?"

Felicity sighed. She had a point. Out of habit, she gestured Katie to precede her from the room. Keeping her maid in front had a tendency to eliminate people bumping into her. But the first servant they encountered stopped and greeted her.

"Mistress, may I have your opinion on the linens?"

Felicity blinked. "The linens?"

"Yes, whether we should continue using the old with his master's parents' initials embroidered on them, or commission a set of new?"

"The old are fine, I'm sure. Now if you'll pardon us, we are headed for a brisk walk in the park." Felicity stepped around the girl, who seemed determined to block their path.

The buck-toothed maid frowned. "Perhaps you can advise me on the silver as well?"

"It can wait," she told the girl firmly. But Felicity was delayed again in the hall when another maid asked about laying out the hearths, and then halfway down the stairs when a footman inquired about uniforms, and then again in the foyer. Too many of the servants took too much notice of her. Such a thing had never, ever, happened to her before.

"If you please," stuttered a scullery girl. "Cook would like to have a word with you about the menu."

Felicity glanced back at Katie, who didn't bother trying to hide her amusement. "I suspect a conspiracy."

Katie nodded and lowered her voice to a whisper. "They can't exactly stop ye, miss. They're just doing their best to follow their master's orders."

Felicity frowned. "I had no idea it would be so annoying to be noticed by the servants."

Both girls looked at her a bit oddly, but Felicity ignored them. "Now, Katie and I are going just across the street to the park. For only a few minutes. There's no need for concern, and I will explain to your master that none of you could stop me. But I will not be a prisoner in my own home, do you understand?"

The girl bobbed her head and backed out of the room, her eyes wide with what Felicity hoped was respect and not fear.

"Now Kate, let us see this park." She lowered her head and hissed, "Hurry, before anyone tries to stop us again."

And with less decorum than she would have liked, they both ran for the door, pushing past the doorman and only pulling up short at the bottom of the steps. Felicity adjusted Daisy around her neck while Katie shoved some stray red locks back into her cap, and with dignity restored, they crossed the street to the park.

"It's quite odd," muttered Felicity, "that Terence's servants take such notice of me. Even at Graystone Castle, I have to be in residence for months before the servants stop overlooking me."

Katie turned a lovely shade of pink. "I must admit, miss, that sometimes even I can forget ye're in the room."

"Why, Katie, you've never mentioned that before."

"I didn't want to hurt yer feelings. Ye've told me time and again how drab ye are and that's why people overlook ye, and I wanted to show ye that it wasn't true."

Felicity picked up her black skirts, which were beginning to acquire a coating of dust from the dirt streets. No cobbled roads for this end of London. "So, why are you mentioning it now?"

"'Cause ye're right, miss. It's very odd the way Sir Terence's servants react to ye, compared to those of Lord Wortley's. Did ye know that they're all shapeshifters?"

Felicity stopped and stared. "Terence's servants?"

"Oh, aye. Weres, the lot of them, down to the scullery maid, whose were-self is a ferret, I believe. Seems like only another shapeshifter wants to hire were-servants."

Felicity stroked Daisy's scales. Yes, the upstairs maid had reminded her of a rabbit, with her large ears and buckteeth. The same way that Terence's thick golden-brown hair reminded her of his lion's mane. But many people had characteristics that were similar to an animal's...

Katie gently grasped her arm and led her out of the street while Felicity stared with unseeing eyes. Could it be just a coincidence that all her husband's new servants had such an awareness of her?

"Weres are immune to magic," she murmured aloud, remembering what Uncle Oliver had told her. And that he'd also admitted he'd never expected her to associate with shapeshifters. Could it be possible that some sort of spell had made people overlook her?

An enchantment that shapeshifters could see past? It seemed quite an outlandish idea. But the more she thought about it, the more she realized how very much it would explain.

Felicity barely noticed the park when they entered, other than to note that the trees and bushes lacked the perfectly sculptured shapes found in the parks near her old home. But the bustle and charm of the neighborhood made up for the lack.

She shook off the dreadful feeling in her stomach and blinked at the colorful cloth gazebos that had been set up along the dirt walkways, with the names of the corresponding shops boldly displayed. Felicity fingered the odd assortment of goods arranged on floating tables and rugs as they walked by: sparkly potions and embroidered charm bags and crystal pendants strung on ribbons.

"They are pretty, aren't they, Katie? Even if they don't hold any real magic."

"Why would ye think that, miss?"

Felicity gazed at the shop owners. "Heavens, they'd have to be descended from aristocracy."

Katie lowered her voice. "Some of them are, though not that ye can tell."

Felicity gave her maid a skeptical look. "Since when did you become such an expert on magic?"

"Not me! I just wanted to know about our new home, and so I asked around this morning—ah, and there's Jane, whose master is really an aristocrat. Do ye mind if I have a word with her?"

"Go on, and take Daisy with you. She could use a snack."

Katie nodded and gathered up the dragonette, who protested with a hiss. "I wouldn't advise making any purchases, though, mistress. Most of them are charlatans."

Felicity tried not to roll her eyes at her maid's dramatic tone, and shooed her off to join the other servant who sat on a bench surrounded by cooing pigeons. The two servants quickly bent their heads together. Daisy looked over at Felicity, then back at the pigeons, swiped her tongue across her scaly lips, and leaped into the middle of the flock.

"I assure you, I am no charlatan," said a voice from beneath a purple and green gazebo.

Felicity colored, embarrassed that someone had overheard her conversation. "I beg your pardon," she mumbled, and tried to hurry past the booth.

A small woman emerged from behind a table and stepped in Felicity's path. Her head barely came to Felicity's waist, and she had the most unusual smell about her, and even though myriad wrinkles creased her face, she was still the most stunning woman Felicity had ever seen.

She found herself smiling at the tiny woman, who returned her friendliness with a snort. "I've been watching for you. Didn't know it would be such a difficult task. So, you're Sir Terence's new lady? Well, now I can understand how you stole his heart, but has he stolen yours as well?" She gestured at her gazebo. "Come inside and sit."

She had a charisma that Felicity found difficult to resist. She went inside and sat.

The old woman picked up a heavy book, the bracelets on her wrists jangling with the movement.

"You know my husband?"

"Better than some, more than you. What's your name?"

Felicity frowned. She felt defensive that this woman thought she knew her husband better than she did. Well, she shouldn't let the truth bother her. With time she would get to know him. But Felicity couldn't help feeling that he kept secrets from her, and so she tolerated the woman's superior attitude in the hopes that she could discover more about him. She squirmed. "Lady Felicity Sey… er, Blackwell—although if you know my husband as well as you profess, shouldn't you have known that as well?"

The woman cackled. "My name's Manda, pleased to meet you. Now let's see what my book can tell me." She stroked the worn cover and breathed Felicity's name, then flipped it open. Her eyes moved as if she read words written there, but Felicity could only see blank pages.

"How do you know the baronet? Is he a customer of yours?"

Manda shrugged. "Of a sort. He's more of a friend, one I would rather not see hurt."

Felicity felt the accusation. "I would never hurt him." She smelled something burning, but all her attention stayed focused on the other woman. "Is your book really magical?"

Manda shook her gray head. "'Course not. But I am."

"What does it say?"

"Ah, now, not anything I wanted to know, as usual. But there seems to be a message for you."

Felicity heard the faint sounds of screaming coming

from behind them. She had hoped for secrets about Terence, not herself. "For me?"

The hostility that Felicity had sensed from the other woman disappeared, to be replaced with a mild confu-. sion. "Mmm. You're very young, aren't you?"

The shop owners nearest them started packing up their wares. They seemed to be in an awful hurry. "Why would it tell you how old I am? I could've just told you that myself."

"Not the way my book could." Manda leaned forward, her beautiful eyes wide with concern. "Listen to the advice of an old woman. The world is neither black nor white, you see. Same with people. You must learn to see beyond the surface of those around you."

Felicity was hypnotized by the other woman's stare. She wanted to dismiss Manda's simple words, but instead she wondered if the woman might be talking about Terence. Who else could she mean?

"I don't know what you're implying." Felicity frowned as people ran past them. She turned, the hubbub around her too loud to ignore, and caught another whiff of smoke. As the crowd cleared, she saw what they had been running from. "Oh dear."

Manda cackled. "Yours, I presume? Your maid was right, most of my neighbors are charlatans, and to see a creature of real magic—that they know they have no defense against—can be a bit unsettling."

Katie had reached them, holding a still smoking Daisy protectively in her arms. "She just wanted a bit of roast pigeon. Who knew what a commotion it would cause?"

Daisy burped a cloud of smoke.

Felicity wagged her finger at the dragonette. "You know you're not supposed to breathe fire in public."

Daisy burped again, this time spewing a few scorched feathers.

Felicity turned on her maid. "Katie, if you hadn't started running, no one might have even noticed."

"Oh, I wasn't running 'cause of Daisy, miss. I was running because of the news Jane told me."

"Nothing could be urgent enough for you to create such a scene."

"But it's about yer aunt and uncle, miss. They've returned to London and taken up residence in yer mansion in Mayfairy."

Felicity forgot all about Manda and her book. "But how could they, unless…"

Katie nodded, setting her cap even more askew. "Yer cousin passed his testing and is now the Duke of Stonehaven."

Felicity took a deep breath. She'd had a feeling that Ralph would be successful. The nightmares he'd sent her had become amazingly strong. She struggled to be happy for him, for he'd restored their family estates. It just seemed all wrong, somehow. She glanced at Manda and the old woman smiled, as if she saw the doubt in Felicity's face and approved.

"But that's good news," said Felicity, lifting her chin. "Why do you look so upset?"

"Because yer aunt and uncle have put out a warrant for Sir Terence's arrest."

"What?" Felicity surged to her feet, taking Daisy into her arms. She petted the scales with shaking hands. "That makes no sense. Why would they do such a thing?"

"Because they say he made off with ye in the middle of the night and they don't know whether ye're dead or alive."

"But I left them a note explaining that Sir Terence and I were getting married." Felicity wrapped Daisy around her neck. "But the baronet will straighten it all out, anyway. He promised to see them today."

"Oh, miss, he may not have a chance, if he's arrested first."

"Goodness. I must see my aunt and uncle immediately, and get this matter straightened out." Perhaps Manda hadn't been referring to Terence after all. Perhaps Felicity's own theory about being under a spell wasn't so fanciful, either. And if that were true, her aunt and uncle must surely know something about it. Felicity narrowed her eyes. "Besides, there's something else I'd like to discuss with my dear family. Katie, call for a cab."

Katie gave a quick glance toward Manda, bobbed her head, and scurried to the street. Felicity gathered her skirts to follow, when the old woman clutched her arm.

"Don't you want to know what else my book said?"

Felicity hesitated in indecision. Hadn't the woman managed to upset her mind enough for one day? Her simple words kept rolling around in her skull, making her world a bit uncertain.

What had happened to the note she'd left for Aunt and Uncle, anyway?

"You'll have to tell me later, Manda. Sir Terence will not spend a moment in a cell, not on my account." Felicity tried to walk away but the old woman wouldn't loosen her grip. For such a tiny thing, she had amazing strength.

"Later will be too late."

Felicity suppressed a roll of her eyes for the second time today. Must everyone be so melodramatic?

"My book cautions you to trust your heart."

"Manda…"

"If you doubt his love for you when he needs it the most, he'll die. And he does love you—trust in that, even when you're surrounded by lies."

Felicity hoped Manda was being melodramatic again. Terence certainly wouldn't die from a stay in Scotland Yard. And her mention of lies… Felicity's stomach twisted at the thought that her family might have lied to her.

"Thank you, Manda. I… I appreciate your concern. I must be off now."

Manda mumbled something about the hastiness of youth, but Felicity had already bolted after Katie, a difficult thing to do in yards of fabric.

The small hansom cab had none of the magical commodities of an aristocratic carriage. No illusions disguised the tattered upholstery or cracked varnish; nothing softened the scraggly coat of the horse or the weathered face of the driver. Felicity sighed. She should just be grateful that she had enough coins in her purse that she didn't have to walk.

Still, the drive gave her too much time to think. Katie stayed quiet during the trip, seemingly as overwhelmed by the day's events as her mistress.

Felicity picked at the folds of her dress. She wanted her life to be predictable, and look what had happened.

She abhorred change, yet had failed her testing and lost everything she'd grown up knowing. Then she'd met Terence and her life had changed even more.

"I have been guilty of doing what everyone has always done to me."

Katie opened her mouth, then shut it.

"Why have I allowed Ralph to terrify me with dreams every night? Why have I overlooked what I didn't want to see?"

Katie shrugged helplessly.

"I'll tell you why," said Felicity. "Because I wanted things to be as I wish, not to see them as they really are." Her voice cracked. "Well, no more. I will have the answers out of my uncle. I am no longer under his rule. If there is a spell on me and he knew about it…"

The cab slowed to a stop in front of her old home in Mayfairy. She stared without regret at the lovely mansion that used to be hers. She had a new home now and a husband who truly loved her.

"I shall have him arrested for misuse of magic."

Katie gasped. She knew as well as Felicity the punishment for such a crime. "But, miss, he's yer uncle—yer family."

"I will give him a chance to make things right first."

She glanced at her maid's pale face, and her heart twisted. Felicity couldn't force her frightened maid to accompany her, but she couldn't leave the girl alone, either. Felicity unwound the dragonette from around her neck and handed her to Katie. "You stay here and take care of Daisy. I will not leave this house until I have some answers, and things might get difficult. I don't need my protective baby firing the curtains."

Katie nodded enthusiastically and burrowed back into the cab's seat. Daisy hissed and squirmed, smoke rising from her nostrils, but Katie held her firmly.

Felicity took a deep breath, went up the steps, and rang the bell.

Fifteen

UNCLE OLIVER SURPRISED HER BY OPENING THE DOOR himself. "We've been expecting you, dear niece. Welcome home."

Some of her resolve faded at the warmth in his voice. She followed him into the peacock parlor, where a lovely tray of tea and scones sat waiting for them. He even poured for her, the corners of his pale gray eyes crinkling from his gentle smile.

Felicity didn't quite know where to start. "Where are all the servants?" she managed to ask.

"They haven't caught up with us yet. They're still transferring our household back to London."

She covered her confusion by sipping her tea. Surely they had kept a skeleton crew here. Everything seemed so ordinary, yet nothing felt right. Felicity took a deep breath.

"I suppose you're wondering," said her uncle, "why we issued a warrant for Sir Terence's arrest."

Felicity decided that she'd follow his lead for the moment. She took a sip from her porcelain cup. "Didn't you get my note?"

"Ah, yes, the note. Did he marry you, then?"

She choked on her tea. "Of course he did. Why would you think otherwise?"

"Given the nature of the beast…" Uncle Oliver shrugged. "We thought it best to put out the word that you'd been kidnapped, just in case."

Felicity's suspicions eased. So that's why they'd done such a thing—to protect her reputation. She felt ashamed of her doubts regarding their actions, and for a moment, she was tempted to let the issue of being enspelled drop.

If she hadn't wondered whether the spell might also be responsible for her shift in attitude, she just might have.

Lord Wortley set down his teacup and leaned toward her. He smelled like cloves and cigar smoke. For some odd reason he sounded terribly disappointed. "Now that we know he has done the honorable thing, I assure you, we will retract our statement."

Felicity nodded, relieved that Terence would no longer be in danger of being thrown in Newgate. Uncle filled her cup again, and she sipped her tea nervously. "Uncle, there's another urgent matter that I wish to discuss with you."

His eyes flicked over her shoulder. "If it involves matters of marriage, perhaps it would be best if you discussed it with your aunt."

Felicity felt the blood rush to her face. An image of Terence leaning over her, his hair falling over his cheekbones in wild disarray, his eyes glazed with passion, came unbidden into her mind. Uncle had managed to distract her again. "No, I have no…

difficulties with my marriage. I assure you, I'm quite happy with it."

Again, he looked disappointed.

"Uncle," she continued, before he could broach some other subject, "something most unusual has happened. Sir Terence's household is comprised of nothing but shapeshifters."

His expression brightened. "My dear, that's something you should have expected. Does it bother you a great deal?"

She realized that he wanted her to be unhappy with her new situation, but she couldn't fathom why. Perhaps he missed her and hoped she had come back to stay. Did they love her so much that they couldn't bear for her to be living elsewhere? Uncle had hinted at such a thing when Terence had first asked for her hand.

She'd been a fool to think that he knew anything about a spell on her. And then Manda's voice echoed in her head. Nothing is black or white.

"No, Uncle, on the contrary. I have found my husband's servants to be quite attentive. Perhaps even excessively so."

"Ah, that's good to hear." But a frown marred his face.

"I cannot walk down a hallway without being curtsied at. I am never overlooked at table. The moment I enter the room, they all come to attention. Don't you think it a bit odd?"

His upper lip had started to sweat, and he looked nervously toward the doorway. "How so?"

Felicity thought she saw a flash of white near the door. But the reaction of her uncle riveted her attention. She felt his change in demeanor, his almost frightened response. She set down her teacup and leaned forward. "I have been overlooked for almost my entire life, Uncle. I've become so accustomed to it that I hadn't realized the extent of it until I lived in a household where everyone could see me."

"Whatever are you talking about? Are you saying that you've felt invisible all these years? That's preposterous! Haven't we always taken care of you, seen to your needs? You wound me, dear girl."

"That's not what I'm talking about. Please don't try to twist things, Uncle. I won't be dissuaded from this line of query, not this time. There is too much evidence that something is gravely wrong. Even you frequently have forgotten my presence in a room. You've seen servants knock me down in the hallways. You've seen guests sit in my lap, unaware that I occupied that same space."

Lord Wortley started to fidget with his tie. "Certainly, it's a bit odd the way some people behave with you. I haven't wanted to hurt your feelings, dear girl, but have you considered that you are just a… forgettable person?"

Felicity felt as if he'd kicked her in the stomach. Before she'd met Terence, she wouldn't have questioned her uncle's sincerity. But her husband had proven to her that she wasn't quite the drab creature her family had led her to believe.

"I suspect that I may be under some sort of spell," Felicity said quite firmly.

Lord Wortley got to his feet and rang the bell-pull. Felicity thought she heard a faint hiss, and glanced around the feather-covered room. Whom did he summon when there were supposedly no servants in the house?

Before she could ask, he said, "I might have known this would be the result of your marriage to that shapeshifter. Has he tried to turn you against your family already?"

Felicity stood. A wave of dizziness washed over her, and she clutched at a chair carved in the likeness of peacock feathers. She had skipped the morning and now the afternoon meal. Perhaps she should eat some of the scones. "This has nothing to do with Terence. It has to do with the truth. You know something, Uncle, and I will not leave until you tell me."

He shook his head sadly. "No, I'm sure you won't."

Aunt Gertrude entered the room, but not the woman Felicity had known her entire life. This woman wore a robe of red satin and her mousy brown hair lay loose around her shoulders, making her look years younger. Felicity had never seen her wear any more jewelry than her favorite pearl necklace, but now when she moved her arms clinked from dozens of gold and gem bracelets.

Her cheeks glowed with such rosy health that she almost looked beautiful.

"She was bound to find out anyway," she said to Uncle Oliver.

"Yes, my dear, quite clever of you to choose the time and place."

Felicity squeezed the chair's back until her fingers hurt. If she didn't know better it would seem that her aunt and uncle had traded roles. As if Aunt Gertrude truly ruled the household. "What are you talking about?"

"A little conversation might just do the trick," said Aunt Gertrude. "Dear niece, wouldn't you rather sit down?"

"No." Felicity wavered a bit, but remained standing.

Her aunt settled herself on her mother's favorite settee and sighed. "I suppose we could discuss your mother Lilly. This is all about her, you know."

Felicity's knees wobbled. She had the strongest desire to flee. She'd been a fool to question the truth about her life. She didn't want to hear anything bad about her mother, she couldn't bear it. But as soon as she'd made the decision to run a chasm materialized between her and the door.

Identical to the one that had appeared on her day of testing, it radiated red heat and sulfurous fumes—and she definitely heard a faint hissing sound.

"Is… is Ralph here?"

Aunt waved her fingers, jewels flashing from every finger. "No, dear, don't worry, he shall never know of this conversation."

Felicity stared at the gaping hole in the floor and realized that Uncle Oliver stood in the middle of it, seemingly floating in midair. Neither of them had the slightest notion that it was there.

"Your mother," continued her aunt, "had too much. Yes, you might object, Oliver, but admit it. It led to her ruin."

Uncle sighed and shuffled his feet.

"Too much power, too much beauty. And it spoiled her. Richard would have been much better off if he'd have kept his word and married me. But your mother always wanted whatever little I managed to have and when she set her cap on your father, well, he didn't stand a chance."

The heat and the fumes of the chasm made Felicity's head spin. "What on earth are you talking about? My father knew you before he met my mother?"

"Of course, dear, but that's all ancient history now. Besides, if Lilly hadn't pursued my Richard, I never would've met dear Oliver. Your mother had begged off from her engagement with him to pursue my beau, so it turned out fairly well. Until they decided to take that dreadful ship."

"It went down in a storm," said Felicity with emphasis. Something of what she knew had to be the truth.

"Yes, but Lilly and Richard were certainly powerful enough to halt such a minor squall. Had your mother not taken another man to her bed and had your father not retaliated by taking to another woman's... well, they would've been together when the thing hit, and could've managed to save the entire ship. As it was—"

"How do you know all of this?"

Aunt waved dismissively. "There were a few survivors. But what's important, dear, is that we didn't want the same thing happening to you. You couldn't help inheriting your parents' good looks, so we put the spell on you for your own protection. So that you would grow up unspoiled and lacking your mother's vanity."

Goodness. Felicity collapsed back into her chair. The chasm vanished and she blinked at her aunt and uncle's concerned faces. They truly believed that they'd done such a dreadful thing for her own good. "Then it's true. I've carried a spell most of my life. But to be so ignored—how could you, Aunt?"

Aunt Gertrude's face crumpled and she blinked back tears. "I had just gotten the relic and really didn't know the extent of its power. I've been trying to find a way to alter the spell ever since I put it on you."

Felicity's mind suddenly felt blanketed in fog. Hadn't Terence mentioned something about relic-magic? She opened her mouth to question her aunt when Uncle Oliver spoke.

"Now, now." He patted his wife's shoulder. "You've done the best you could. And look at our niece. How modest and humble she is. We couldn't have gone too far wrong."

Aunt sniffed and gave him a watery smile. "She is the sweetest thing, isn't she? Nothing like my sister." She got up and held out her hand. "Come along, Felicity. It's time to go now."

Felicity stared at the rings on her aunt's fingers. They glittered with hypnotic fascination. The dizziness had gotten worse, and she felt so weak. "Go where?"

Uncle Oliver tsked, and dragged her to her feet. He supported one side of her, while Aunt supported the other, and they half carried her from the room.

"We're forced to protect you again," said Aunt.

They walked through the hallway towards the kitchen.

"Do we have to tell her all of it?" asked Uncle. "The poor dear has had enough of a shock today."

Aunt Gertrude started to puff from the exertion of hauling Felicity along. "It's best she get it all in one dose, don't you think?"

"What are you talking about?" Felicity heard the slur of her own words. Why did she feel so strange?

The last time she'd felt like this was when she'd had the fever, and Uncle Oliver had given her a potion to help her sleep. "What did you put in my tea?"

"Nothing harmful, I assure you," replied Uncle. "We knew this would come as something of a shock, so I just gave you a potion to keep you calm."

Felicity felt more than calm. She felt like melted butter. Her eyes kept crossing, and for a moment she thought she saw opal scales and petal-soft wings. When she'd managed to focus again, she realized they'd taken her into the kitchen. How very odd.

"Where are we going?"

They dragged her into the muggy washroom. The smell of lye stung her nostrils.

"To the cellar," puffed Aunt Gertrude.

Felicity attempted to struggle. Did they think she'd trust them, after lying to her all these years? Just because they thought it had been for her own good didn't mean that they were right. "Terence."

"Ah, but he's exactly why we're hiding you away," explained Uncle Oliver, who seemed to have more breath for explanations. "He's a spy for the prince, you see. And he wants to steal your aunt's relic. We can't allow him to do that." He dropped her arm and she stumbled. He went to the back of the washroom and stuck his fingers between two bricks. The wall swung open and Uncle lit a candle.

Felicity tried to concentrate. Too many things were happening too quickly, and her mind felt just as melted as her muscles. Since when had there been a door in the washroom? And why would they think Terence wanted to steal their relic? That he was some kind of secret spy? She'd more likely believe that he was the bastard son of the prince.

"Ridi-klous," she said, her tongue unable to twist out the word properly.

Aunt and Uncle traded knowing glances, and Felicity blinked. Gracious, what had Terence said about a relic anyway? She tried to get past her memories of sweaty limbs and tangled sheets and delicious pleasure. She did recall that he'd asked if she'd ever heard of relic-magic and something about it being too powerful.

Uncle patted her hand. "Don't you see, Felicity? Without the relic, Ralph wouldn't be able to keep the title. These lands rightfully belong to our child. The relic was put into your aunt's hands for just that purpose."

Felicity swung her head around drunkenly to stare into her aunt's glittering eyes. Aunt Gertrude nodded. "The only reason Sir Terence courted you was to get close to the family. He's a relic-hunter, dear, a spy for the prince. The crown doesn't want anyone else to have magic stronger than their own, and Merlin's relics threaten their supremacy."

Uncle entered the black opening, and Aunt gave her a little push to follow him down the stairs. Felicity's legs moved as sluggishly as her mind. Weren't Merlin's thirteen relics supposed to contain evil magic? She'd always thought they were just a myth to scare children.

Yet, if they weren't a myth, and the prince coveted the relics, didn't it follow that it would be against the laws of the crown to possess one? That Aunt and Uncle used a magic they weren't entitled to?

She'd known that Terence kept secrets from her,

but she thought they'd be ones similar to not knowing that he had any sisters.

Not that everything he'd ever told her had been a lie.

Ridiculous, she said again to herself. She would just go ask Terence instead of letting her imagination run wild.

Felicity tripped on the earthen stairs and slammed face-first into Uncle's back. She felt Aunt's fingers dig into the waistband of her skirt and tug her upright.

"You're lying," she gasped. "Just like you lied about the spell you put on me. I shall go ask Terence for an ecshplana… explanashun."

"We don't blame you for not trusting us," huffed her aunt, her breath hot against the back of Felicity's head. "But if you think about it, you'll understand that we're right. Why would he start courting a girl with no dowry or magic?"

"He took advantage of your vulnerability," said Uncle from in front of her. "But we suspected something wrong right away. Made a few inquiries at my gentlemen's club—and a few other, less seemly places. Paid off, though. His family has spied for the royals for generations. Why do you think those shape-shifting baronets are tolerated by the gentry? Because the prince says so, that's why. They help him by sniffing out relics, then stealing them. Royals are too scared to do their own dirty work, because only shapeshifters are immune to relic-magic."

Felicity wanted him to stop talking. She wanted to turn around and run to Terence and demand an explanation. But her legs would not cooperate. Instead they followed wherever her aunt and uncle led, and she couldn't stop them.

She could only fight against her inner doubts. She'd suspected from the beginning that Terence had pursued her too quickly, had professed his love too lightly. Oh, she'd suspected him, but had refused to look too deeply. She had wanted him to love her and had overlooked anything else to the contrary.

"But he didn't have to marry me." Now, that truth they surely couldn't dispute.

They had reached a cellar; old bottles of dusty wine lay about the cool chamber. Felicity didn't feel too surprised when Uncle pushed several bricks in a pattern that seemed vaguely familiar, and another wall slid open.

Uncle mumbled a counter-spell to dismiss the wards, and Felicity thought she saw another flash of pearly white disappear into the tunnel behind Uncle's back.

"Sir Terence could see past the spell on you," accused her aunt. "We think it's possible that he couldn't resist the temptation to, well, you know…"

Felicity laughed—a high-pitched sound that echoed down the dark tunnel in the wall. She'd been so worried about her drab looks, about enticing him to her bed. And now they told her that he'd married her because he couldn't resist her beauty. They allowed her a few moments of hysterics, until she managed to wipe the tears from her eyes and straighten up again.

"You're not going to retract your statement to Scotland Yard, are you? You're going to hide me away so that they will keep him in Newgate."

"He'll spend the rest of his life in a cell," assured

Uncle Oliver. "Your impulsive marriage gave us just the opportunity we needed to get rid of him."

"But you can't keep me hidden away forever."

"Why ever not?" said Aunt, giving Felicity a little prod forward. "Sorcerers have been hiding in the Underground for centuries."

Felicity spun around in an effort to run back the way they'd come, away from that dark tunnel where Uncle Oliver waited. Even if Terence had used her to find the relic, even if his service to the royals was more important than some foolish girl's heart, she would never be responsible for putting him in some dreadful prison. And she'd rather endure the patronizing look on his face as he explained that he'd never loved her than be imprisoned in the Underground.

They'd made her doubt him. But how could she not doubt everyone and everything when she'd just discovered that those dearest to her had lied?

Uncle moved faster than she could have imagined. He grasped her from behind, wrapped his arms around her and squeezed her so hard she heard the muscles in her back pop. He laid his scratchy cheek next to her soft one. "Your strength is no match for mine, dear girl. Can't you see we are doing what's best for the entire family? Since you lost us the title, don't you think it's fair that you help us let your cousin keep it?"

Felicity tried to take a breath against his vise-like grip. He spoke of being fair when he knew that she'd been enspelled most of her life? When he intended to imprison both her and her husband forever?

She stomped on his toes with her heel. He grunted

but only tightened his grip. The room spun crazily, and Felicity wondered if it wouldn't be simpler for them just to kill her. The thought that she felt them capable of such a horrible thing made her heart break. And made her freeze in terror.

"I remain," she whispered breathlessly, "loyal to this family."

Uncle kissed her cheek. "Good girl."

Felicity marveled at his tone of voice. He believed that she'd been irrational and had finally come to her senses. They thought their actions were truly for her own good, or at least, the greater good of the family. Had her aunt and uncle been blinded by their lust for power, or were they simply mad?

Uncle Oliver released her and took up his candle, stepping into the dark tunnel. Felicity meekly followed, while inside she raged against her helplessness. If only she'd inherited her parents' powers, she might have been able to fight them. She tried to feel that shred of magic that she'd managed to summon once or twice... but finally gave up in hopeless frustration.

The tunnel sloped downward; it twisted and turned until she had no idea of the direction they traveled. They wouldn't need to lock her in a cell to imprison her down here.

"What is this place?" she asked.

"Oh," puffed Aunt Gertrude, replying as if they still retained their old relationship. "They call it the Underground, but we call it the Maze."

"You mean the underground railway tunnels?"

"Well, dear, that's how it started. Then some wise magician decided it would be a perfect place to, um, have a private residence. So, they started tunneling, and well, there's an entire city here now."

Felicity stumbled. How had she managed to get through life being so ignorant? Not that she'd ever wanted to know about relics, or undergrounds, or gambling dens or any of the aristocracy's vices. Had she been kept purposely sheltered from them, or had she overlooked their presence in her quest for the perfect world? Perhaps a bit of both.

Felicity decided that she wouldn't hide from the world again, even if they never removed the spell on her. She would no longer accept her invisibility, she vowed, even though the decision had come too late to really matter. What kind of miserable life could she have in this Underground?

No, no. She would find some way to escape. She held on to that hope while they journeyed deeper beneath the earth.

The walls of the tunnel expanded and Felicity blinked at the sudden brilliance. Fairylights winked from the ceiling of a cavern, like starlight in a true sky. The ground sloped down from them, and she gasped at the expanse of the chamber. The roofs of houses and shops seemed to go on for miles, a network of small streams running through and between them like the pattern of a crazy quilt.

"This is the marketplace," said Uncle. "And like the East End, it's best you never go there."

Had he forgotten that she lived in the East End now? Felicity swayed on her feet. Had she forgotten that it had all been a lie?

They skirted the edges of the city, so Felicity only faintly heard the cries of children, the raucous shouts of drunken men and the high-pitched laughter of female companions. The stench of the place drifted toward her, and she wrinkled her nose. Thank goodness she didn't have to smell it at close quarters.

They entered another tunnel, then another. She kept seeing flashes of white at the edges of her vision, but since Aunt and Uncle didn't mention it, neither did she. She recalled the image of Uncle floating in midair, and felt positive neither one of them had been aware of the chasm, either. And if Ralph hadn't been home, where had the illusion come from anyway?

A bit of panic stirred Felicity's belly, and she shook her head in another attempt to clear it. If only she had some magic herself, perhaps she could solve some of these mysteries. No wonder commoners felt so frightened of the aristocracy. Bad enough to hold all the power, but when that power couldn't even be understood…

"Aah, here we are," announced Uncle. "It would've been much easier to transport us here, Gertrude. Your face is quite flushed."

"How many times," panted her aunt, "do I have to tell you that we can't risk draining her?"

Felicity blinked. Hard. "Draining whom of what?"

Aunt patted her shoulder. "The relic, dear. For some silly reason I always refer to it as a female. It has to have time to… replenish itself."

Uncle Oliver sniffed and pushed open an iron gate. The tunnel had opened onto a large, tall cave—small when compared to the city one, but still, when the gate's hinges squeaked, it echoed repeatedly off the walls.

Felicity pinched her arm through the material of

her sleeve. It barely hurt, so she knew the potion still affected her. She struggled to free her mind of its grip. "How did you find the relic anyway, Aunt?"

They started up the cobbled pathway to the front door of a house that resembled something from a gargoyle's dreams. Constructed of black stone that seemed to swallow the already faint glow of the fairy-lights, it resembled the walls of the cave with its craggy lines and misshapen windows.

Uncle lifted an eyebrow at Aunt, who shrugged. "Your uncle found a very old manuscript while pursuing his charming hobby of deciphering ancient codes. What a surprise to discover that it had been written by one of Merlin's very own apprentices, who'd stolen one of the relics and had hidden it himself. Tomb-raiding is not likely something I'll ever do again, but it was worth it."

Uncle turned the knob of the front door, and it creaked open. Felicity could sense the wardings on it. She cringed as she crossed the threshold, even though she knew Uncle had lifted them before she went in.

Uncle spoke a word, and fairylights illuminated the entry hall. The mansion lacked the gaslight sconces of the city above. Could it be possible that the entire Underground ran strictly on magic alone?

Felicity stared in dismay at the black stone floors and walls. Everything had been constructed to absorb the light. She fought against the feeling that the stone would absorb her into it, as well.

Aunt Gertrude's bracelets tinkled as she raised her fingers to her pearl necklace, something Felicity had always noted as a nervous habit.

"There you are," said her aunt as two ghostly figures entered the hall. "It's about time."

Felicity suppressed a scream. She feared, at first, that she'd met the gargoyles who had dreamed up this ghastly mansion. She decided on closer inspection that they might be just incredibly ugly human beings.

"Take my dear niece to the tower room and make her comfortable. Provide for her needs, and don't let her wander off. I wouldn't want her becoming lost in these catacombs."

A warning… or a threat? Felicity frowned at her aunt's choice of words. Despite her efforts, her head had become fuzzier with each passing moment, and she realized that she didn't quite know where she was, nor why she might be here. She rubbed her temple. "I feel so sleepy."

Uncle Oliver nodded, his forehead creased in sympathy. "No wonder, after the miles you've just walked. Not to mention the shock of learning that your husband deceived you so thoroughly."

"And the potion you gave me," added Felicity.

"Barely gave you a drop, my girl. Now, off to bed. Aunt and I have some unfinished business to attend to."

"You're leaving me here?"

Aunt Gertrude looked down at her dirty skirts in dismay. "There's no help for it. But don't worry, Cleo and Chloe will take good care of you."

That's what Felicity feared. She wanted to follow Aunt and Uncle out of this place, but the two servants had replaced them by taking each of her arms, and her legs still only wanted to move where they were led.

The door closed behind them with a resounding

thud, and Felicity gave in to the pull of the servants on her arms. They led her up a curving staircase, and unless it had been crafted by magic, the number of steps told her that the ceiling of the cave had been taller than she'd realized.

The servants dropped her arms to push open two double doors, and Felicity sank to the floor. They hurried back to help her up, and when she murmured her thanks, they leered at her in what she hoped might be smiles.

Although her room had been constructed of the same black stone, the walls had been relieved of complete darkness by tapestries woven in pale creams. Felicity glanced at them only a moment, her attention riveted by a large four-poster bed. It lacked any ornate embellishments, but made up for it by boasting fluffy, feather-stuffed bedding.

Cleo left, but Chloe stayed and helped her out of her gown, so Felicity surmised that Cleo was male. With their half-bald heads and shriveled features, she hadn't been sure.

"Have you served here long?" she ventured.

Chloe turned and stared at her with fathomless black eyes.

"Can you speak?"

The servant cackled, a sound Felicity would rather not have heard repeated, and so she gave up her questions and resigned herself to Chloe's silent ministrations.

Felicity crawled beneath the linens, studying the room and its furnishings. It appeared as if it had been designed for her and had only been waiting for her to occupy it.

But Uncle's potion finally overwhelmed her, and her eyelids closed of their own accord. She dreamt of a lion that leapt beneath a golden sun. He asked her to run across the moors with him, and like a child she scrambled onto his back, her face pressed into his thick mane, and flew across the heather as if her lion had sported wings. But then he stumbled, and she fell off his back into a pool of black sludge.

The lion turned into a man and stood at the edge of the pool, laughing while she cried out to him.

She understood that he'd purposefully thrown her into the pool, and she struggled against inhaling the stuff into her lungs, against swallowing it down her throat.

She knew he wouldn't save her, and her heart broke with a resounding crack, and she gave up the struggle, no longer caring. Then the blackness changed into a pearly white fire, and welcomed her. Since she no longer struggled, she no longer felt any pain.

But when the pearly fire retreated, she realized that unlike the blackness, it had taken a part of her with it.

Sixteen

TERENCE DUCKED INTO THE COACH AND NARROWED his eyes at Bentley, daring him to say a word about last night. But Bentley had other things on his mind.

"My contact has been waiting to meet with you."

Terence grunted. "I had a better idea."

Bentley twitched his nose.

"My wife seems to think that her cousin, Ralph Wortley, is responsible for her nightmares. It made me wonder that he qualified for the dukedom within a few weeks of Felicity losing it."

Bentley tilted his head. "I see where you're going. It's uncommon for power to fall to another line, or even skip a generation."

"True. And we're running out of time. I think I need to have a little chat with this Ralph. I thought that the residual stink of relic magic on him was an overflow from Felicity. But now I'm not so sure."

"One way to find out." Bentley raised his voice to the coachman. "Driver, take us to Spellsinger Gardens."

Terence raised a golden brow in inquiry.

Bentley twitched a shrug. "It's what you pay me

for, isn't it? Ralph's been spending a lot of time celebrating in the Gardens since he passed his testing."

Terence crossed his arms over his chest and settled back for the ride. The morning air flowed through the windows and played with his hair. It reminded him of the way Felicity seemed to enjoy burying her fingers in it; and that led to visions of her lavender eyes glazed with passion, her full lips parted in a moan of delight, the feel of her encasing him as he felt his own release.

He shifted where he sat.

"Are you sure," asked Bentley, bringing a screeching halt to Terence's pleasant thoughts, "that your desire for the girl isn't affecting your judgment, sir?"

Terence clenched his fists. He should've known Bentley wouldn't leave it alone. "Desire, hell. I'm in love with the chit. What do you say to that, old friend?"

"I'd say we're in a lot of trouble. I knew once you had her…" Bentley sighed. "I tried to stop you."

Terence almost laughed. Bentley had argued with him most of last night, pointing out every logical reason for him to keep his hands off the girl until they'd found the relic. When his friend realized that no argument in the world could stop him, he'd plied him with brandy, hoping to get him drunk enough to pass out. "Since when have you ever known me to succumb to liquor?"

"Never. But it was the only thing I could think of."

This time, Terence did laugh. He slapped Bentley on the shoulder. "Admit it, man, there's not a thing you could've done."

"No, she's had you under her spell since the moment you met her."

"May I remind you that we're immune to magic?"

"Not that kind of spell." Bentley wiggled in his coat. "Don't you wonder what she'll do when she finds out you've been lying to her?"

"Worse. I wonder what I'll do if I find out she's been lying to me."

That ended their discussion until they reached the Gardens. Terence got out of the coach and strolled through the pavilions, his eyes sharp for any sign of Felicity's cousin. The boy had made himself scarce after their first meeting at the ball, slipping out of the house whenever Terence came to visit. He thought Ralph might even be afraid of him. When Bentley made a few discreet inquiries, then guided them to a huge willow tree, Terence realized he'd been right.

Bentley pulled back the heavy curtain of hanging branches to reveal a cozy haven padded with thick moss and speckled with filtered sunlight. Ralph's naked skin looked impossibly white against the dark green, as did the even whiter complexion of his companions.

The look in the young man's eyes when he saw Terence's face changed from wicked passion to absolute panic. Ralph scrambled for his clothing, but the two female nymphs just smiled slyly at him.

Terence could only detect the faintest traces of relic-magic on Ralph. He allowed himself to half shift, just a ghost of an outline of his lion-self, just enough to scare the nymphs back up into their tree.

Terence went straight to the point. "What do you know about the relic?"

Ralph's mouth dropped open. It appeared that the question was the last thing he'd expected to hear, and this convinced Terence, more than words could have, that the current Duke of Stonehaven had no idea what the baronet was talking about.

"What relic?" Ralph asked as he struggled into his clothing.

Terence frowned. It had been a long shot anyway, that the young man would have known anything. He growled in frustration. Ralph shuddered at the sound. Terence shifted again to his lion-form and swiped a paw with claws extended at the boy.

Terence marveled at how much the feint frightened Ralph. Maybe this trip wouldn't be such a waste after all. He shifted to human, curved his mouth into a half smile, and stepped back, holding the branches for Ralph to exit. "I would appreciate any information you could give me."

"S-such as?" Ralph emerged from the canopy and blinked at the sudden light. He appeared to be eager to help Terence… or maybe just to get rid of him.

"You've never heard of Merlin's thirteen relics?"

Ralph shrugged. "Everybody knows that old legend."

"Have you ever seen your mother or father use any type of gem as the focal point of their powers?"

Ralph pulled at his ear. "Father dabbles in potions and charms and old manuscripts. Mother doesn't have any power to speak of." He spoke with an arrogance that his recent rise to the dukedom made possible.

Terence grunted with frustration. "What do you know about the Underground entrance in your cellar?"

That rocked the boy. "There is no—by Jove! There's no entrance to the Underground at my mansion."

Bentley pressed the advantage, his ears twitching

forward in eagerness. "Then what about the visions that you've been tormenting your cousin with? I suppose you know nothing of them as well?"

Ralph turned red and hunched his shoulders. "I've never sent her any illusions, scary or otherwise. I just let her think that because…" He cleared his throat. "Well, because she had everything. The title, the lands. But now that I've got them, well, it's not as jolly as I thought it would be."

Terence exchanged a look of irritation with Bentley.

"Do you have any idea who might be sending them to her?"

"How would I know? She's had them ever since her parents died on that ship. Father says she brings them on herself."

Which meant that she was the one using the relic. Terence refused to believe it. The boy really didn't know anything, and they'd wasted their time seeking him out. And he still had the meeting with Lord and Lady Wortley.

"I'm sure I don't need to warn you not to divulge anything we've discussed here to anyone else."

"It's not like anyone would actually believe any of this."

"You'd be surprised."

Bentley jabbed his thumb over his shoulder. "Something's going on."

"I say," squeaked Ralph, "it's the police. But they know better than to come here."

Terence glanced over his shoulder. Several uniformed officers seemed to be routing the place, even though Scotland Yard usually turned a blind eye to the Gardens in deference to the prince. "Something out of the ordinary must have brought them."

"Uh, Sir Terence," said the Duke of Stonehaven.

"What is it?" Terence replied rather distractedly. It wasn't every day one saw naked bodies leaping over shrubs and fountains. Most amusing.

"It's possible, um, that they might be looking for you."

Bentley grabbed Ralph by his coat lapels. "Why?"

Terence resisted the urge to shift. The police did seem to be combing the area, as if looking for someone.

"It's not my fault," yelped Ralph.

"Hurry up and explain, Your Grace," snarled Terence. "I'd like to know what I'm running from before I start." With a grunt of annoyance, Terence pushed Ralph back under the sheltering canopy of the willow and ducked in behind him.

Bentley followed and kept watch through the branches. "We've got about one minute."

"Since my dunce of a cousin left no note when she eloped with you, my parents were concerned," the duke said in a rush. "They notified the authorities that Felicity had been kidnapped. Just to protect her reputation, mind. As soon as they speak to her and she confirms the marriage, they said they'd drop any charges."

"Bloody hell," muttered Terence. He couldn't fault Lord and Lady Wortley for their concern; however, he specifically recalled that Felicity had indeed left her aunt and uncle a message. But to have him thrown in a cell just to protect the girl's reputation... oh, yes, he definitely needed to have a chat with them.

Raised voices sounded outside their screen of leaves, and Terence angrily pushed through the branches and walked toward the closest policeman. It would save him some time to just avoid them, but he'd be hanged if he ran. Bentley shook his head with disgust, but followed, the duke trailing behind.

"I heard you were looking for me." Terence eyed the officer's badge. "Inspector Scrugs, how can I be of assistance?"

The man studied Terence's confident face for a few moments in shocked silence. "Sir Terence Blackwell?"

"Indeed."

"There appears to be a misunderstanding regarding the niece of Viscount Wortley. I'd like to take you in for questioning, if it's not too much of an inconvenience."

Terence appreciated his veil of politeness. "Ah, but I'm afraid it is. I'm rather pressed for time at the moment. Perhaps we can clear this matter up right now."

The inspector rubbed the end of his bulbous nose. "And how might we accomplish that?"

Four other uniformed men joined the group. If Terence had not been so confident, he might have felt uncomfortable. "Quite simply. Just send one of your men to my home, and my wife will explain the situation."

"We've already done that, sir. It appears she's not there."

Terence mentally cursed. Hadn't he told her not to leave the house? Couldn't she follow one simple order? "I assume you spoke with my staff then and verified that I did marry the girl. So you can drop all this."

"That's not the issue at the moment. Your servants confirmed that someone matching the description of Miss Felicity Seymour did spend the evening in your home and that she left this morning to visit her aunt and uncle. However, Lord and Lady Wortley deny having seen her since you abducted her. So as of this moment, she's a missing person." The inspector waved at another group of officers, who surrounded the rear of their party. "I apologize Sir Terence, but until we locate the girl, we'll have to hold you on charges of kidnapping, and if Lady Wortley is to be believed, suspicion of murder."

"This is ridiculous!" Ralph puffed up his chest. "I say, inspector, do you know who I am?"

The officer nodded. "Congratulations on your recent attainment, Your Grace."

"Yes, yes, thank you." Ralph attempted to look like a man of the world.

"His grace was aware of my engagement to Miss Seymour," Terence interjected. "This is all a misunderstanding on the part of his mother and father. My wife is probably off shopping somewhere, unaware of the difficulty she's created."

The officer shrugged. "It may be just as you say, sir. But until I can verify her whereabouts… Well, perhaps it would be helpful if his grace accompanies us."

Ralph sputtered while Terence's mind churned. Even though he told her he'd see to it, it would be just like Felicity to visit her aunt and uncle to ease their minds. Had something happened to her on the way to see them? Terence felt a frisson of concern.

"I smell a rat," he murmured over his shoulder to Bentley. "And it's not you."

"This is a setup," agreed his friend. "But whose?"

Terence smoothed his hair away from his face. He

knew what Bentley implied. Was Felicity involved with this, or simply a pawn of Lord and Lady Wortley's?

Terence raised his voice. "It seems that I will be unavoidably delayed, after all. I am at your service, Inspector Scrugs." He turned a sardonic smile toward Ralph. "As, I am sure, is his grace."

The officer let out a breath of relief and waved the other policemen off. "Arrest who you can while we're here."

The men's faces lit up, and they turned to look for the nearest naked woman.

"If you will be so kind, Sir Terence?"

Terence grabbed Ralph's arm and strolled toward his coach, Bentley following. The efficient inspector had already parked a police wagon in front of and behind his conveyance. It appeared that they would have a close escort to the station.

"I have a favor to ask," said Terence to the Duke of Stonehaven after they'd settled into the carriage. Ralph narrowed his eyes. Terence lowered his voice. "I would prefer that no one get hurt. I need a distraction."

Ralph blinked. "What kind of distraction?"

"Ah, well, just use your imagination."

"B-but when?"

The carriage rattled over Spellsinger Bridge. "Right about now would be most convenient."

"You could've given me a bit more warning," muttered Ralph. But he quickly closed his eyes in concentration. He opened them for a moment. "This could be fun."

"Quite."

Ralph closed his eyes again.

The light streaming through the windows turned black, as if a blanket had been thrown over the sun. Terence heard the policemen's horses scream, and his own carriage slowed. He raised a brow at Bentley, who snapped a smile and leaned out the window.

"Your Grace, are those insects?"

Ralph opened his eyes and grinned sheepishly. "I still have difficulty summoning enough power to change anything larger than a bug, and I figured an illusion wouldn't do."

Terence stuck his head out his own window. A cloud of black specks swirled around their escort's horses, and as far down the road as he could see. But his own conveyance held a circle of immunity, and his horses only snorted in confusion at the chaos around them.

Despite the driver's best efforts, the police coach in front of them jerked forward, the horses finally bolting at the thousands of tiny bites on their hides.

Terence settled back in his seat. "Well done, Lord Wortley." He knocked on the wall behind him. "Drive on. To number three, Gargoyle Square."

Ralph smiled with arrogance at Terence's compliment, until Bentley groaned.

"Your Grace, the entire city will be picking flies out of their soup for days. Why couldn't you have just made them an illusion?"

"Then the police would've suspected him," replied Terence. The coach that had been behind them passed them on the open road, covered in a black cloud that made them blind to all around them. "An illusion couldn't be refuted as magical assistance, but a sudden swarm of flies? The Thames breeds them in droves."

Bentley shrugged an agreement. "They'll be suspicious, but it'll be deuced difficult to prove anything. Well done, man."

Ralph's arrogant grin returned and stayed plastered to his face until they reached his home.

After several tries at the door's bell, the duke finally fished a key from his pocket. "I wonder where Wimpole's gotten to? The servants should have returned from the country estate by now."

Terence pushed his way past the smaller man into the mansion and shifted, his nose and ears straining, before shifting back to human again. "There are only two people here. Upstairs."

"I say," protested Ralph. "You can't just go barging into their private quarters—"

Terence climbed the stairs two at a time. He hoped that one of the two people he'd sensed in the house would be Felicity; otherwise, he feared that this unusual feeling of panic in his gut might get even worse.

Terence quietly opened the door to the Wortleys' bedchamber and beheld the couple in the oddest tableau. Lord Wortley lounged atop rumpled bedcovers, his linen shirt open to expose a surprisingly muscled torso. Terence had glimpsed Felicity's aunt only a few times, but his memory of her warred with the image of the woman who sat on the bare floor in the middle of the room.

"What's the matter, love?" asked Viscount Wortley, his voice thick with the aftermath of an obviously successful bout of lovemaking.

Felicity's aunt clutched a glowing object that

hung around her neck. "Ralph's playing with magic again—or it's that potion you gave the—"

They sensed Terence's presence at the same time, both of them turning surprised faces in his direction.

Viscount Wortley sat up. "I say, Sir Terence, what's the meaning of this?"

The aunt didn't bother with questions. With her eyes gleaming and her unbound hair swirling around her face, she mumbled a few words. The darkness that surrounded her coalesced into her open hands, and she flung it at him.

Terence blocked most of the doorway and didn't bother to duck, since the spell couldn't harm him. Bentley and Ralph had just reached the top of the landing. Bentley tackled Ralph and covered the young man's body with his own, trying to protect him but possibly suffocating him in the process.

Terence focused his attention on his wife's aunt and uncle. He needn't wonder about their involvement with the relic anymore, for the glowing pearl around the woman's neck reeked of enough magic to make him choke. What startled him into immobility was the sudden feel of Felicity in the room. But he knew it to be empty except for Lord and Lady Wortley.

"Where is she?" he growled. The relic sat right in front of him for the taking, but all he could think about was his wife.

"Somewhere safe from you," answered Lord Wortley, rolling from the bed and coming up with a knife in his fist. He took a defensive stance in front of his wife, waving the knife with a practiced ease that told Terence he knew how to use it.

"You can't have it," screeched the aunt. "I know you've come to steal it, but it's mine."

Terence growled. "I don't want your stupid relic."

He heard Bentley grunt and a smothered gasp from Ralph.

"All I want is my wife."

Wortley snorted and rocked on the balls of his bare feet.

"I'll leave you alone," continued Terence, "if you just return Felicity to me. You can leave London with the relic, go where no one would ever find you." To his surprise, he realized that he meant every word. Since he'd become aware of his family's mission, he'd been obsessed with becoming the best relic-hunter the crown had ever employed. And now it no longer seemed to matter. Felicity had become the most important thing in the world to him.

The woman peeked around her husband's leg. "Oh, but you can't have her either, Sir Terence. We need her, you see."

Terence shook his head. The woman spoke to him as if they were seated across from each other at a tea party. For that matter, despite the threatening look in Lord Wortley's eyes, his voice sounded just as congenial.

"Gertrude, dear, if you don't do something soon, I'll be forced to fight like a common ruffian."

"You forget, Oliver darling, that shapeshifters are immune to magic. What do you suggest I do?"

"Increase my odds," he replied, and lunged for Terence.

At the same moment, objects from around the room flew toward the doorway. Terence didn't move while his gaze frantically searched the room. He could feel Felicity stronger than ever.

"For God's sake, duck," screamed Bentley as a chamber pot flew right at Terence's face.

Terence shook himself from his stupor, ducked, and came up with Lord Wortley's knife arm in his grasp. He twisted, yanking the man's arm behind him, and held it upward in a bruising lock.

"Where is she?" he demanded again, stretching the man's muscles painfully. He hesitated to hurt Felicity's uncle, even though it might be the death of him.

Terence's close proximity to the man kept him safe from the flying projectiles, but a fireplace poker flew past him into the hall, and he heard an agonized squeak from Bentley.

"Really, Gertrude," panted Lord Wortley. "It's worth the risk."

Terence heard the woman sigh from behind him.

"I suppose you're right," she calmly agreed. And they both disappeared.

But not before Terence felt Felicity's presence again, so strong that he needed only to reach out to touch her.

His fingers closed on empty air.

Terence turned to Bentley. "How bad is it?"

His friend rolled off the young duke and twitched. "Just a flesh wound."

Ralph's face was slightly blue, and he gasped for air. His eyes widened when he caught sight of the blood dripping down Bentley's sleeve.

"Your parents are using the magic of a relic," said Terence.

Ralph's eyes widened even further. "I don't understand—"

Terence slashed his hand through the air like a knife. "Enough. Come with me." He grabbed Ralph's arm. "You'll be all right?" he called to Bentley as he dragged the duke down the stairs.

Bentley shuddered as he tore off a strip of his shirt and wrapped it around the wound. But he met Terence's eyes and nodded his agreement.

Terence led Ralph into the kitchen, through the washroom and to the apparently solid wall at the back. It took him a few minutes to find the hidden mechanism again, but finally the brick wall slid open.

Ralph gaped.

"They don't have a relic," grated Terence. "The house doesn't have an entrance into the Underground either, does it?"

"I... I..."

"If I weren't so worried about your cousin, I might feel sorry for you. But I don't have the time."

Terence took a candle out of a wall sconce and gestured for Ralph to follow him. The boy stayed hard on his heels down the stairs, until they reached the wine cellar.

"No wonder they never told me about this place," breathed the young duke. "Look at all the wine!"

"That's not what they were hiding," Terence snapped. "Don't you feel the wards?"

Ralph closed his eyes, then shuddered.

Terence nodded. "But I can't find the door."

"Ah." Ralph peered at the brick wall. "Father spoke often of secret passageways and the clever tricks that sorcerers use to keep them concealed. Did you feel for another hidden latch?"

Terence swiped his fingers through his hair. Even if they located the door and Felicity's aunt and uncle had taken her underground as he suspected, how would he ever find her? What if Lord and Lady Wortley were taking her even deeper into the Underground right now?

Terence almost jumped at the sound of Bentley's voice behind him. "He can't find it either, can he?"

Ralph cocked his head, squinting at the brick wall. "I say, do you notice that some of the bricks are numbered? Now, the fifth one from the bottom has a small two inscribed in it, and the third one from the top has a small nine." He pushed at the bricks. "Not those then—yes, that's it! Very clever for Father to have used Maximillian's Code as a mundane lock."

"What are you talking about?" asked Bentley.

Terence just watched the boy with narrowed eyes.

"See here," continued the duke. "We just start at the center point, hmm, let me count the bricks. Right here. Now, we take five twice, and count down, then move over two, count over nine, three times, move back three... Yes, push this, and this, and then..."

With a rattle, something shifted, and a portion of the brick wall swung into the room.

Ralph took a step back, for as soon as the door opened, his uncle's wards crackled with warning.

Terence shifted and plunged into the dark tunnel, his nose up and eagerly searching for the smell of Felicity. But... nothing. Nothing at all, not even a whiff of the relic. He roared with frustration, rattling the tunnel walls and sending gravel down on his head. To have come so close and still fail! Without a scent to follow, they could wander through the tunnels forever.

Terence clawed at the walls in frustration, raking long gashes through the rock. After he'd vented his fury, Bentley called into the darkness from the open door. "There's no help for it then. We must meet with my contact."

Terence swung his head and moaned, forcing his animal nature to calm.

He would find his wife. He must.

Seventeen

TERENCE FLEW ACROSS THE ROOFTOPS, WATCHING carefully for weak patches and holes. When one ventured this deeply into the true slums of the East Side, one did not go in a coach, unless one wanted to get robbed. Or on foot, for the same reason. With Bentley in rat-form securely buried in his mane, leaping across dilapidated rooftops seemed a safer proposition.

But his instincts had taken over the run, and Terence had too much time to think. To worry about why Felicity's aunt and uncle seemed so determined to keep them apart. Did they truly want to protect her, or was there a more sinister reason? Even if they managed to keep him in prison, they had to know that he'd report them to the prince, and another shapeshifter would come for their relic. Did they think to hold Felicity as hostage? The prince would sacrifice her—regretfully of course, but he'd do worse to recover a relic.

Terence had to find Felicity before the prince got wind of what had happened.

He had to find her because he had no idea what her

aunt and uncle might be capable of. The way they'd acted in that room had struck him that they might be a bit mad, whether from using the relic or wanting to keep what it offered, he couldn't be sure.

He had to find Felicity because he loved her.

Terence's front paw sank into a soft spot, and he hop-skipped over to another roof before that one caved in from his weight. Bentley gave a disgusted squeak, but Terence ignored him.

Although Terence had been frustrated that the discovery of the mansion's doorway into the Underground had been nothing but a waste of time, Bentley had pointed out that it did prove one thing: Ralph was completely innocent of his parents' activities. And therefore, it was possible that Felicity was as well.

But why would he feel Felicity's presence so strongly when he'd been in the room with her aunt and uncle? She had to be tangled up in the use of the relic in some way.

Not that it mattered, mused Terence, leaping over a chimney spout. The girl could be guilty of any crime imaginable, and it still wouldn't change the fact that he loved her. Had this been the way Thomas had felt when he'd given up his life for Alicia?

Because he knew he'd give up his own for Felicity, without a moment's hesitation.

He winced at a sudden yank of his fur and studied his location. Yes, they stood near the junction of Goblinwell Railway and Witchcomb Crossing. The slums of London didn't have addresses, just general locations.

Terence leapt to the littered ground and shifted

back to human after Bentley had scrambled out of his mane. Bentley shifted as well and wasted no time in pulling his knife from out of his boot top, only wincing slightly from the injury to his arm. His friend scanned the area suspiciously.

"Follow me," he whispered, and Terence hid a smile. Had Bentley just given him an order? He couldn't really blame him though, after the way Terence had frozen when they'd confronted Lord and Lady Wortley.

Terence followed his friend, both of them keeping to the shadows, their footsteps soundless in the foggy night.

"Here," muttered Bentley, stopping in front of a shack which appeared to be in better condition that its neighbors. A small shingle with the outline of a needle and thread advertised that this home served as a shop, as well.

Terence shouldered his friend aside and opened the door. The shop consisted of a tiny front room with bolts of cloth taking up most of the space, and a curtained doorway that he assumed led into the private quarters. He could only assume because he didn't make it that far. The familiar sound of a gun being cocked froze him in his tracks. The business-end of the weapon poked through the curtain.

"It has silver bullets," said a woman's voice. "So be you human or otherwise, there ain't enough here worth stealing to shed blood over."

"Mildred," squeaked Bentley from behind him. "Don't shoot. It's Bentley Poole."

The barrel of the gun lowered a fraction. "Bentley?"

"Please forgive us for sneaking in on you, but

knocking on your door at this time of night would've caused more commotion than…"

"Cor, it is you!" The gun disappeared, a match lit a candle, and the curtain parted. "Only Bentley Poole would sneak into a house at night and then apologize for it."

Terence studied Mildred. She looked small but stout, with yellow-blonde hair and enormous blue eyes. He had a feeling her soft appearance hid an inner strength as tough as steel.

Terence kept his voice neutral. "We need a guide."

"Do you, now?" she replied, keeping her eyes riveted to Bentley's narrow face. "I haven't been to the Underground in years, but if the price is right…"

"How much?" Terence asked.

Mildred lifted the curtain and gestured them into the other room, setting the candleholder on a small table. She named a price that made Terence raise a brow. High enough to be worthwhile, but not so much that he couldn't easily afford it. The network of intelligence within the lower classes always astonished him.

"Still hunting relics, eh?" asked Mildred.

"Not this time," Terence growled. "I'm hunting my wife."

"Aah." Mildred stood and slipped behind a changing screen. "Well, that's a little different, ain't it? Bentley, hand me them trousers. I'm not about to go traipsing through those tunnels in my nightdress."

Bentley picked up a pair of trousers from a stack folded neatly in a mending basket and tossed them over the screen. She reappeared in a ruffled blouse tucked incongruously into the waist of the trousers.

She wrapped a belt around her, tucked her gun beneath it, and covered it all with a wool mantel. She took a lantern and matches and looked questioningly at Terence. "Did you bring a mount?"

Terence stood and shifted, his heavy front paws hitting the warped slats of the floor with a thud.

Mildred jumped, but Bentley touched Terence's back. "Just sit here, and keep your knees up, so your feet don't drag."

Mildred took a deep breath and nodded.

Now that Terence wore his animal-self, the impatience to find Felicity became even more overwhelming. He snarled at Bentley, who quickly shifted and crawled up into Terence's mane. Mildred shook herself, gingerly hiked a leg over Terence's back, and drew up her knees. "Are you sure you can take my weight? I'm rather heavy."

Terence answered by leaping for the door, pushing it open as he fled into the night. Mildred plastered herself to his back, her fingers clutching his mane with a death-grip. "Follow the Goblinwell rails."

When they reached an abandoned theater, Mildred told him to turn right. He followed a footpath between years of accumulated cast-offs—old shoes, chairs, and items whose original purpose he couldn't even guess at. Then Mildred told him to turn again, and he picked his way through the broken stones of an old building until they came to a graveyard.

She asked him to stop and tumbled off his back. Her legs wobbled when she stood, and she pushed a hand into the small of her back. "Thank you, Sir Terence. That was certainly the most exhilarating ride I've had in quite a while."

Bentley slid out of his mane, and they both shifted back to human.

"Why are we stopping?" growled Terence.

Mildred walked over to a mausoleum, reached up, and pulled the big toe of a statue of a gargoyle that sat atop it. The earth shook as the stone door slid open. She lit her lantern and went inside. Terence and Bentley exchanged a glance of loathing, then followed.

The air felt twice as cold as it did outside, and the hairs on the back of Terence's neck stood up. When Mildred slid the top of a coffin aside, he almost pounced on her. Leave it to the denizens of the Underground to disrespect the dead. But they were half dead themselves, living beneath the earth, so he shouldn't have been surprised.

Mildred reached into the box and pulled something. Again Terence heard stone shift, and a black square appeared at the foot of the coffin. Bentley followed her down into the blackness without hesitation, but Terence had to grit his teeth and force his limbs down the rusty ladder. His lion-self hated to go beneath the earth, since he ruled in the open plains and sunshine. He broke out in a sweat as he fought the animal part of his nature.

The ladder ended in a narrow dirt tunnel. Unlike the large stone entrance in Viscount Wortley's mansion, the confines of this passageway made Terence feel trapped. Made him aware of the heavy earth that grew denser above his head as they descended. His shoulders scraped the sides of the wall again and again, and he cursed with each contact.

"It'll widen out soon," promised Mildred, her voice

dulled as if the earth sucked the vibrancy from it. "Bentley, stay close with your knife at the ready. We shouldn't run into anyone else at this hour, but those in the Underground have a tendency to ignore our time schedules. It's not like they have daylight to follow.

"Oh, and Sir Terence, I suppose I needn't warn you to watch your back?"

Terence grunted.

Mildred led them through the narrow tunnels. As soon as they widened, Terence shifted and Mildred straddled his back again, Bentley quickly shifting and crawling into his mane. Terence sprang forward, keeping his leaps low, covering as much ground as he possibly could. Mildred held the lantern beside his head, indicating by a swing which path to take. Terence's feline vision had no trouble negotiating the tunnels, and he kept up his swift pace with little trouble. After several hours Mildred's grip slackened from fatigue, but he refused to stop until she made him. It seemed as if a lifetime had passed since he'd last been with Felicity, and he couldn't bear any more delay.

Mildred stopped him by the simple expediency of falling off his back. Terence let his tongue loll and his ribs heave while she recovered enough to scramble to her feet.

"We're at the city," she announced.

Terence and Bentley shifted to human and strode to the end of the passage. After the darkness of their journey, Terence had to narrow his eyes at the brilliance of the fairylights that illuminated the ceiling of a cavern larger than he would hazard to guess. He might've thought that he looked at the slums of

London's East End had it not been for the smell of the
place. Even the Thames at its worst had never reeked
like this.

"Now what?" asked Bentley.

"We'll have to ask around, find someone who can
tell us the way to Viscount Wortley's lair."

"You mean she's not in the city?" snapped Mildred.

"She's down here somewhere," said Bentley, "and I'm
sure I can manage to persuade some helpful citizen—"

"Not unless you want a knife between your ribs," she
replied. "The sorcerers who live here value their privacy."

"I'll find her," growled Terence. "Bentley, is there
somewhere safe you can take Mildred?"

His friend wiggled his nose. "You're not going
without me."

Mildred started walking down a dusty path. "I'll
take you to the tavern where my sister works. I'll wait
there for you until you bring your wife. You'll need
me to guide you back up."

Terence didn't comprehend the magnitude of their
task until they reached the twisting streets and he
saw how many tunnels branched into the city. The
sorcerers who hid in the Underground controlled the
city, and he couldn't imagine any one of the citizens
revealing their secret lairs.

A spider web of streams flowed through the city,
taking some of the garbage out of it. They left Mildred
at the fifth tavern by the thirteenth stream they
crossed. She made them repeat the directions to be
sure they could find her again. All the buildings looked
alike, formed of irregular stones that Terence guessed
had been acquired from the tunneling. And most of

them seemed to be comprised of taverns and alehouses and gambling dens.

"Now what?" Bentley asked again, after Mildred closed the door.

Terence surveyed the empty streets. "What's the matter with you? That's the second time you've asked me that, and you're the one who usually has ten wild plans for me to choose from."

Bentley twitched his mustache, his black eyes glittering in the dim light. "Sorry. I just never expected—"

Terence clapped his friend on the shoulder. "Quiet. Do you hear that? That hissing sounds familiar. It sounds like—"

"A very angry dragonette."

Terence had already shifted before the words were out of Bentley's mouth, and he sprang down the street before he realized that he'd left his friend to try and follow in human form.

Terence bounded to a rooftop and fell through the thin cloth covering it. He landed on his feet, naturally, but had managed to rap his head on a protruding beam on the way down. He shook his mane, uttering a rumble of confusion. Of course, he should've guessed that without the threat of rain or snow, the city had no need of sturdy roofs.

He leaped through the door before most of the occupants of the small home had a chance to react. Even then, he heard neither screams nor curses behind him. He could only wonder at what the citizens were used to, that a lion crashing through their roof brought no undue alarm.

A flash of white fire through the alley of two

buildings led him to Daisy. His head still ached, and he had to blink twice to clear his double vision. The dragonette had been backed up to a wall by a ring of men, all of them brandishing swords or pistols, except for the center man, who held out empty hands and shouted at his henchmen.

"No, you fools! I want it alive. Don't you know what this lizard's worth?"

Terence ignored him, for the sorcerer had no power to hurt him, but bullets and pistols were altogether different. He let out a roar that rattled the stones of the nearby buildings and charged forward, hoping to knock down the men with guns first. At the same time the sorcerer released the spell he'd been casting at Daisy, and the little dragonette whined at whatever hit her.

Terence had two men unconscious with his first leap. He snarled and sliced flesh before another man could get off a shot, but the fourth one managed to pull the trigger before Terence could take him down. The bullet had fortunately not been made of silver, and he only felt a brief burst of discomfort from its passing.

The sorcerer raised his hands toward the dragonette again, and Terence couldn't ignore him any longer. Daisy's normally opalescent hide had dulled to ashen gray, and her gouts of fire had trickled to a mere puff of smoke.

Terence tensed his back legs and exposed his fangs in a snarl. He felt the slice of a blade across his ribs right as he leapt, and at least a part of it had been forged with silver, for it ripped his flesh open with a cold burn. He didn't allow the pain to interfere with his target though, and he smashed right into the sorcerer's chest, sending the man onto his back. The sorcerer's head smacked the ground with a dull thud, and his head sagged to the left, revealing a blood-soaked rock beneath.

Terence spun, ready to confront the rest of the pack. Bentley saluted him with the blade of a bloody sword, his lean body surrounded by fallen men. Terence grunted and shifted back to human, stanching the flow of blood on his side with his hand. He took a step toward Daisy, but the dragonette launched herself at him, curling around his neck and whimpering with happiness.

"It's all right, girl," whispered Terence. "Daddy's—er—I'm here."

Eighteen

FELICITY WOKE FEELING AS IF A PART OF HER SOUL HAD been ripped away. She glanced around the strange room and tried to sit up, but her muscles wouldn't work, and it was all she could do just to keep her eyes open. Her mind was clear, so it couldn't be Uncle's potion still affecting her. The last time she'd felt this weak had been when Terence had stolen her away from Uncle Oliver's manor in Sussex.

And had married her.

Felicity groaned when the memories of how and why she'd come to this place returned to her. Could Terence have been lying to her the entire time? She dreaded the answer but knew she must get to the truth.

"Miss?"

Felicity almost groaned again at the sound of her friend's voice. "Katie? Is that you?"

A dark form broke away from the shadowed corner of the room. Katie's red-rimmed eyes blinked at her with happiness as she grabbed Felicity's shoulders. "Ye're alive!"

"Well, of course I am. Have we any water? My mouth feels like it's full of cotton."

Her maid lifted Felicity by the shoulders and stuffed several pillows behind her, managing to keep her in a semi-upright position. She held a crystal goblet to Felicity's lips, and the liquid tasted like the sweetest of wines.

"I couldn't see ye breathing," babbled Katie. "And I didn't have a mirror to hold under yer nose, and ye haven't moved for the longest time. Yer aunt and uncle insisted ye needed me, so I followed them down into this graveyard of a place…"

Felicity followed her maid's movements around the room. Besides her mouth, it seemed that her eyes were the only parts of her working right now.

"Where's Daisy?"

Fresh tears slid down Katie's face. "She ran off just after you got out of the carriage, miss. I tried to stop her, but she lit my sleeve on fire. Why are we here?" She shuddered. "I don't like this place."

"Neither do I. The sooner we leave it, the better."

Katie wrung her hands. "We'd never find our way up to the surface, miss. Yer aunt and uncle told me so. We'd get lost in the tunnels and starve to death before we found our way out. Besides," she fingered a black collar around her neck, "yer aunt put this on me."

Felicity blinked. "What is it?"

"Yer uncle called it insurance. He said if either ye or I went wandering, it would tighten like a noose."

Felicity's mouth dropped open. "Surely, they were just trying to frighten you."

Katie fingered the collar. "But why? Why would they want to keep us prisoners?"

"They seem to believe that Terence is a spy. And that he wants to steal their relic from them." She just couldn't say she doubted Terence had ever loved her. "Maybe they brought you here too because they were afraid that you could testify that you saw me go into the mansion and not come out. And then the police would release Terence... oh, Katie, there's still a lot I don't understand. But it's important for us to get out of here. Can you help me get dressed?"

Katie nodded enthusiastically, her red curls bobbing around her freckled face. But after several hours of tugging and pulling, she'd only managed to get Felicity half clothed.

Felicity stared at her maid in frustration. "I don't feel ill, just like I have no strength at all. Blast! What is wrong with me?"

Felicity closed her eyes. She could feel sparks inside of her, like when she'd tried to gather enough magic for her testing. So she concentrated on willing those sparks of strength to her muscles and managed to move her arms.

Felicity opened her eyes in surprise, and then was distracted by the look on her maid's face. "Poor Katie, you look so miserable. I'm sorry I ever asked you to stay with me."

The Irish girl snapped her spine rigid. "Don't say such a thing, miss. If I hadn't been such a coward and stayed in the carriage, and if ye hadn't tried to protect me by giving me Daisy, ye might not be in this mess. I won't fail ye again, miss. Sorry I am that I acted so silly about this." She fingered the black collar again. "Did I see ye move yer arms, then?"

Felicity nodded and grinned when she realized she'd managed that as well. With a bit more time, she'd be able to walk, and somehow they'd figure out a way through the labyrinth of this Underground. She glanced out the one large window in the room. It opened onto the cave's walls, which lay only a few feet from them, like a black void. She wondered how the inhabitants of the city could live in such perpetual darkness.

Katie had just managed to drag Felicity's skirt up to her waist when the sound of a lion's roar made the black stone walls shake. Her maid slapped her hands to her ears, and Felicity smiled.

"It's Sir Terence," breathed Katie, when the echoes of the roar had faded. "He's come to rescue us!"

Felicity nodded. She had no doubt who'd uttered that roar of challenge. "So it seems. I think I have the strength to put on my blouse, Katie."

Katie quickly helped her into the sleeves. While she did up the pearl buttons, Felicity tried to wiggle her toes. If she could just get the strength back in her legs, she wouldn't feel at such a disadvantage when she confronted Terence.

The wooden doors of her chamber shuddered from a blow.

"Are they locked, Katie?" At her maid's nod, Felicity fell back against the pillows. "We'll just wait then, shall we?"

The double doors shuddered again, the wood splintering as several claws pierced it. With a final crack they split apart, and her lion bounded into the room, his fangs exposed and his golden eyes ablaze with challenge. Katie sucked in a breath and backed away, but Felicity just grinned helplessly. This lion had been her rescuer, saving her from the monsters in her dreams.

Terence padded toward Felicity, grumbling low in his throat. Bentley appeared behind the lion, a twitching sword in his hand, an opal white dragonette wrapped around his neck.

Daisy uncoiled herself and skittered across the room, her filmy wings flowing behind her. She scrambled up the bed with a hiss of delight, burrowing beneath Felicity's neck, her raspy tongue stealing licks as she did so.

"Daisy, my baby. I was so worried about you! Where have you been?"

"She followed you," answered Bentley. "Without her to lead us, I don't think we would've found you."

So Felicity *had* seen flashes of white in the tunnels. She gently petted the cool scales of her dragonette. "Good girl," she murmured.

The lion reached her side and pushed up against her, moaning low in his throat. Felicity couldn't resist running her fingers through his thick mane just once, and noticed the line of scarlet across his ribs. "You've been hurt!"

Terence shifted to human, and she caught her breath. She'd forgotten how handsome he was, and when he spoke, she couldn't help the little thrill that coursed through her at the sound of his deep voice.

"It looks worse than it is." He reached out and stroked the hair off her forehead. "I was afraid I might never see you again."

Felicity needed to know the truth. She hardened her resolve and batted his hand away. "Me? Or the relic?"

Terence looked startled for a moment, then shook his golden mane. "We don't have much time," he growled. "I'd rather have you safely away before I confront your family again. What have they told you?"

Felicity's eyes burned and she blinked furiously. So, he wasn't going to deny it. She braced herself. "That you're a spy for the prince and you only courted me to find your precious relic." Anger replaced her fear. "That you, sir, are a consummate liar."

Daisy hissed. Katie sucked in a breath. Bentley turned and stood under the sill of the broken door, as if he thought he might need to stand guard for a while.

Terence scowled. "Guilty as charged."

Felicity's hand flopped back down to the bedding. She'd thought... no, she'd hoped that her aunt and uncle had lied about him, just as they'd lied about the spell on her. At his words, her stomach dropped with such a dreadful feeling of desolation and humiliation that she wanted to jump from the bed and hit him. But her body still wouldn't cooperate, and so she took a deep breath and glared into his dratted lovely eyes. She'd withstood her aunt and uncle's betrayal. She'd withstand this one as well.

Terence dropped to his knees, encased her hand with both of his own, and studied her face intently. "But that's only how it started. The spell you carried had the taint of relic-magic, and it seemed an easy thing just to court you to find out more. But don't you see that I could have devised other ways to investigate it? I think I fell in love with you the first time I saw you. I just wouldn't admit it to myself."

Felicity felt herself drowning in his eyes, felt his

words wrapping around her like a soft, woolen cloak. No, she wouldn't allow herself to be so easily led. Not ever again.

"You let me make a fool òf myself over you." She tried to twist her hand from his grip, but he wouldn't let her.

Katie gasped again, and Bentley strode over and dragged the maid to his position by the door, turning both of their backs to the room.

Terence leaned forward and put his lips against her ear, his breath warm as a caress, his musky smell filling her senses. "If I fooled you into thinking I courted you only for the relic, I fooled myself as well. My brother was betrayed by a woman who used the power of a relic, and I just couldn't be sure if you were involved in the use of it."

Felicity pulled her head away and struggled to sit up. Only her stubborn legs now remained useless. How dare he think that she could be involved with forbidden magic? By the startled look on his handsome face, she realized that he wasn't even aware that he'd just insulted her.

Terence let go of her hands and enfolded her in his arms, stroking the back of her hair. "But don't you see? I dòn't care anymore. I love you just the way you are—good or evil."

Felicity fought the desire to scream that she was a good person, blast it. If he didn't know that already, it was his fault, not hers. "If I had the strength, I'd punch you in the nose."

He backed away, studying her inert body with a frown of concern. "You're still angry, and I don't blame you. But you have to trust me, at least a little bit, to get you out of here."

Felicity shivered. The room seemed colder than before he'd wrapped his warmth around her. She wished she didn't have to look at his handsome face. It made her want to apologize for her anger. To do anything for his love. But she'd vowed never to be that simpleton of a girl again, and if she allowed herself to fall under the spell of his silken words so easily, she'd forever be that pliable girl. "I can take care of myself just fine."

Terence cocked his head, his eyes suddenly intense. "Get up out of that bed, then."

"I will when I'm good and ready." Felicity crossed her arms over her bosom.

"Right," snorted Terence. "You've been ill again, haven't you?"

"It's no concern of yours if I have."

He ignored her. "Bentley, she has no strength again. She's never struck me as a sickly person."

Bentley gave up his post by the door, looking at the two of them as if trying to determine if they were friends or enemies. His black eyes finally settled on Felicity. "No. She's a healthy enough girl, ordinarily."

"She's just weak," continued Terence. "As if the life had been sucked out of her."

"Or the magic?"

The two of them bantered back and forth, and Felicity found herself getting annoyed.

"It's only happened twice," said Terence.

"That we know of," interjected Bentley.

"Yes, and think about it. The first time, Ralph passed his testing."

"That would strain anyone's magical resources."

"And Lord Oliver, he said the transference spell took a lot of power."

"Do you really think it's possible, sir?"

Terence raked his hand through his hair in frustration, wincing at the pull of his injury. "It makes more sense than I'd like to admit. I wonder if her nightmares are tied up in this somehow?"

Felicity's stomach twisted. She would no longer tolerate people speaking around her as if she were invisible. She'd had enough of that her entire life. "What are you two talking about?"

The look of eager curiosity faded from Terence's eyes to be replaced with a warmth that made Felicity squirm.

"We'll discuss it when I get you out of here. I promise. But for now," he leaned over and picked her up in his arms, "your safety is more important."

Daisy gave a satisfied hiss of delight, and Felicity sighed with annoyance. She did need his help, and despite his lies, she trusted him to protect her.

Terence grunted from the pain in his rib.

"I don't want to hurt you," she said.

Surprisingly, he smiled. "Does that mean that you forgive me?"

"Certainly not. Now put me down."

He lowered her to the floor, and Felicity sighed with relief when her legs managed to support her. She unwrapped Daisy from around her neck.

"Lead the way home, baby," she murmured. Felicity didn't look at anyone. "It's time to go."

"Oh, but my dear," said a voice from the doorway, "I don't think it's wise for you to go anywhere."

Felicity swayed, her footsteps halting at the sight of Uncle Oliver standing casually atop the ruins of the wooden door, his hand tenderly placed on Katie's shoulder.

Terence shifted to lion and Bentley took a step forward. Daisy spat flame at Uncle's boot.

"I wouldn't do that if I were you," admonished Lord Oliver. "It would be dreadfully foolish of them, wouldn't it, dear?"

Aunt Gertrude swept into the room, still in her odd sorcerer's outfit. Her hand cradled the large pearl on her necklace. "Horribly unwise. And wouldn't you like to know why, Sir Terence?"

Terence shifted back to human as quickly as he'd become his lion-self. "There are many things I'd like to know," he said. "Is it possible that you're willing to tell me?"

Aunt Gertrude cackled, such a grand imitation of an evil witch that Daisy hissed and Felicity backed up a step. Her aunt and uncle looked quite calm, as if they were attending an evening soiree, but Uncle's grip on Katie's shoulder had tightened until his fingers turned white.

"Oh, wouldn't you like to know all our secrets," crowed Aunt. "But I'll not have you spoiling my niece's innocence, Sir Terence. At least, no more than you already have."

The pearl in Aunt's hands started to glow, and Felicity's knees wobbled beneath her.

"Felicity?" whispered Terence, as he stared at the pearl. He quickly turned and stared down at her face. "Felicity?"

She nodded, reassuring him that she still stood next to him, not beside her aunt. Because she understood his confusion. She, too, felt as if a part of herself lay across the room inside the pearl in Aunt's hand.

Uncle Oliver shook his head, and Aunt covered the glowing object beneath her robe. Felicity didn't have time to wonder about it, though, because Katie had started to choke.

Felicity took a step toward her maid.

"Now, now," chided Uncle. "All of you stay where you are. Yes, even you, dear niece. Until we get rid of these spies, it's best if you stay out of the way."

Katie started to choke in earnest, her breath laboring to get past the pressure of the collar around her throat.

"It's for the best," assured Uncle Oliver. Then he turned his attention toward Terence. "As you can see, should you threaten either myself or my wife, this young maid will die. Don't you think my niece might look with disfavor on the man who killed her dearest friend?"

Terence snarled, but didn't move. "It's you using Felicity's magic that will be the death of her friend, Lord Oliver. Not I."

Felicity's knees buckled and she sank to the floor, her skirts whispering around her in the sudden silence of the room. Daisy seemed to have taken her cues from Terence until now, for she broke her frozen stance to clamber back up around her mistress's neck.

Aunt Gertrude looked frightened. "Felicity, dear, he doesn't know what he's talking about. You have no magic. It all went to Ralph, as it should have."

Felicity felt the cold stone of the floor beneath her hands, the comforting weight of her dragonette around her neck, her thoughts swirling with confusion.

"Dear niece," said Uncle Oliver. "This man has done nothing but lie to you from the moment you met him. If the girl should die, it'll be his fault, not yours. Don't let him allow any guilt to fall on your shoulders." He looked at Terence, his face twisting in a sneer. "Now, get out of my home!"

Terence held out his hands and backed up, Bentley copying his movements. "Felicity," he murmured. "I felt you in the relic. Somehow they have a part of you. Fight them."

"Shut up," shouted Aunt Gertrude, her plump shoulders quivering with rage. "The magic doesn't belong to her, it never did. My sister always had everything, but not anymore. Never again."

Felicity stared at her aunt. The pearl had fallen out of her cloak, and glowed softly, as if beckoning to Felicity. She raised her hand, remembering her last dream, when she'd given herself up to the blackness and had felt a part of her soul taken from her.

Katie dropped to her knees, her terrified eyes at a level with her mistress's. She wheezed, clutching at the collar around her neck with both hands. Felicity reached for the tiny sparks of power within her and tried to halt the squeezing of that noose.

For a moment, the pressure seemed to ease, for Katie gave her a half smile of relief.

Then Aunt cupped the pearl, and the collar tightened even more, and Katie choked.

"Really, gentlemen," said Uncle Oliver, his voice quite cool. "If you don't leave within the next few minutes, the girl won't have a chance." He stood aside and nodded toward the open door.

Terence and Bentley began edging their way out of the room.

"You can't keep her ignorant forever," Terence said. "She'll find out the pearl relic steals magic—and that you've been draining her for years. And not only do you transfer her power to Ralph, but you tap into it yourself, don't you? No wonder she has bouts of weakness—you don't give her enough time to regenerate her magic."

"Shut up," hissed Aunt Gertrude. "She won't listen to you. She knows you're nothing but a liar."

"What I can't figure out," continued Terence, "is how her nightmares fit into all of this. But maybe Felicity will be able to."

Felicity didn't want to believe that Terence might be right, that her aunt and uncle had purposely stolen her birthright. But she recalled what Aunt Gertrude had said about draining her, and maybe she'd truly meant herself and not the relic. Felicity stared at the blue-tinged face of her maid, the only person she could truly call her friend. Could it be possible her magic had crafted that collar? That she'd always had magic, and it had been stolen from her?

Manda's words seemed to echo in her head. If you doubt his love for you, he'll die. Despite his lie, did she believe that Terence truly loved her?

Felicity raised her hand again toward the glowing pearl. She reached out for it, like she did when trying to summon the paltry bit of magic inside of her. If the relic had only held her magic, perhaps she wouldn't have been able to access it, but in her dream, she'd given herself up to the blackness and it had changed into a pearly white fire. Somehow the relic had taken a part of her soul with her magic that time. And it was easy to call that back to her.

"No," screamed Aunt Gertrude. "Oliver, stop her. She's stealing her power back."

The tapestries on the walls snapped off, the bedding rose to attention, the glass goblet wavered in midair as Aunt Gertrude clutched at the pearl and tried to make the magic turn them into weapons.

The pressure of the collar around Katie's neck eased. With relief, Felicity heard her friend gasp a breath.

Daisy hissed and spewed fire at Uncle Oliver's lunge in her direction. Terence shifted and pounced in front of her dragonette, favoring his injured side, but shielding them both. Bentley shifted as well, his rat-form skittering under Aunt Gertrude's skirts, making her scream even harder.

Distracting her aunt and uncle.

The tapestries and beddings fluttered harmlessly to the floor. The goblet shattered into a thousand pieces.

With a sigh, Felicity waved her hand, and the piece of her soul flew back to fuse inside her, making her feel whole again. Unbidden, her magic came with it, filling her up with a strength that pulled her to her feet. If she hadn't given up herself to the blackness so that it took a part of her soul with it, would she have been able to call her magic back to her?

It didn't matter, for it was hers now. Felicity held out her arms, reveling in the feeling of rightness. Yes, the magic had always been her legacy.

Aunt lay on the floor whimpering, Bentley back in human form holding his sword point to her throat, daring her to move. Terence had Uncle Oliver pinned to the ground with one giant paw, his golden lion's eyes watching her with admiration.

"That's the real reason you put a spell on me," murmured Felicity. "If no one could remember me, then Ralph could take my title without anyone wondering about the true heir." Her voice rose. "I'm stealing nothing. I'm only taking back what was stolen from me. You say you did it in the name of love, in the name of family. But some things are black and white. And what you've done is evil."

She quickly strode over to her dear Katie and laid her hand on the collar. She remembered the lessons that her uncle had taught her. Lessons he'd only pretended that she'd ever have the opportunity to use. The metal shivered beneath her touch, then parted into separate pieces that transformed into perfectly cut and faceted sapphires.

Felicity felt the sudden drain of her strength. She would have to learn how and when to use her newly restored powers. "Keep them," she told Katie. "They're real and will be your dowry."

Katie's eyes widened, and her mouth gaped, but she still struggled to regain her breath and didn't respond.

"That was unwise," snorted Bentley.

Felicity shrugged. "I'm new to this magic business."

"Well, she's not." Bentley jerked his head down at her aunt. "Can't you feel it?"

Yes, now that he'd made her aware of it, Felicity could feel the slow tugging at her magical reserves. And could see the hazy outline of a monster forming in front of her. Daisy hissed and squirmed around her neck, and Felicity felt the little dragonette protecting her, just as she always had in her dreams.

Of course! Her dreams had come when the relic stole her power, and since her magic was mixed up in it, it responded to her imagination, transforming the magical attack into monsters.

But Aunt had used the relic for a long time, and her magic seemed to be torn between the two of them, making the monster howl in confusion.

Bentley tried to keep his sword across Aunt's throat, and wrestle the pearl from her at the same time. Terence growled in frustration, obviously wanting to help, yet reluctant to release Uncle. Aunt's madness gave her strength, however, and Bentley couldn't unwind her fingers from around the relic with just one hand.

The monster lumbered toward Terence, thick talons extended toward her lion. Aunt Gertrude had taken control of the apparition.

"No," screamed Felicity, struggling to call back her magic. Her nightmare. Remembering all the times Terence had protected her.

Terence gave a woof of surprise, the hackles on his back raising, his claws extended to fight off this new threat. Felicity saw Uncle take advantage of the distraction, saw the glitter of a knife being raised toward Terence's soft underbelly.

Felicity frantically tried to think of what to do. The more she fought against her aunt's control, the weaker she became.

Felicity gathered what power remained within her. And she shoved it back at the relic, pushing the magic from her. She could almost see the sparkle of it as it surged across the room, toward the white pearl that Aunt refused to let go of.

Felicity's head swam with dizziness.

She could hear Aunt Gertrude's screams and Bentley's curses. The monster imploded just as it swiped a talon at Terence's shaggy head, barely ruffling his golden mane.

Uncle Oliver turned and dropped the knife when he saw the light that sprayed out from between Aunt's fingers. "Let it go, Gertrude!"

But Aunt held on, screaming that she wouldn't let go, her body convulsing with the backwash of power from the relic. Bentley flew off her, as if he'd been hit with a bolt of lightning. And Aunt went still, her cries abruptly silenced.

Something shattered inside Felicity. Ah, the spell that she'd carried all these years. Only now that it was gone did she become aware of the heavy burden it had been.

Terence shifted back to human and took his prone friend's shoulders in his hands. "Bentley, are you all right?"

Bentley's eyes fluttered open. His dark brown hair stuck out from his head in spikes, and his entire body twitched three times before it stilled. "That was an experience I never want to repeat."

Terence grunted in relief.

"Gertrude," cried Uncle Oliver, falling to his knees at her side, smothering his face in her bosom. "My dear, dear wife. Why didn't you let it go?"

Felicity got to her feet, her knees shaking not from weakness, but from fear. Daisy hissed a warning, but she ignored it. When she stood over her aunt's dead body, she stared for a very long time at the woman who she'd thought had loved her.

Uncle Oliver kept patting Aunt Gertrude's face, his sobs rising and falling like a madman's. He didn't try to stop Felicity when she reached down and took the pearl from her aunt's limp hand. During the struggle the chain that held it had broken, and it came easily into her grasp. But it no longer shone white; instead it glistened a dull black.

Terence helped a ragged-looking Bentley to his feet, then turned and held out his hand to Felicity.

Felicity dropped the pearl into his palm. "Here. Isn't this what you wanted?"

Terence tossed the black pearl across the room and took her gently by the shoulders, his golden eyes glowing with such intensity that she couldn't look away. "No. I only want you."

He revealed his soul to her with his eyes.

A thousand images flitted through Felicity's mind, but the one that she kept focusing on was their first dinner together in his home. He'd noticed that she didn't liked peas. Perhaps it had all started with a lie, but only a man in love with his wife would care about something so inconsequential.

She rested her cheek against his chest with a sigh, and his strong arms folded around her. "You shall never lie to me again."

"Never," he agreed, his words muffled in her hair.

"And you shall spend the rest of our lives making up for lying to me."

She felt his grin against her scalp. "Yes, dearest. The rest of our lives."

Nineteen

FELICITY RAN UP THE STAIRS TO THEIR BEDROOM, lifting armfuls of the silk fabric of her ball gown to avoid tripping. She staggered to a halt in front of the door, mindful of the day of her first testing. But no bubbling chasm awaited her, and she crossed the solid floor, shaking her head at her caution.

It had been three months since Terence had rescued her, and everything had changed. She just couldn't quite get used to it. Illusions no longer haunted her days. From her studies she surmised that Ralph had indeed been innocent of them and that the relic had created those gaping chasms.

Felicity wrapped the shawl around her bare shoulders and glanced at her reflection in the mirror. The breaking of the spell had made her all too visible to others, another change that she had difficulty adjusting to. Oh, she appreciated not being sat on anymore; she just didn't want people staring at her all the time.

She reached up and pulled down one of her husband's cravats that had been slung carelessly over the top of the mirror, and smiled. Sharing a bedroom with Terence was one change that had been nothing but pleasure.

"Felicity," called her husband from downstairs. "We're going to be late."

Her heart did that wonderful flip at the sound of his voice, and she hurried out of the room. She saw a flash of white linen from the corner of her eye, heard muffled giggles, and tiptoed around the large vase that sat at the corner of the landing.

"Girls, what are you doing up this late?"

Rianna emerged first, her golden curls a lighter hue of Terence's, and then little Lonna followed, her rosebud of a mouth curled into a guilty smile.

"We just wanted to see your dress," said Rianna.

Lonna held up her pudgy arms. "An' get our kiss goo'night."

Felicity squatted and held out her arms, gathering the girls into a hug. Her sisters. She wondered how long it would take to get used to this wonderful change.

"You look beautiful," said Rianna, her golden eyes wistful. "Will you dance every dance?"

"I'll try," promised Felicity.

Lonna lowered her voice to a conspiratorial whisper. "An' are you gonna show him tonight?"

Felicity nodded. Both girls shifted a bit with excitement, their silky fur brushing her arms.

"I promise to tell you everything in the morning, if you promise to go right to bed."

They both sighed, looking so forlorn that Felicity's heart twisted. She patted the cool scales around her neck. "Daisy, how would you like to snuggle with the girls this evening?"

Her dragonette hissed with delight, and scrambled down her skirts, bounding into the girl's room. Felicity laughed, watching the girls now eagerly run off to bed.

Still smiling, she headed down the stairs, slowing her steps as she reached the landing, watching the fire light up in her husband's golden eyes.

"You look enchanting," he growled. "Instead of fighting off people from crashing into you, I'll have to fend off the young bucks from falling in love with you."

Felicity laughed. "No one would dare approach me with you at my side. Your scowl is absolutely ferocious."

He grunted, but she caught the flicker of a smile on his lips. Lips that could make her forget time and place, that made her long to touch them right this very minute…

Oh, dear.

"Come along, Katie," said Felicity.

The Irish girl hovered behind the coat rack. "Oh, miss. I just can't go among all them lords and ladies. I'm sure I'll make a fool of myself."

"Nonsense," sniffed Felicity. "You will just have to get used to your new status as my companion sooner or later. Come now, let me have a look at you."

Katie stumbled over her skirts, but managed a small curtsy. A tight bun contained her wild red hair, except for a fall of curls surrounding her forehead. The soft blue of her gown brought out the same color in her hazel eyes, and the simple cut of the dress reflected her modest status.

"You look absolutely lovely and will get along splendidly, I'm sure." Without another word Felicity took Katie's hand, and dragged her out to the waiting coach.

"Oh, miss!"

"Now, Katie, it's just an illusion. We won't really fly to the ball." Felicity couldn't suppress a tiny bit of pride however, and studied the coach and four. The dragons that pulled it looked suspiciously like Daisy. The carriage looked like a crystal jewel, the facets of the design reflecting rainbows of color along the cobbled streets.

Felicity settled herself on the velvet cushions next to Katie, admiring the way the crystal made a sparkling wonderland on the inside. Terence sat across from them, watching her with golden eyes that held a wicked gleam. She knew that look, and the promise it held for her later this evening. Felicity couldn't help fidgeting in her seat, and gave him such a scowl that he laughed aloud.

It seemed but a moment before their carriage slowed to a stop in front of the gates of Buckingham Palace, and Felicity couldn't help comparing this night to her first ball, when she'd failed the testing. The prince had given this ball in her husband's honor, and the spell upon her had been broken when Aunt had died, so everyone would be sure to notice her.

Why then didn't she want to go in?

She peeked at Terence beneath her lashes. She felt nervous about her plan, that's why. She couldn't be sure how he would react. The moment they'd pulled up to the gates, he'd shuttered his face, looking bored and a bit defensive. It strengthened her resolve to carry out her plan.

Katie sat beside her solid as a stone, and when Felicity looked at her terrified face, she couldn't help giggling.

"Aren't we a pair," she said. "Come along, Katie, we've faced worse than a mere ball, now, haven't we?"

Katie let herself be led along the golden path.

"The first time I was here, they'd turned the ballroom into a huge pirate ship, complete with ocean waves and eye-patched servants. I wonder what they've done this evening?"

Felicity noticed with relief that her comments seemed to bring Katie out of her daze. The Irish girl craned her neck to see beyond the line of people, past the shimmering gates of the entrance.

"Miss, those are Saint Peter's pearly gates."

"That would be a bit of a stretch," replied Felicity. "The aristocracy all in heaven?"

Katie laughed and Terence grunted. But when they passed the luminescent gates, they all realized that the ballroom had indeed been transformed into a heavenly realm.

Their names were announced as soon as they passed the threshold, and Felicity stepped onto a puffy white cloud amidst a sudden silence. Even the lovely strains of the harp had ceased. She dared to look up, and it seemed that every eye in the room was trained on her party.

Specifically, on her.

She lifted her chin, trying to stare them all down. Really, she could get used to people noticing her, but when men stopped and stared on the street and carriages collided because the occupants had stopped to stare at her, well, it was just too much.

Terence pulled her closer, and the warm, solid feel of him helped her gather her courage.

The clouds appeared to float at different levels, eventually meeting up with another puff of white before meandering off again. Felicity saw a few brave souls step off over the seeming black abyss, but instead of plummeting down to earth, they just floated to the next cloud. As this had a tendency to expose under-garments to those below, she noticed that only men had the temerity to take the leap.

A top-hatted gentleman stepped into the abyss toward their own cloud. "May I have the honor of this first dance?"

Her heart did a flip. Felicity looked up into the glittering eyes of Prince Albert, England's crown prince.

"With your permission, of course, Sir Terence."

Her husband nodded with a grim smile, and Felicity took the prince's pudgy hand. Although several clouds supporting the musicians floated around, the huge cloud comprising the main dance floor appeared to be stationary. Prince Albert swept her through the white fluff, curls of tiny hurricanes appearing between the waltzing couples. She couldn't help noting how finely he danced.

"I've been meaning to speak with you," he said, grasping her hand and turning her in a circle as the dance required. "It appears that you've been of great service to the crown. Is there some boon I can grant you?"

Felicity swallowed. "I... well, I've been meaning to speak with you about something."

Prince Albert grinned, his cheeks pink with the exertion of the dance. "Anything, my dear."

They parted and she curtsied while he bowed. "I do not wish to go through my testing tomorrow."

"That's not a boon, that's a sacrifice. Why would you wish such a thing?"

They clasped hands again, skipping down the center of the row of other dancers.

"I wish to be my husband's wife, Your Highness."

Albert frowned, then a slow grin spread across his face. "I think I understand. But... are you sure I can't offer you something else? A castle, perhaps?"

Felicity smiled, thinking he meant it as a jest, but when he spun her again, she looked into his earnest face and realized he'd been quite serious. "My husband's home is enough for me, Your Highness. But there is something I would wish from you."

Prince Albert's frown deepened, as if he were afraid to ask what she might want that would be of more value to her than a castle.

They parted, taking a spin with the dancers on their right, and then came together again. "My parents," she blurted. "I would most gratefully wish to speak with you of their relationship."

"Is that all?" The Prince beamed at her. "My dear girl, they were the closest of my friends, as I hope someday you will be, as well. What would you wish to know?"

"Oh, everything," sighed Felicity.

"That would take some time. You must visit me at your earliest convenience, when we will have the leisure for a long discussion."

The dance ended, and the prince escorted her back to the edge of the cloud.

"In the meantime," said Felicity, before she lost the courage, "can you tell me, did they love each other very much?"

His eyebrows rose. "Yes, they did, until the very last. A sailor told me that they'd stood together at the bow of the ship, hands clasped, trying to calm the wind and water when they were swept overboard."

Felicity's eyes stung. So her aunt had lied about her parents, as well. "Thank you, Your Highness. You cannot know what that knowledge means to me."

He picked up her hand and kissed it. "Remember, you must visit soon." And then he walked away.

Felicity scanned the room, meeting the gaze of her husband's golden eyes. He looked impatient and irritated, as if he wanted to pull her back to his side, but held himself in check.

"Cousin, may I have the honor of this dance?"

Felicity blinked.

She'd planned on seeking out Ralph this evening, but never imagined that he'd approach her. He hated to dance with her.

She stared at Terence. He glanced at Ralph, then shrugged. Felicity sighed. Her husband had become more reserved the closer it came to her day of testing. He constantly bullied the household staff about seeing to her needs, complained that his home wasn't good enough for her, and worried about her position in society. As if it truly mattered.

Felicity allowed Ralph to escort her back onto the dance floor. He held her rather awkwardly, stepping on her toes more than once.

"I wanted to apologize," he said.

She studied her cousin's face. He'd matured a great deal since Aunt's death. "But, Ralph, you needn't. The nightmares and illusions had all been a product of the relic. And I know you were completely innocent of Aunt and Uncle's doings."

Ralph heaved a sigh of relief. "I want you to know that I went to the crown and confessed the entire affair. And I'll willingly give up the title and lands as soon as you pass your testing tomorrow."

Ralph twirled her, and Felicity saw a golden pair of eyes follow her movements. "That won't be necessary."

"What?"

"I'm not going to my testing."

Ralph stumbled and stepped on her hem, making her stumble as well. "But I don't understand."

"You don't need to. But, Ralph, would you carry the title of duke-of-honor, holding it for my children?"

"Well, yes, of course, but I still don't see why you don't want to take what's rightfully yours."

Felicity sighed. Ralph had matured, but he would always remain spoiled and arrogant. He simply wouldn't understand. She quickly changed the subject. "How is Uncle Oliver?"

He stepped on her hem again, but she managed to keep her balance. It was the first time she'd asked about Uncle, since that night in the Underground.

"He's in a private asylum just outside of London, and he's quite mad," replied Ralph. "I have to tell you, I admire those relic-hunters. It's not that the relics are evil, mind you, but the power they possess is just too much for us ordinary mortals—the world would be better off without Merlin's relics."

Felicity heartily agreed with her cousin, for once.

The song ended, and Ralph escorted her off the dance floor, and Felicity noticed Katie with a young man, whose wide smile and merry eyes never left her freckled face.

Felicity grinned as she floated back to her impatient husband, but it faded as she noticed the group of young gentlemen who made a wide circle around Terence. She could hear their whispers quite clearly.

"Who is he?"

"...husband."

"The shapeshifter?"

"...dirty animal."

Felicity bridled at their tone. She fought the urge to defend him, to tell the louts that this man saved their sorry selves from evil magic. That they should be offering to shake his hand, not backing away from him as if his touch would soil their clothing.

But her husband should have defended himself. Instead he chose to ignore them, amused by Felicity's anger on his behalf.

Terence's eyes lit as she slid her hand into his. He swept her onto the dance floor, his arm wrapping easily around her waist, his movements in perfect harmony with hers. Felicity had thought she'd enjoyed dancing with the prince, but it was nothing when compared to moving across the floor with her husband. Every nerve in her body sang, every brush of his skin against her own made her senses explode. She felt as if she truly danced on a cloud, her feet never quite touching the floor.

His eyes never left hers, and time and again, she felt her lips drawn to his, as if some force kept pulling them together. But it wouldn't be proper for them to kiss in front of all these strangers, would it?

The song ended, the strains of the harp fading into silence. And she remembered that Terence cared little for propriety.

He kissed her with a passion that had several ladies gasping and the entire assembly staring. Felicity wrapped her arms eagerly around his shoulders, opening her mouth with a groan. He bent her backwards, his hands hot against her back, his mouth delving, searching. Branding her as his own.

When he finally stood her back on her feet, Felicity's knees wobbled and she struggled to breathe.

"Let's go home."

He cocked a golden brow, his mouth curled in a rather smug grin. "Are you sure?"

Felicity answered his grin with one of her own. "I have something to show you."

❦

Terence didn't give her a chance to show him her surprise until much later. As soon as they entered the bedroom, he took her into his arms, his body enfolding her own, and kissed her senseless.

He growled in his throat, sounding more animal than man, but Felicity felt no fear. Instead, a thrill of anticipation went through her. He always seemed to hold a part of himself back, and tonight she sensed he wouldn't.

He managed to rip the clothes from her body— popping off every button and sending them rolling about the room—without injuring her in the slightest. But she couldn't even manage his coat, his shoulders too wide for the fabric to slide easily over.

He treated his garments as roughly as her own, until the heat of his skin covered her body. His touch had a gentle reverence to it, sliding over every inch of her, as if memorizing the way she felt in his arms.

His hand slid between her legs, making her knees buckle, and he set her on the bed, his fingers moving all the while, his mouth sucking at her breasts and then lips and then back again to her breasts.

Felicity felt on the edge of exploding when he took his hand away and plunged himself inside of her. Feverishly, wildly, he took her, each stroke claiming her as his own. She couldn't think and didn't care, her climax ripping through her at the same time as his. When they finally tumbled back to earth, they twisted their legs and arms around each other as if to keep their bodies fused into one.

"Did I hurt you?" he murmured.

Felicity smiled. "No. Did I hurt you?"

His chuckle sent shivers of pleasure down her spine.

Felicity took a deep breath. "I have something to show you."

"I thought you just did."

Felicity slapped at his hand. She felt excited and nervous and afraid all at the same time. She crawled out from beneath the bedclothes, and rose to her hands and knees.

Terence grinned. "I like it already."

"Stop. This is serious. You know that I've been teaching Lonna and Rianna to keep their human shape?"

He nodded, crossing his arms behind his head, a frown starting to form on his brow.

"Well, they've been teaching me something, too."

Felicity closed her eyes. She couldn't do it as effort-lessly as Terence; it wasn't her true nature. She had to concentrate to form the vision of a lioness in her mind, had to change each individual muscle and tendon and hair. And it hurt a bit.

She let out a plaintive mew, and Terence surged upright in bed. Quickly, she leaped down and peeked in the mirror, making sure she'd arranged all the parts correctly. She stared at the whiskers sprouting from her lioness nose, and lolled her tongue with a grin. Except for the blackness of her fur, and her violet eyes, she looked just like Lonna and Rianna. But a lot larger.

She bounded back onto the bed, and grunted at her husband's open-mouthed surprise. She licked his cheek.

"How… why?"

Felicity changed herself back to human. Thankfully, it took a lot less effort. She answered his ques-tions in a roundabout way. "I'm not going to my testing tomorrow."

His amazement turned quickly to anger, and she could see the bunch of his muscles. "Why not?"

"Ralph is going to hold the lands in honor for our children. Assuming that one of them will inherit my magic." She tapped a finger against her cheek. "Although, I won't be unhappy if they all turn out to be weres."

Terence sprang to his feet, his naked, glorious body distracting Felicity for a moment.

"I won't let you do it," he growled. "I won't let you give up everything! You deserve so much more than I can give you, and I won't stand by and watch you throw it all away."

"I'll still have my magic. No one can ever take that away from me again."

He brought his face close to hers. "I repeat. I will not let you give up everything for me."

Felicity knew he'd feel this way. She knew he'd be angry. But she'd prepared for this. "Is that what you think? That I'm doing all of this for you?"

That set him back a few steps. He raked his hands through his thick hair, his anger overcome with confusion.

"I want to be a relic-hunter."

"You what?"

"I want to be part of your work. And the only way I can do that is to become a baroness. It's going to be hard enough to convince the prince to accept me as it is."

"Accept you? Dearest, you're not immune to magic. I would spend the entire time worrying about you. Besides, there's never been a non-were relic-hunter before. I can't even imagine…"

Felicity got up and kissed him, the tips of her breasts brushing against the hairs of his chest. His arms caught her up and pressed her body against the hot length of him.

"I love you," he growled. "Are you sure you're not just doing this for me?"

Felicity smiled, wanting to be truthful, knowing the harm that lies could cause. "Maybe just a little. But you see, I've always wondered what it would be like to bound across the rooftops of London in the moonlight."

A joy she'd never seen before transformed his face, and he shifted so quickly she felt him change in her arms. Terence paced the room while she changed herself as well, and she knew the moment she'd completed her transformation, because he pushed against her, making those soft moaning noises and pushing against her until she fell over. He nudged her to her paws with his nose, and led her up the attic stairs and onto the roof.

And showed her exactly what it was like to leap across moonlit rooftops.

Double Enchantment

AVAILABLE MARCH 2013
FROM SOURCEBOOKS CASABLANCA

London, 1848
Where magic has never died…

LADY JASMINA KARLYLE SNUCK INTO HER MOTHER'S bedroom like a thief. To her dismay, she realized that she was getting quite skilled at breaking and entering. Jasmina ignored the illusion of slobbering, snarling wolves that her mother had set to protect the chamber from intruders, and began to search the contents of several bandboxes.

She carefully set aside a lovely bonnet decorated with iridescent feathers, a lacquered fan painted with swans, several lace-trimmed handkerchiefs and a beaded reticule. A glitter of red caught her eye, and she scrabbled for it, scowling with disappointment when she held it up and realized it was only a jeweled button.

She put everything back into the bandbox and opened the lid of another. It was astonishing, really, how clever her mother could be when she set her mind to it. Illusory boxes were interspersed with the real ones, so that her collection looked double.

Fortunately, Jasmina had searched her mother's belongings often enough that she knew where the real items were stored.

The door rattled and Jasmina spun guiltily, waving her fingers with the absent-minded habit she'd developed whenever she cast a spell. She couldn't quite make herself invisible, but her spell would cause whoever entered the room to overlook her presence.

Despite being her mother's maid for forty years, dear Nanette took one glance at the snarling wolves and slammed the door shut again.

Jasmina smiled and continued her search. Nothing in the larger boxes! She moved her search to the smaller, decorative boxes that littered Mother's chiffonier. She shook her head with frustration. There was still the wardrobe to search, and the washing stand cupboard, then beneath the canopied bed—and she hadn't even checked Mother's dressing room yet.

And all for an ugly brooch that looked exactly like—

Jasmina blinked. Nestled among other jewelry, in a pretty box decorated with tiny abalone shells, lay the Duchess of Hagersham's brooch. Her instincts had been correct. Last evening at the Hagersham dinner, her mother *had* been admiring the duke's new gift to his wife with a little too much avarice.

Jasmina held the brooch up to the candlelight, and the large garnet in the center of the piece danced with reflected light. The jewel itself was quite stunning, but the silver figures carved around the sides of it leered grotesquely at her. Ugly little creatures with the most shocking anatomically correct details.

Whatever had possessed her mother to "borrow" it?

Jasmina froze. She could hear the pounding of her heart and realized that the snarling of the wolves had stopped, which could only mean—

"Lucy." Aunt Ettie's voice carried through the closed door. "Are you getting ready for the ball so soon?"

Mother answered, but Jasmina didn't hear the reply. Jasmina shoved the brooch into the pocket sewn into the seam of her dress and sprinted across the room as quickly as her petticoats would allow. Her mother always noticed her, no matter how strongly she cast her spell. She slipped inside the connecting door to Mother's dressing room just as the bedroom door opened and sighed with relief. Her mother hadn't caught her, thank heavens, which meant she wouldn't have to bear another scene with Mother weeping excuses.

Jasmina crept out the main door and into the hallway and around the stairwell to the safety of her own bedroom. She collapsed on her bed, fighting for breath against the confines of her corset, and dissolved her spell.

A soft tapping on her door, and Aunt Ettie entered. "Well, were we right?"

Jasmina nodded, staring into emerald green eyes that matched her own. But the resemblance stopped there, for Aunt's features were sharp and intelligent, whereas Jasmina's matched those of her mother: soft and innocent.

"Oh dear." Aunt settled her skirts over the arms of the dressing table chair. "My silly, foolish sister. I don't suppose we should tell your father this time?"

Jasmina rose and smoothed the wrinkles from the counterpane before she carefully rolled it to the foot of the bed. "We have been over this before." Even Aunt Ettie sometimes forgot that Jasmina's doll-like features hid a keen intelligence and a will of iron. "Father wouldn't have the slightest idea how to handle the situation, short of locking Mother away. And it's a woman's duty to keep a man's house a refuge against the rest of the world. Since Mother is unable to do so, that task falls to me."

"I just wish I could do more." Aunt tucked a stray lock of prematurely gray hair back into her severe coiffure.

"Dear Aunt Henrietta, you have already given up all of your prospects to keep our family secret safe. And my magic makes it so much easier to handle the situation."

"I suppose you're right. But it means you shall miss the queen's ball tonight."

Jasmina shrugged and presented her back to her aunt, who began to unbutton the back of her gown.

"If only my sister weren't so…" Aunt left her thought unspoken and pushed the bodice of Jasmina's dress forward. "She insists she's only 'borrowing' from people, and that she has every intention of returning the item right away. She just forgets to."

Jasmina tugged at her sleeves, hearing the frustration in Aunt's voice. She had tried talking to Mother about it as well.

"And then somehow," continued her aunt, "she turns it around and makes me feel guilty. As if it's all my fault, and I'm being quite vulgar for even mentioning it."

"I just think it's something she can't control, and it frightens her," replied Jasmina. "That's why she needs me." Jasmina gasped with relief as the stays of her corset were loosened. "All that matters is keeping Mother and Father happy."

"But you, Jaz. I'm afraid that you'll sacrifice all of your happiness for their own."

"On the contrary. Can you imagine our social standing if Mother's...eccentricity was known?"

Aunt sniffed. "That wasn't quite what I meant."

The door flew open and the subject of their discussion sailed into the room. Mother looked stunning in a pale green ball gown that matched the color of her eyes. Her blonde hair, a shade darker than Jasmina's, was decorated with diamond-studded pins that matched the elegant necklace around her throat. A natural pink blush complemented her smooth complexion, and she'd used only a hint of illusion to smooth the wrinkles from around her eyes. "Jasmina, dear, what are you wearing to the..."

Jasmina stepped out of the puddle of her dress and petticoats and staggered over to her bed, the back of her hand pressed to her forehead.

Mother's full lips puckered in a charming frown. "Whatever is the matter, dear?"

"My head...hurts dreadfully." Jasmina collapsed onto the bedding.

Aunt Henrietta raised a brow at her from behind Mother's back. Jasmina coughed to hide a smile. Mother backed up a step. "I hope it's not catching. You know how susceptible I am to the slightest thing."

"I'm sure it's nothing serious, Lucy," replied Aunt Ettie. "But it seems wise to keep Jasmina at home this evening."

About the Author

Kathryne Kennedy is an award-winning author acclaimed for her world building and known for blending genres to create groundbreaking stories. *Enchanting the Lady* is the first book in her popular *Relics of Merlin* series. Her magical new series, *The Elven Lords*, includes *The Fire Lord's Lover*, *The Lady of the Storm*, and *The Lord of Illusion*. She's lived in Guam, Okinawa, and several states in the United States and currently lives in Arizona with her wonderful family—which includes two very tiny Chihuahuas. She loves to hear from readers and welcomes you to visit her website where she has ongoing contests at: www.KathryneKennedy.com.